Unfinished Business

———

Marie Norling

This is a work of fiction. The dialogue and characters are products of the author's imagination. Any resemblance to living persons is entirely coincidental.

Copyright © 2022 by Wayne McCreedy

Published in the United States of America

All rights reserved. This book, or parts thereof, may not be reproduced in any form without expressed written permission of Wayne McCreedy.

ISBN: 978-1-939917-35-5

Available from:
   Amazon.com
   Barnes & Noble.com

> To my husband, The Responsible Man

ONE

I was pumped.

The morning's weather was so perfect—the early spring air perfumed by lilacs and daffodils trumpeting an end to winter in D.C.— that my jogging partner and I had added a couple more miles to our pre-work run. Now I was standing at my kitchen counter, hair still damp from the shower, skimming *The Washington Post* while scarfing down a bowl of yogurt and fresh blueberries to make up the time well spent on those extra miles. The day seemed to shimmer with possibilities.

Flipping open the "Style" section to the second page, I raised the spoon for another bite. But at the glimpse of a small black-and-white photograph in the visiting celebrity segment, my breath knotted in my throat. I sat abruptly, luckily catching the edge of a stool.

The spoon, still clutched in my hand, hovered in front of me like a jittery hummingbird. Not moving my eyes from the photo, I lowered the utensil to the bowl until it struck the dish, clanking sharply and jolting me free from my fixation.

It wasn't that I had never seen a picture of this man in the paper before, but these stock headshots unnerved me. They captured his good looks but never his vitality.

And it didn't help that whenever I unexpectedly saw his photograph, I was immediately reminded of my brother, Alex, even though he'd been dead now for over ten years. On cue, tears welled up behind my eyelids.

I squeezed my eyes shut before the salty droplets could ruin the little mascara I had on. Then, after a few seconds, I went back to studying the picture. No, an action shot was required to convey this man's inner fire. Perhaps a photo of him commanding the stage, guitar in hand, belting out vocals. Then his energy would explode off the page.

Tanner Edward Daulton. Rock musician. Front man for two of the most iconic post-grunge rock bands of the twenty-first century. Everyone called him Teddie or Teddie D, but I'd always called him Tanner—his given name and his mother's surname.

According to the article, he was in town to appear before Congress to advocate for increasing the use of drug courts to divert nonviolent drug offenders into treatment programs. Over the years, he'd rolled into D.C. for many causes, the most frequent visits being to wounded military personnel at Walter Reed Medical Center.

Sighing, I touched my fingertip to the picture. He looked so familiar, even though it had been twelve years—and four months—since I'd seen him face-to-face. But who's counting?

The one major change in his appearance was the trimmed facial stubble he was sporting. It was very L.A., but I had to confess the beard looked perfect on him, giving his handsome features the edge befitting a rocker.

Brushing the beard with my forefinger, my breath quickened as I imagined the sensation of the bristly scruff against my skin. But cold reality kicked in swiftly—all I felt was the grainy surface of the newsprint.

I snatched my hand from the page. Once upon a time, though,

that same touch on his skin would have inflamed not only my fingers but my body.

Whenever Tanner came to D.C., I'd wonder whether he thought of calling. He could have easily gotten my number from the couple who had been our best friends in California. Sometimes I was even surprised when he didn't call.

Then I would remember.

I had walked out on him.

TWO

"Morning, Jessie," Stephanie greeted me as I arrived at the office a little late, having foolishly lingered over Tanner's picture. "What a nice day?"

Our receptionist converses in "upspeak." When she first joined us, I initially had responded with an answer when, in fact, there had been no question.

"Perfect." At least weather-wise.

Two years out of college and in the midst of career decisions, Stephanie had recently asked me to mentor her. I had eagerly accepted. At some point, we would address the upspeak. It's tough enough being a woman in business without being perceived as tentative.

The mentoring, however, had been put on hold.

"How's the condo?" I asked.

"We're supposed to get the results of the radon testing today or tomorrow? And tomorrow we'll walk through with the home inspector. Thanks for recommending someone?"

Stephanie and her boyfriend, Joe, were buying their first place together. They'd found a condo in Arlington, Virginia, near a Metro station. Before signing a contract, they'd asked me to check out the unit, a foreclosure that had sat empty for over a year. The "as-is" price was well below their budget.

After my walk-through, I noted there were cosmetic issues but that the bones looked good. I wrote up a list of items needing repair—frayed wallpaper in the guest bathroom, broken tile in the foyer, walls requiring a fresh coat of paint, etc.—so they could try to negotiate a lower price. Banks, however, are notorious for refusing to haggle on foreclosures.

"Good. If you have questions about either report, give me a call this weekend."

"Thanks for all your help, Jessie?"

I work at Pearce & Associates, an architecture firm located in downtown Washington, D.C. It's a small regional firm—fifteen people tops. I've been at the company for over seven years, having obtained my master of architecture degree and architect's license in Los Angeles.

Not quite two years ago, my boss, Evan Pearce, promoted me to Director of Design, which means the architecture staff work under my guidance. Evan also said I was on track to be his first partner.

Elation had rocketed through me. I'd wanted to be an architect since I was thirteen. My parents are professors at Brown University, in Providence, Rhode Island. Growing up, I'd spent many weekends with my family exploring the nearby town of Newport with its robber-baron mansions. Those grand mansions may epitomize conspicuous consumption but their marvelous craftsmanship and architectural details are what had inspired me.

Becoming a partner with Evan would be the culmination of those early dreams.

Pearce Hartley & Associates.

The name sounded glorious.

I dropped my briefcase in my office and headed out to the bullpen.

Every morning, I checked with the staff, from our two project managers to the junior architects and interns, about unresolved issues. It was my responsibility to ensure that each project progressed smoothly and on schedule.

Examining a drawing prepared by one of the junior architects for the cross-section of an exterior wall, I noticed the design could channel rainwater into the wall system. Normally I'd have used this as a teaching moment; instead, I simply corrected the drawing.

That photograph of Tanner had thrown me off my game. I grabbed a cup of coffee and headed back to my office which, in addition to exterior windows, had an interior wall of glass overlooking the bullpen. Maybe I could forget the earlier heartburn if I focused on my latest project—expanding a public library in Montgomery County, Maryland, northwest of D.C.

The extension would, among other improvements, house a new technology center, bringing the library into the twenty-first century. Libraries are among my favorite buildings to design as they are so often the hearts of their communities.

But not today apparently. After an hour at my desk and repeated doses of caffeine, I still couldn't focus.

Besides, I was being watched.

Sitting smack-dab in the middle of the bookcases lining the

wall opposite my desk was a brown teddy bear. Alongside were souvenirs from vacations—like a six-inch high Eiffel Tower and a Leaning Tower of Pisa, kitschy icons that architects love to collect. The bear, though, had pride of place. He was about fifteen inches tall, wearing a slick yellow raincoat and rain hat, and was staring at me, unrelentingly, with glassy black eyes.

The bear had been a gift from Tanner on the return from his first road trip—twenty-eight days traveling the Northwest with his first band, mPulse. The bear came from his hometown of Seattle, one of the stops on the trio's itinerary.

From then on, Tanner had brought back a namesake bear from each trip, promising that they would keep me safe while he was on the road. And they had, perched vigilantly on the dresser in our bedroom. When Tanner was away, the growing pack of bruins was one of the last things I looked at before turning off the light at night. I'd fall asleep imagining where the next one would come from. Those teddy bears had been my most valued possessions—representing Tanner's safe return from each journey.

But it wasn't only seeing that beloved bear on the shelf—sometimes a too potent reminder of the past—that bothered me today.

It was that I had turned thirty-six the previous week.

To celebrate, my best friend, Charlene Adkins, would be taking me to dinner later at Rasika, one of the best Indian restaurants in the country. A meal there is a sensory indulgence, the food bursting with exotic aromas and flavors and rich earthy colors. But even the restaurant was making me think of Tanner. On tight budgets in L.A.—as I had started my three-year graduate program in architecture and Tanner had launched his career, we had eaten a lot of ethnic food,

Indian a particular favorite.

Should I cancel? I didn't want to waste my birthday dinner wallowing in messy memories triggered by that photo. But then Charlene did have a knack for lightening my mood.

I stared out the window at the ever-changing cinematic show on the metallic-sheathed office building opposite, which mirrored the clouds overhead as if part of its skin, and tried to quell memories and emotions.

On reflection, I decided that my disquiet probably owed less to that picture of Tanner and more to the fact that my birthday had underscored the fact that things weren't turning out quite as expected—at least not in my personal life.

Mid-afternoon, Evan knocked on my door jamb. "Got a minute, Jessie?"

In his mid-forties, Evan was the rainmaker for the company, bringing in new business. Even better, his reputation for quality and attention to detail kept clients returning. He was my mentor and role model.

"Of course."

Settling into a chair in front of my desk, he tried, without success, to repress a grin.

"What's up, Evan?"

"Have you heard that the D.C. government is sponsoring an architectural Ideas Competition?"

I shook my head but couldn't stop the beginning of an ear-to-ear smile.

"It starts in two weeks," he continued. "The city wants to

generate ideas for the use of a downtown site they own. Would you be interested?" Certain of my response, Evan let his grin off the leash.

I laughed. "You know me. I'm always up for a competition." Competitions have been an integral part of architecture tradition for well over two thousand years. And I love being part of the tradition.

"Then check out the website over the weekend and we'll talk about it on Monday."

An Ideas Competition!

Now that was a birthday present.

THREE

Walking to the restaurant, I suddenly realized I was looking forward to dinner with my best friend. The conversation with Evan had put the bounce back into my step and returned Tanner to the cobwebs.

At the corner I spotted Charlene heading toward me on D Street. She was easy to pick out at six-feet-one, with short, platinum-blond hair and a lean athletic build. She moved with a long, rolling stride, almost a swagger, that reminded me of a gunslinger in an old TV western—an apt image as she is a formidable litigator. We'd met at a pick-up volleyball game on the National Mall shortly after I moved to D.C.

I waved and waited for her.

As we were being shown to our seats at Rasika, the walls of the restaurant started spinning madly around me, the contrails left by their orbit visible. I stumbled in confusion and awkwardly righted myself on the top edge of a banquette, apologizing to the startled occupant.

Whether I first saw him or sensed him, I'm not sure. Or perhaps I had unconsciously teased his voice out from the cacophony of conversations ricocheting off the walls, the familiar tenor catching me by surprise and catapulting me off-balance.

Even with his back to me—his table located at the rear of the dining room for privacy—I'd have recognized the silhouette anywhere: the shape of his head, the broad swimmer's shoulders, and the long-limbed torso. I knew every inch of that six-foot-three body—at least I had.

Initially my heart fluttered at his proximity and then went into full-out A-fib, my chest feeling as though it would burst from too many heartbeats. I blindly followed Charlene to our table, simply trying to breathe.

Once seated, though, I couldn't focus on the menu. I glanced up at my friend. She was oblivious to my distress. A staunch meat-and-potatoes gal, she was scrutinizing the offerings for the least spicy entrée.

I casually lowered my menu to the table. "Excuse me a minute, Charlene."

She nodded, not bothering to look up.

In a trance, I moved towards the man's table, a hapless moth to the shimmering flame.

I wondered if he would recognize me after all these years. Back when we'd been together, I'd had long hair with bangs. Now I wore it shoulder-length and parted to one side. With age, the color had also gone a deeper blond. And he certainly wasn't accustomed to seeing me in a suit and heels.

A server, who had just refilled the man's water glass, tried to wave me off as I approached the table but I was on autopilot, barely conscious of what I was doing, barely aware of anyone else in the restaurant.

Seeing him was like hearing a favorite song. One I recognized as soon as I heard the opening few notes, one I knew all the words to, and one forever part of my soul and my bones.

I pulled up alongside his right elbow. He looked wonderful. Perhaps he was a little more muscular than when I had known him; either he kept in very good shape for his concerts or his lanky body had filled in with age.

What hadn't changed was the strength of his life force, already resonating through my body. The sensation almost brought me to my knees.

Everything about him registered in seconds with an overwhelming sense of familiarity. His elegant, long fingers with their calloused tips—those fingers that had once known my body as thoroughly as they had known his guitars. His distinctive scent—masculine and fresh, reminding me of musk and the evergreen trees that thrive in the Northwest where he'd grown up—though perhaps that was a trick of memory. I inhaled again anyway.

But there was also that well-manicured stubble, exotic in its unfamiliarity. I wanted to touch it as I had his photograph earlier in the day . . . to render the unfamiliar familiar.

Yet, dressed as he was in his customary public uniform of dark blue jeans and a black T-shirt, a black sports coat draped over his chair, it all felt normal. My breathing stabilized and my heart settled down.

Chatting with his three dining companions (two men, one woman), the man hadn't glanced up at me—his presumably gawking fan—for he wasn't in public mode. Anyone else would have been intimidated by that formidable persona but I knew exactly how to get his attention.

Leaning in close and whispering so only he could hear, I breathed his name, "Tanner."

His body froze for an instant but as he raised his dark brown eyes to my "emerald" ones (he had always likened my eyes to gems) a smile swept across his face and was echoed in his own lustrous eyes.

Tanner's joy at seeing me was so natural that I couldn't help but smile back. His grin had always been irresistible, a bona fide force of nature. I basked in its glow.

"Jessie?"

My name on his lips sounded sweet. A thousand emotions, memories, and sensations danced through me at the single word.

Tanner started to rise from his chair.

With my left hand, I motioned for him to stay seated.

With my right hand—and still beaming at him, I grabbed his water glass and tossed the chilled liquid onto his chest. He and I watched as the silvery, crazed cubes of ice bounced down his shirtfront onto his jeans, followed by rivulets of water.

I hoped it was a very expensive bottle of water.

The liquid immediately soaked into his dark clothes, creating sodden, spreading splotches. The drenched shirt became plastered to his torso, revealing the hard muscles of his abdomen—a bonus I hadn't counted on.

He stared up at me, stunned.

I leaned in, amazed at his nearness, and hissed in his ear, "That was for my brother."

Tanner, suspended halfway out of his chair, grabbed for napkins. The two men at the table rose.

Turning to them, I said, "Don't bother. I'm leaving."

I stormed off. I was not some hapless moth. I was an avenging Valkyrie, aglow with righteousness.

Behind me I heard Tanner say, "It's okay. Just an occupational hazard."

He was wrong. I wasn't an occupational hazard. This was personal.

Waiters hurried past me with towels. I sidestepped them on the way back to my table. Only to find Charlene watching me, her mouth agape. No words came out. Truly a first.

"Charlene, grab your bag. It's your lucky night. We're leaving."

She complied without a sound.

Before departing I tossed a wad of cash on the table for the nuisance factor. As I headed for the front door, I turned around for one last satisfying look at the commotion.

Though briskly drying himself with towels, Tanner was staring at me. I was certain that he'd be glowering, daggers hurtling at me from dark, unforgiving eyes.

Instead he appeared . . . confused.

FOUR

"What. The. Fuck?"

Charlene had found her voice.

I didn't respond. Instead I walked faster, limbs shaking from adrenaline.

"Do you know who that was?"

"Of course," I growled. Did she think I was an idiot? Although given what I had just done, perhaps there was some truth to the notion.

"What in the world did Teddie Daulton ever do to you? Write a song you didn't like?"

I didn't answer.

"Or, perhaps he paired words that didn't rhyme?"

I continued to ignore her.

"Oh, I know. He must have slandered architects."

As the adrenaline started to abate, regret started to kick in. What had I been thinking? But that was the problem—I hadn't been. I had been driven solely by hurt and disappointment.

Passing several restaurants, I slowed down as I caught the solacing whiff of a traditional wood oven. Comfort food. I could use some.

"If it was slander, I might be able to sue him," Charlene added.

She was jerking my chain. "It wasn't about me," I replied self-righteously. "It was about my brother."

That brought her up short. "Your brother? What in the world does Teddie Daulton have to do with your brother? Your brother died a long time ago—before we even met."

The heavenly aroma of pizza was making me salivate. I checked out the restaurant through the window. Plenty of empty tables.

"I'm starving. Is it okay if we get something to eat here? I didn't realize drenching someone would whet my appetite."

Charlene gazed at me in disbelief and then burst out laughing.

I could see the humor in the situation—it wasn't like me to commit such an outrageous act, much less in public. I always keep my cool. But right now, I was closer to tears than laughter.

I walked into the pizzeria, Charlene following, and found a table in the far corner. The waiter came over with menus but I shook my head.

"A large pizza. Olives, green peppers, onions, mushrooms. Topped with sausage."

I looked at Charlene.

"Extra cheese."

I nodded at the waiter. "Lots of cheese."

Nothing offsets a funk as much as the unctuous sensation of warm, melted cheese in your mouth, softened but still stringy—even as you feel it clog your arteries on its way down your esophagus. Maybe all the grease would smother the still-flaming anger in my stomach as well as the prickly beginnings of shame, like slurry dropped onto a forest fire to extinguish it.

But that would be too easy.

As soon as the server turned his back, Charlene leaned forward. "So, what does Teddie Daulton have to do with your brother?"

By now, I repented the whole misdeed. And although I was still shaking, it was no longer from a surplus of adrenaline but its lack: chills coursed through my body and my muscles and tendons hadn't the strength to keep my bones connected. I buttoned my suit jacket and wrapped my arms around my chest to keep from shivering.

Suddenly sirens shrieked nearby.

I winced and the hairs on the back of my neck recoiled in tandem. Great. My sense of guilt was obviously overdeveloped.

Once the police cars sped past, lights blazing, just another staple of the electric urban night, I reluctantly answered, voice cracking. "Nothing . . . and everything."

Charlene gave me the stink eye. "Stop being dramatic. Start at the beginning. How do you know Teddie D?"

I sighed. My friend had been a lawyer too long. Born in South Carolina, she could be all southern hospitality and charm and then, when you weren't paying attention, go for the jugular.

"Tanner—uh, Teddie and I met in Chicago. In our last year at college. I was applying to graduate schools for a master's program in architecture. He was a history major. By the way, his first name's Tanner."

She didn't respond, only gesturing with her hands for me to hurry along.

Oh well, I didn't want to prolong the story either. "We met at one of his gigs."

That previous summer a blues bassist had joined Tanner's college band. The trio's styles had coalesced: the energy of rock and grunge, the honesty of the blues, and the tunefulness of post-grunge producing a singular sound.

The band, mPulse, played every weekend at different clubs in Chicago. Tanner played guitar and sang lead vocals, Mike was on drums, and Ron was on bass. Given the rock groups popular in the late 1990s, the three-man lineup was a bit retro, though there is certainly a tradition of power trios in rock history. One such trio, Nirvana, was from Tanner's hometown; he was fourteen when Nirvana's seminal album, *Nevermind*, came out.

"My roommate's boyfriend, a friend of Tanner's, invited me to one of the band's gigs in November to celebrate completing my graduate school applications. Between sets, Tanner joined us and we chatted for about twenty minutes." What I remembered most about that evening was how much the man had made me laugh and his energy on and off the stage.

The next morning Tanner called and we met mid-afternoon for coffee. Just as the evening before, he made me laugh, but that afternoon I detected the intensity beneath the surface. It was an irresistible combination. Coffee stretched to dinner, followed by more coffee.

On the midnight walk back to my dorm (hadn't the stars seemed more brilliant that night?), he asked me to call him Tanner. I sensed it was a gift—a glimpse, perhaps, of his true self. We kissed before parting—a soft, lingering kiss, full of promises. It was a small moment filled with enormous potential.

"We hit it off," I continued. Which meant we fell head-over-heels, which wasn't typical of me. But Tanner had this life force—the élan vital, perhaps—that my body and spirit resonated with. Even this evening, standing next to him at the restaurant, I had experienced his presence in my bones. My ability to feel his energy was like a sixth sense, a recognition of something fundamental within him, the place from which his creativity arose, perhaps. Even our decade plus apart hadn't diminished my awareness of that energy—or the thrill.

"After I received acceptances from graduate schools, Tanner and

I discussed cities that could work for both of us, finally agreeing on Los Angeles. Tanner and his bandmates could pursue their music careers there while I attended UCLA."

The waiter brought over the just-out-of-the-oven pizza, with its consoling yeasty aroma. I dug in, finishing the first slice before saying another word. The cheese was already starting to work its magic, both calming and comforting me.

"What happened in L.A.?" Charlene prodded, only halfway through her first piece of pizza.

"We rented an old apartment near campus. For Tanner and his bandmates those first months in L.A. were about getting to know the local club owners and promoters.

"Then, to jump-start the second part of their plan, the guys self-recorded an album, a combination of grunge and rock covers along with several of Tanner's original songs. They felt their music needed to be experienced live, though, so they grew their base the old-fashioned way—by touring, using the demo to secure bookings."

Although mPulse had been playing clubs in L.A. on a regular basis, Tanner felt that initial road trip was the first real step in establishing his career. Yet he had apologized profusely when he set off, wanting to be there for my first day of graduate school, only a few days later. I assured him the timing was perfect—that we were starting our journey together.

After loading his equipment into the van, Tanner pulled me to him and we danced gleefully over the sidewalk and street as he sang, every step and dip filled with joy and excitement about the future. Pedestrians, dog-walkers, and drivers passing by stared, undoubtedly thinking us drunk despite the early hour.

The dance came to an end at the driver's door, where we kissed. That kiss, too, was extraordinary, full of promises like the first kiss in Chicago, but this time filled with dreams as well. I felt lucky to be with Tanner at the moment he embarked on his musical quest. I could no longer imagine a life without him.

"How long were you together?"

"A little over two years. We split up before mPulse signed its first recording contract."

"What happened?" Charlene was like a dog with a bone. I wondered if this was her persona when grilling someone in the witness box. The poor soul would probably confess just to get away from the unrelenting barrage of questions.

I sighed. "Tanner was starting out in his career and I was in architecture school. We had . . . different priorities." I almost laughed at the absurdity that four words could encapsulate the collapse of our relationship. The speed and ease of our intimacy had always made the relationship feel inevitable. But perhaps there's a price to pay when something of such value comes so effortlessly.

"Why in the world haven't you mentioned him?" Charlene's voice was rising along with her eyebrows.

My jaw clenched. Really? Both Charlene and I were private people. She held secrets she hadn't shared with me. For example, she never talked about the divorce that had left her with sole custody of a young daughter while she was still in law school. But that was fine. If she ever wanted to talk, she knew I'd be there for her.

"Gee, Charlene, how clichéd is it to fall for a rock musician—"

"Don't you mean rock god?" she interjected.

For the first time since the "unfortunate event," I laughed. "Not when I knew him. And remember that by the time I moved to D.C., Tanner was well in the past—along with two ex-wives and a son. There simply wasn't a story to tell."

But clichés and time weren't the real reasons I hadn't spoken of Tanner.

It was because he had broken my heart.

Meanwhile, Charlene's steel-blue eyes kept getting wider. "Nothing to tell! You lived with Teddie Daulton!"

Heat rose quickly to my face. "Charlene. Shh." I glanced around the near-empty restaurant.

Lowering her voice, she added, "For crying out loud, you had sex with the man. I've invited you to his concerts every time he's come to town and you've never joined me—and certainly never hinted that you knew him."

I shrugged. I had never gone with anyone to one of Tanner's concerts.

But I did go on my own when he formed his second band, In This Together. For a short time, I could forget our past and simply be in the moment, reveling in his energy. I always left early, though, never wanting to watch Tanner walk off the stage at the end of the evening.

"Doesn't mean I didn't go," I muttered, just to be annoying.

She gave me a look that jackhammered my eyeballs and frontal lobe. "Well, you've got no excuse for not going with me in the future. But what I don't get is the connection between Teddie D and your brother?"

My brother, Alex, and I had been very close growing up, despite his being three years older. At the time of his death, Alex was in a surgical residency, planning to join an international health organization aiding places afflicted by war, epidemic, or natural disaster.

He had died in a skiing accident in Vermont, a little less than a year after I left Tanner. He was making a run down a double black diamond trail. The snow had been too icy, too slick, for him to maintain his line.

It was an incredible shock. Only two weeks before, he and I'd been celebrating Thanksgiving at our parents' home in Rhode Island. He had been so full of life.

I played with the handle on my coffee cup, not meeting Charlene's eyes. My chest ached from all the dredged-up emotions. "Alex came out twice to L.A. to visit us. The two guys bonded immediately." They even phoned each other, particularly when Tanner was on the road.

When my relationship with Tanner started to unravel, Alex was the only person I'd confided in. He offered to talk to Tanner but I refused. It was reassuring to know my big brother was willing to intercede, but it would have been pointless.

Tanner and I split at the beginning of 2001. By the end of that awful year, Alex was gone, too. Over the years I'd come to conflate the loss of the two of them, always feeling them entwined.

"I didn't hear from Tanner when Alex died. I've never been able to forgive him for that." Then I added softly, more to myself than Charlene, "And I had needed his words of comfort."

Sure, Tanner and I hadn't spoken in almost a year when Alex passed. And it was a crazy time for Tanner: mPulse had signed their first recording contract; the tabloids were full of stories about the band's outrageous behavior on the road; and in November it was reported that Tanner was to be a father. Still, I never doubted that I'd hear from him because he had loved Alex.

So, when the weeks went by after Alex's death with no word, I was increasingly hurt. How could Tanner have moved on so quickly? It wasn't until Tanner's marriage early the following year and the subsequent birth of his son that I finally accepted that our relationship was over.

Charlene wiped some wayward pizza sauce off her fingers with a napkin. "If the two of you weren't talking, are you sure he knew of your brother's death?" Charlene—the voice of reason.

"Oh, yes. Our best friends told him."

For a while I had continued to hear about Tanner from those friends: Alan Ritter, a fabulous musician with one foot in traditional American music and the other in rock, and his wife, Trish Dumont, a landscape painter. Alan didn't tour frequently anymore as he was now in high demand as a music producer. After Tanner and I separated they remained friends with both of us, for which I'd always been grateful.

Charlene shook her head. "I'm so sorry, Jessie. That's a lot of grief to have carried around for so many years. No wonder you were upset when you saw him."

"What's odd, Charlene, is that I had no intention of throwing water on him when I walked over. I simply couldn't pass up the opportunity to see him face-to-face." Perhaps if I hadn't spotted that photo of him in the paper and obsessed about him all day, I'd have been more rational.

"Well, I'm sure it's an encounter he won't forget. How many women can say that?" Charlene laughed and patted my hand as if now a co-conspirator in the misadventure. "By the way, how serious were the two of you?"

I looked down at my plate. An untouched slice of pizza rested on it. The sight of the congealing cheese made my stomach churn. But I knew it wasn't the food that was causing my heartburn. It was the answer to her question.

"A-house-filled-with-light,-happiness,-and-three-children serious."

FIVE

By the time I arrived home, I had a splitting headache. I grabbed two aspirins and a glass of water from my bathroom on the third floor and headed across the hall to my office.

Gulping down the tablets and setting the glass on an end table, I perched on the edge of my prized black leather Eames chair, an architectural icon that usually made me feel better just for being ensconced in it. Tonight, though, I sat on it with my head in my hands, elbows on knees, and felt sick, clammy . . . and mortified.

Why had I confronted Tanner? Our relationship was ancient history. Nothing would change. And I certainly didn't feel better—except for those few peculiar seconds hurling the water at him, when adrenaline had been in control. I didn't even know what had driven me to do it. Anger? Hurt? Temporary insanity?

I suppose in a way it was funny—or perhaps ironic. For sometimes I would fantasize that were Tanner and I to ever meet again, I would, of course, look stunning, be free from the musty memories and emotions of our past, and exude confidence and satisfaction with my life. Certainly not the harridan I had been this evening.

Sometimes reality sucks.

I rose from the chair and searched the bookshelves until I found an old photo album. Sitting back down, I paged through photographs from my undergraduate days in Chicago.

The first picture I found of Tanner was a solo shot. His hair was a little darker now, and shorter. But his eyes were the same—rich roasted-coffee brown, intense. No, maybe "passionate" was a better word. "Intense" might connote darkness, and there had been no darkness back then.

There were also a few more creases around those intelligent eyes now than in the picture. Laugh lines, I hoped.

Here were a couple of photos of us with friends, and another of just Tanner and me. A group of us had gone downtown one Saturday. I had talked everyone into taking an architectural sightseeing cruise up the Chicago River. Our friends had been good sports, though I was the only one listening to the guide. I had been quite happy studying the skyline punctuated with buildings designed by well-known twentieth-century architects. In one of the pictures, my long blond hair was whipping around in the wind and Tanner was trying to catch the ends and tuck the hair inside my jacket. We were both laughing.

In another photo, we were at a party celebrating the end of the fall term. Tanner had his arm around my waist and I was leaning into him. We made a good-looking couple: my five-foot-ten paired well with his height, my willowy figure (according to friends) suited his broad-shouldered, elongated body, and my blond hair contrasted nicely with his dark hair.

I traced his face with my forefinger. Had it been love at first sight?

I don't think so. After all, how can you love someone without first knowing their values, both big and small? How they treat people? How they deal with the rough patches in life? What their biases and blind spots are? Are they generous of heart, time, and money? Or, do they cheat on taxes, complain about restaurant service as an excuse to leave a paltry tip, and speed when driving because their time is more important than others' safety?

But those first months together had been exhilarating . . . and terrifying. Like jumping off a high cliff into unknown churning waves below—a leap full of adrenaline and blind faith.

Love had snuck in during the quiet moments. Sharing a sofa with Tanner and feeling his support, though no words were spoken. Admiring his work ethos. Respecting the people he surrounded himself with and marveling at the extent of his loyalty to them and theirs to him. Wanting to share the important—and not so important—things in my life with him. Knowing he trusted and respected me. Loving how he made me laugh, even when I was angry.

Several of our friends suggested that Tanner and I were a case of opposites attracting, but I never thought that. At heart, Tanner and I shared the same values and attitudes about people, work, life, and ethics. Our differences were in how we approached life. He was a dreamer, I was practical; he was an optimist, I was a realist; he was spontaneous, I was a planner; he operated from instinct, or maybe his life force, and I operated from my brain (well, except for architecture and Tanner, when I operated from my heart). Together we created balance and were better for it.

I continued going through the photos. They brought back such joyful memories, when everything about the other person was new and exciting, every word and gesture a marvelous revelation to be turned over, examined, and savored.

On one page, I had placed a short review of a performance by mPulse at a club in Chicago. As I reread the review my chest tightened. The music critic had been amazingly prescient about the future of this "up-and-coming" alt-rock trio.

I loved watching Tanner take command of a venue, especially with his latest band. Tanner would stand there for a moment collecting himself, spotlights blazing down on him, and then he would strike the first notes on his guitar and his life force would let loose, detonating goose bumps along my arms. Barely a few bars in and he had hooked the audience.

He stalked and prowled the stage like a panther. His bandmates were equally animated, leaping, strutting, moving to and away from each other all evening. It was like watching subatomic particles, in constant motion, being attracted or repulsed—a fitting image given that rock concerts are ultimately about energy and connection.

Oh, here was my favorite picture: an enlarged image of Tanner, sitting on a stool, with a guitar. His head was bent over the fingerboard, working on a new song. Something about the curve of his neck as he leaned forward had thrilled me. I remembered wanting to trace the curve with my fingers, just as I had wanted to stroke his beard in the paper this morning.

This photo had always been a compelling image; it became even more so after I encountered a quotation of Beethoven's: "Music is the mediator between the spiritual and the sensual life." In this image, Tanner manifested that musical bridge between the two worlds of the spiritual and the physical, the creative and the flesh.

The picture had sat on our dresser in L.A. alongside the teddy bears—all magical amulets to guarantee Tanner's safe return from his road trips.

In these photographs, Tanner and I were twenty-one. We were so happy—and so naïve. What was that line from Pearl Jam? "Is it so wrong to think that Love can keep us safe?"

I closed the album and placed it back on the shelf. Too many misgivings, too much sorrow.

And what made the memories all the worse was that I always experienced the pain of losing Tanner twice: once, when I physically left him, and earlier, when I'd lost him to drugs.

SIX

After tossing and turning all night, I forced myself to crawl out of bed in the morning and took a long shower to clean off the residue of last night's lunacy. Like Lady Macbeth, though, I wasn't able to scrub off yesterday's madness.

Tired, I opted not to go to the office that Saturday morning to play catch-up. Maybe after substantial infusions of caffeine I'd have a better chance of concentrating on work in the afternoon. Instead, I put on a pair of black yoga pants and a purple tunic T-shirt and wandered around the house, moving winter clothes into storage and pulling out spring and summer items. Tangled up in cobwebbed memories, though, I found myself sometimes going up or down staircases with nothing in my hands, having forgotten my destination.

I was on the second floor, heading up to my bedroom on the third level for more sweaters, when the doorbell rang.

Good ole Charlene. Checking on me after last night's fiasco.

Padding downstairs, barefoot, I felt a bit better, a little less harsh with myself. With time, I'd be able to stow this ludicrous event away in that crowded storeroom in my brain packed with cartons of other Tanner memorabilia. Maybe I could even laugh about it with Charlene this morning.

I opened the front door.

It wasn't Charlene.

I tried slamming the door but Tanner's elbow blocked it. The acrid taste of last night reappeared in my stomach.

"Go away, Tanner," I sputtered through the crack.

"Not until we talk."

I peeked out. When I'd last seen him in the restaurant, he had looked confused. Not now. This morning he was incensed, the usual warmth of his dark eyes turned hard and cold.

I had my left hand on the door jamb and my right on the inside doorknob, my body blocking the opening. Tanner could have easily shoved the door open but, ever the gentleman, he was waiting for an invitation.

He'd be a long time waiting. "I've got nothing to say."

"That's funny. Last night you seemed to have plenty to say—I just don't have a clue what you meant. I'm standing here until you let me in."

I considered my options. Maybe if Tanner got what he wanted, he'd leave.

"If you want an apology, then I'm sorry." But I couldn't meet his eyes.

He scoffed. "What I want is an explanation. I did a lot of foolish things back in those days, but I can't imagine what I did to your brother that would have triggered last night."

How could he not have a clue? My heart pounded at his callousness.

"I take my apology back." But the words sounded like those of a petulant five-year-old, hardly the high ground I was aiming for.

"Open this door, Jessie. I went to a lot of trouble to get your address."

My turn to mock. "What did you do? Call Trish?"

A vein popped out on his neck. Score one for me.

"Well, yes," he conceded. "But only because I thought you lived in Virginia and couldn't find you online."

When I first moved to the D.C. area, I had rented a townhouse in Virginia. How did he know that?

"Too bad your extensive efforts were wasted." Sarcasm added prickles to the words. "You had nothing to say when my brother died, so it's a little late to talk now."

The pressure Tanner had been exerting on the door lessened for a moment.

Aha, I had hit a nerve.

But when Tanner responded, his face and voice reflected confusion. "What are you talking about? I gave you my condolences."

"No, you didn't."

"Of course, I did!" he snapped.

I sagged against the door jamb, my anger and self-righteousness dissipating as I realized he was telling the truth.

"What do you mean?" I whispered.

"I'm talking about the letter I wrote when I heard about Alex."

I couldn't breathe.

Tanner realized something had changed and released his weight against the door.

I could barely get the words out. "I never received a letter."

"May I come in?" The sharpness had vanished from his voice.

I stepped away from the door. He turned back toward a taxi idling at the curb, which I hadn't noticed, and motioned for it to leave.

When Tanner faced me again, he looked stricken, his face mirroring what I felt. Whatever we thought we knew with such conviction wasn't true.

I pivoted and headed down the hall to the stairs. Tanner closed the door behind him and followed without a word.

On the second floor, I took a seat in the living room on the sofa in front of the rear floor-to-ceiling windows and motioned for him to take the longer sofa at a right angle to mine. The sunshine from the windows behind me would illuminate his face but leave mine in shadow.

I tucked my feet under me, making myself smaller, less of a target for whatever he had to say. Tanner, on the other hand, seemed to expand as he sat down, taking over the sofa the way he took over a stage.

He looked wonderful—except for the fresh pain etched into his face. He had on dark jeans, a luscious navy sweater (cashmere, perhaps?), and a brown leather bomber jacket. Briefly, I wondered if he had dressed with the intent of distracting me. Well, he wouldn't find me swooning just because he had rocker clothes on.

I said nothing. He had come to my house. He could begin the conversation. Besides, my body was still reeling from what he'd said.

In the silence, he swiped a hand through his hair, a tell-tale sign he was rattled.

I wasn't any calmer, though, my hands clasped so tightly I was afraid the fingernails would draw blood.

"Jessie." This morning my name sounded bittersweet on his lips. "When Trish told me about Alex's death, I was devastated. I knew how close you two were. How close your family was.

"My immediate reaction was to go see you, to tell you how sorry I was, for you and your parents. But Trish said you had already flown home for the funeral. With time to reflect, I decided you might not want to see me anyway . . . since I was still using."

Yes. All the touring had taken a toll on Tanner. He'd always needed solitude after performances to reenergize. The downtime wasn't a nicety, though, but a necessity for his well-being. It was how he rekindled his creativity, restored his energy, and grounded himself.

Instead, what he had to look forward to on the road was mind-numbing and bone-wearying travel, repeated day after day, week after week, and always in the company of others. Under the pressures of touring, his energy reserves had dried up, sacrificed to an insatiable audience. And rather than deal with the problem, Tanner had taken an uncharacteristic short cut. For when it came to his music, Tanner had always worked long and hard. There had been no short cuts. But on the road, he eventually resorted to amphetamines to ignite the fire needed to perform every night.

While the drugs might have seemed like a quick solution for coping with the demands of the road, over time the quick fix became the bigger problem. The last eleven months we were together I'd watched as amphetamines and alcohol took hold of Tanner. He needed the amphetamines to get up and the alcohol to smooth out the descent; it became an unending cycle of highs and lows.

I'd tried everything I could think of to help, my efforts escalating as Tanner's drug use escalated. I even attended Al-Anon meetings weekly, sometimes more. But the drugs had a far more powerful hold on him than any words, alternatives, or future I could offer.

Finally, I realized that I couldn't let his addiction control me as well, so, during Christmas break of my second year in school, while Tanner was on a road trip, I'd packed up my things and left . . . but always feeling I had abandoned him.

Simply thinking about the past made my chest tighten. All the losses—Tanner's health, our relationship, my brother—had been unbearable at times. The weight of the grief sometimes pressed so heavily on my chest at night that I couldn't breathe and would get up from bed to sleep upright in a chair.

I inhaled deeply and refocused on the man sitting in front of me, concentrating on his energy. As Tanner became addicted, the drugs had wreaked havoc on his life force. Sometimes I could barely feel it, weakened as it was by competing stimulants and depressants, his body literally at war with itself, ricocheting from one extreme to the other to find the bright spot.

Sitting here now, though, I felt his internal fire burning strong and steady—as when I had first known him. So strong, in fact, that I scooted back on the couch, worried his energy might make me shaky given that I was no longer used to it.

"I wrote a letter instead. Telling you what your brother meant to me. That I saw Alex's love for life reflected in you. And how sad it was that he couldn't be there to watch you flourish in your career."

He paused for a moment as though replaying the letter in his mind—like a song he might have written.

"I never got a letter." Sorrow and disappointment seeped into my voice. I grabbed a nearby throw pillow and hugged it to my body, like a shield.

Tanner sounded almost as upset. "It's my fault. You didn't leave your new address and I was too proud to ask Trish for it." But resentment had also crept into his words.

I didn't defend myself. There was plenty of blame and guilt to go around. It had been a cowardly thing for me to do, moving out while he was on a three-week tour.

And the reason I hadn't left a forwarding address? If he had visited me, still abusing drugs, and asked me to return, I would have. And I wouldn't have had the strength to leave him a second time.

Even after moving out, I continued to attend Al-Anon for another year-and-a-half—the irony of my own addiction not escaping me.

"I took the letter to your studio on campus," he explained, finally getting his voice under control. "I put it on your drafting table so it would be the first thing you saw when you got back to campus."

"There . . . there was no letter on my table when I got back." I could barely whisper.

His face paled, his dark eyes and beard standing out in stark contrast. "I don't understand. Your classmate said she would make sure you got it."

A chill went down my spine and I felt cold in my bones.

"Which classmate?" I asked softly.

"You know, that woman who—" He was at a loss of words for how to describe her.

"Do you mean Dana Reardon?" My voice was an octave lower as I tried to control my anger.

Dana had always been fascinated with Tanner, flirting with him when he'd stopped by the studio to bring me dinner or a snack before a gig so I could keep working. She had never understood boundaries. While the flirting hadn't bothered me, it had exasperated Tanner. He thought it showed a lack of respect for me and he always turned away quickly to engage someone else.

"Yes." He nodded vehemently. "She said she'd take care of the letter."

"I guess she did," I said with such acerbity that I wouldn't have been surprised if an ulcer had formed in my mouth.

His hand was flying through his hair. "She didn't give it to you? Why? I told her it was about your brother."

I shrugged my shoulders. I was sick to my stomach that someone had deprived me of something I had needed so desperately. "Who knows? I'm sure she had a rationalization for her behavior—she always did. By that time, she knew we had broken up. Maybe she figured I didn't need to be reminded of the past, even if it was a sympathy letter." Or, more likely, she had relished the power of having deprived us of the communication.

"How could I have been so stupid?" Tanner asked. "I should have known better than to trust her. But then Dana shouldn't have been involved in the first place. The fault was my foolish pride—I hadn't wanted Trish to know you didn't trust me with your address."

His shoulders slumped against the sofa. "How can I apologize for my stupidity?"

"Well, it's not any worse than my ambushing you in public last night. When I walked over to your table, it wasn't my intention to embarrass you. But . . . something snapped."

Tanner forced a smile. "It could have been worse."

That was generous. "Do I need to write a letter of apology to your friends so they needn't fear going out to dinner with you?" I responded, half-kidding.

He shook his head. "Not friends, colleagues—with the organization I was in D.C. for. No need to apologize. They'll have a great tale to replay at dinner parties, thanks to you. With each telling, the event will become more epic. A thwarted groupie. A jilted mistress."

"A stalker ignoring the many restraining orders," I chimed in.

He snorted. "An entire pitcher of water. No, hot coffee. Third degree burns. Scarred for life. Probably deserved it—you know rock stars."

We shared a smile.

Then Tanner stopped smiling. "Is there anything I can do to make up for my mistake?"

I hesitated, embarrassed by my neediness. "Can you . . . can you tell me what Alex meant to you?"

Tanner is a wonderful wordsmith and storyteller, two of the reasons he's such a great songwriter. In just a few lines, he can tell a story, color a moment, recreate a memory, evoke a sizzling emotion, or offer a sense of commonality and community for someone feeling alone. By finding the emotional heart of a story he shares in your sorrow, your joy, and your anguish.

That morning Tanner gave me the healing words I had needed so long ago. How much he enjoyed knowing Alex. How he looked forward to having him as a brother-in-law. How impressed he was with Alex's dedication and career. How smart he was, how compassionate. How similar the two of us were—not only in appearance but in our humor, focus, and sense of purpose.

Then he paused, his expression uncertain.

"Go ahead, Tanner. Say what's on your mind."

"I'm afraid it'll sound selfish." After a long sigh, though, he continued, "When I heard the news from Trish, one of the first things that hit me was that I would never have the chance to regain Alex's trust, to redeem myself in his eyes.

"You may not know this, but Alex kept in touch after you left. The first time he phoned, he said that you'd told him about the drugs and that he was disappointed in me. Yet he continued to check in, asking if there was anything he could do for me or anyone he could refer me to for the substance abuse. He told me that when I was ready, he would be there. He never said 'if' but always 'when'—as though he never doubted me.

"Alex's belief in me is one of the reasons I advocate treatment for nonviolent drug offenders, instead of jail. I try to pay his kindness forward."

I couldn't breathe. I hadn't known any of this. But that was my brother. Tanner may have hurt me but Alex would try his damnedest to help, knowing I'd loved Tanner.

Clutching the pillow now like a life raft, I started blubbering. I had waited a long time to hear Tanner's words of consolation. As I repeatedly wiped my eyes with my tunic, it became almost as waterlogged as Tanner's shirt from the night before.

Tanner sat quietly on the sofa, letting me grieve. But as my long-held emotions about the past started to catch up with reality, my heart began to lighten.

When I had myself under control, Tanner said, "I don't mean to make you sad, Jessie. I've been clean for more than seven years, but not a day goes by that I don't think about your brother's offers of help. And I'll always regret disappointing him."

I met his eyes. "No, I'm glad you told me. And I think Alex would be impressed by the person you've become and all the good work you do for others. When he and I talked initially about your addiction, he offered to come out to California to defend my honor—an offer which seemed to include doing bodily harm." Tanner's eyebrows shot up. "I'm so glad he got past it."

"He did say on more than one occasion he should kick my butt, but I thought that was a figure of speech." Tanner started to laugh.

I couldn't help but laugh as well—at Tanner's naïveté. "Nope, Alex meant it. Be glad I have excellent powers of persuasion or your nose might not be quite so perfect."

Had I just said that?

Now it was my turn to apologize. "I'm sorry, too, that I doubted you would write. I knew Trish had told you of Alex's passing. But I wasn't thinking straight and so much was going on in your life just then—you know, the recording contract . . . and everything. Not hearing from you didn't totally surprise me, but it hurt."

Our separation (which I never imagined would be permanent), the tabloid stories, followed by the announcement of his child-to-be, the marriage to his first wife, and my brother's death, had all taken place within eighteen months. For years afterward, all I'd done was grieve. I had never been able to separate out the individual strands of my sorrow, to make peace with each event. It was all one big muddle of emotions I hadn't been able to push through.

My body sagged in relief. Maybe now I could finally tease my brother out from all the other entanglements. Maybe I could finally have closure, knowing that Tanner had not forgotten Alex and that Alex had forgiven Tanner.

Lost in my thoughts, I surfaced to find Tanner glancing warily around. Did he think some male was about to lumber downstairs at the sound of my tears?

"Uh, am I keeping you from anything?" he asked, rubbing the back of his neck.

"Not really. I was feeling sorry for myself this morning, just moping around the house. You know, the anticlimax after an exhausting performance the night before."

He grinned. That was one of the things I'd loved about Tanner—he always got my humor.

And the truth was that I wasn't ready for him to leave. The conversation about Alex had been a gift. Maybe we could be civil to one another despite the past—at least for a little while longer.

"Would you like something to drink?"

With a sigh of relief, Tanner answered, "Coffee would be great."

SEVEN

I rose from the sofa and Tanner followed, finally taking off his jacket. I took it from him and hung it on the back of a dining room chair.

Fingering the scrumptiously soft coat made my imagination race.

Maybe he'd forget the jacket when he returned to the hotel. This coat could be the compounded interest on the favorite cobalt-blue shirt of his I'd been tempted to take when I'd left but hadn't—not wanting to turn my leaving into a pathetic breakup trope. Still, there were many sleepless nights afterwards when I had ached for something that would give me a physical connection with him.

Tanner took a seat at the breakfast counter, while I poured water into the coffeemaker—with a trembling hand—and added the ground beans. Let's hope I wouldn't do something stupid, like spill coffee on the counter—or worse, on him.

As the coffee started to drip, its familiar aroma soothing, I placed a plate of biscotti on the counter in front of Tanner to ward off lunchtime hunger pangs.

I had just pulled two mugs from the cabinet when my home phone rang. I shook my head at Tanner to indicate that I wasn't going to pick up.

The answering machine clicked on. "Jessie? This is Stephanie? We just got the report back on the radon test—"

Her voice was frantic. I put the mugs down and picked up the phone, turning my back on Tanner as I walked into the living room.

"Hey, Stephanie. What's going on?"

"The report came back and the condo's radon level is elevated?"

That didn't surprise me. Radon is a naturally occurring radioactive gas released from the soil. Most of us are exposed to it daily when we go outside, but the gas disperses rapidly in air so it's not an issue. When a house is built on a concrete slab, though, with no crawl space underneath to provide an escape for the gas, radon can enter the house through settlement cracks in the slab. Once in the house, the gas is confined and the levels become elevated. In high amounts, radon can cause lung cancer.

Because I hadn't seen any signs of remediation on the interior or exterior of the first-floor unit, I had tried to prepare Stephanie for this possibility.

"I'm sorry, Stephanie. But it can be remediated, usually at the condo association's expense. Your agent should call the association's management company, tell them the results, and then find out if the association is responsible for the remediation."

I glanced at Tanner as I paced. He was pouring the brewed coffee into the mugs just fine.

"Have you done the walk-through with the home inspector yet?" I asked.

"No. That's at two."

"Before you worry too much about this, see what he has to say. If he finds equipment that needs to be replaced, you may want to rethink things. But in case you decide to move forward, I'll email you some information on radon later."

"Thanks so much, Jessie. You're right. We'll wait until we have all the information before we . . . panic?"

I laughed. "I'm glad you still have your sense of humor. Things will work out—eventually."

I walked back into the kitchen, replaced the phone, and then took a seat in front of the second mug Tanner had placed on the counter. "Sorry about that."

"Moonlighting as a real estate agent now?"

He was kidding—Tanner knew very well where my passion lay.

"No. Still love the day job. That was the receptionist at my office.

She and her boyfriend are buying their first place. I'm just trying to help them make an informed decision."

"She's lucky. So where do you work now?"

I took a big sip of coffee. "Downtown, at Pearce & Associates."

"Do you like the work?"

"Love it. Particularly the variety. Primarily institutional buildings, like campus buildings, libraries, and churches, as well as one-of-a-kind residences." And, to let him know I had done fine without him, I added, "A couple of years ago my boss, Evan, placed me in charge of the architecture staff—Director, Architecture and Design."

His face erupted in a smile. "That's wonderful. Congratulations! 'Director' sounds so . . . responsible."

"Thanks. I enjoy the role and I'm good at it." It had been tough initially, though, as others had been at the company longer than I. "But it's definitely not as glamorous a job title as 'Rock Star.'"

He gave me a dirty look.

I grinned, happy I could still needle him.

And, since I wasn't above boasting, I continued, "In fact, Evan and I have talked about my becoming a partner."

"Wow. That's great."

Too quickly, a creased brow replaced his congratulatory smile. "But didn't you talk about having your own firm?"

Damn him. The comment stung—I had wanted that at one time. Why had I needed to brag? Now I had to justify my choices. I dunked a biscotti in the coffee and took a bite, giving me time to consider my answer.

"I've had eleven years to learn the realities of the business. I couldn't ask for a better mentor or a company with a better reputation."

My bland response was intended to squelch more questions.

Tanner, too, crunched a bit of cookie. More than likely, he was parsing his words as carefully as I was—not that we were being entirely successful. There was an edge to this conversation that hadn't been there while we were talking about Alex. But why would I expect otherwise, given how things had ended?

"Every so often I ask Trish how you're doing," he said. "She always tells me you're fine, but never gives details. It's good to hear you're happy in your career."

Trish had done the right thing. She wasn't an intermediary.

"So, are you married?" he continued, glancing at my ring finger.

Trying for casual, I answered, "No."

"Have you ever been married?"

I didn't remember him being so annoying.

"No."

"Why not?"

"Why have you been married multiple times?"

He laughed. "You're right. I was being rude. But I am curious—why haven't you married?"

"Just hasn't happened." I got up to refill his empty cup.

"But you've had relationships?"

"Not as many as you, if the tabloids are the least bit factual."

The barb didn't faze him.

In fact, a slight smile hovered at the corners of his mouth.

"So why aren't you married?" he pressed.

As I handed him the mug, my fingers brushed his. The tips felt as if they'd passed through flames, the heat spreading up my arm.

Disconcerted, I responded too hastily. "None of the relationships seemed particularly . . . sponge-worthy."

He chortled, catching the reference to an episode of Seinfeld, one of his favorite TV shows.

That answer, however, was only partially true.

I'd often thought that one of the reasons so many musicians used drugs was that the world must seem a dull and drab place once you've stood on stage with adrenaline coursing through your body. And that was how I felt in my early days with Tanner. No one else had ever inspired the same passion and joy.

"What's the real reason?" he pressed.

"Are you married? If not, are you dating?" I countered.

Tanner accepted the challenge. "I've been married twice and divorced twice. It's not a great record. Besides, I don't want to introduce anyone to Jason unless I'm serious."

Jason. His son. My stomach did a somersault. Hunger pains or not, the biscotti wasn't helping.

"At least I have a fighting chance of getting it right now that I'm clean. Your turn."

From the glint in his eyes, I knew it was a dare. Well, my response would be as evasive as his.

"I date. But I'm a bit agnostic about love."

His look of amusement evaporated. "Jessie—"

"How old is your son?"

Not that I didn't know for certain, thanks again to Dana.

I had been in my studio at school, working all night on my final design project—a performing and visual arts complex—for the juried review later in the day. The project was the culmination of my three-year master's program.

Mid-morning, Dana had approached. "Have you heard the news?"

"What news?" I asked, looking up, bone-tired and bleary-eyed from the last push to complete the drawings.

Waiting a beat to make sure she had my attention, Dana replied, "Teddie Daulton's wife just had a baby. A son."

Her words pierced my body like a thousand shards of glass. I wanted to crumple to the ground and roll up in a ball to contain the grief and keep from bleeding out.

Instead, I replied, "Good for him," and turned back to my drawing.

As Dana walked away, her drooping shoulders shouting disappointment at not getting a rise out of me, my hand automatically continued to fill in the shadows on the site plan cast by the interconnected buildings so that the rendering would read three-dimensionally. My body and heart, however, had gone numb.

The birth of Tanner's son—a graduation present for completing my master's degree.

"Jason will be eleven in June," Tanner answered. "I spend as much time with him as I can when I'm not on the road." As he spoke of his son, Tanner's face and voice brightened.

"I always thought you would make a great father, Tanner." Whoops. Heat crawled up my neck. To distract him, I asked if he had any pictures.

Tanner smiled self-consciously but pulled out his cell phone. "I think he looks a little like me."

I examined the pictures closely. His son's coloring was similar but his hair was straighter—Tanner's had a slight wave to it, looking perfectly styled within minutes of taking a shower.

"He definitely has your eyes." I would have known immediately he was Tanner's child. Gut-punched by the idea, I almost dropped the phone. "The girls are going to fall head-over-heels for him. You're going to have your hands full."

His eyes widened. "You think?"

"Oh, yeah. Trust me. Though it seems like poetic justice, doesn't it?" I laughed. Karma could be a bitch.

At first, he didn't get my joke, and then he looked embarrassed. "I guess I need to have a talk with my son."

"You'll need several."

This time he grinned wryly, his mouth slightly twisted. "Great. Won't that be fun? Can parents have their pasts legally sealed from their kids? I haven't been the best role model."

"Maybe that's your hook?"

He snorted. "Then the conversations should go really well."

I handed Tanner back his phone. "Is Jason musical?"

"Not so far. Maybe he'll be more like his mother and go into business."

His first wife had worked on the financial side of the company that had given mPulse its first recording contract. I grabbed another biscotti.

Tanner's voice turned serious. "That period was one of the darkest in my life. I was trying to fill the hole you'd left, and with the band's first taste of success we were taking increasingly foolish risks. Your brother's death, though, made me try to do the right thing at the time."

My stomach corkscrewed on the cookie, even though I had no idea what he was talking about.

Seeing my blank expression, Tanner leaned towards me, almost as if he were trying to cushion me from his next words—so he wouldn't have to speak so loudly, so the words wouldn't wound quite so deeply.

"I married my first wife, Nadine, because she was pregnant, not because I loved her. Five years older than I, her biological clock was ticking. Unfortunately, I didn't know I was to be the sperm donor. She'd told me she was on birth control but wasn't. Unbelievably stupid, right? She knew I didn't love her, but I tried to do the right thing for Jason—to give him a family."

I couldn't speak. I believe Tanner was trying to offer me some comfort for that time long ago, but the words slashed at my heart anyway. He hadn't loved her, yet he had married her. Breathing was nearly impossible.

"Because of Jason I tried abstaining from drugs a couple of times but it never lasted. And the marriage ultimately couldn't endure Nadine's lies or my drug use, nor was it a healthy environment for Jason. But I am so grateful for him."

It felt like a confession. Did he want absolution? Well, I couldn't grant him that. Even though we hadn't talked in over a year, his marriage had hit me hard as I had still felt connected to him. But the marriage severed that link—plus, it made me realize how stupid I was to have expected otherwise.

But his son was innocent. "You know, Tanner, I'm glad something good came out of that tumultuous time and that you've been able to enjoy a relationship with Jason. It sounds like he's the one constant in your life."

His concerned coffee-brown eyes went all puppy-dog soft. "You know, he has been. I hadn't thought of it that way. I disappointed so many people when I was on drugs, but I tried hard to maintain a relationship with Jason."

I wonder how my brother would feel about inspiring Tanner to do the honorable thing by marrying Nadine, while his sister waited foolishly in the wings. That was a whole lot of irony.

Yet Tanner had tried to make a go of it for his son and that mattered a great deal.

I put down my cup and rose. It was time to get Tanner back to his hotel. I was exhausted—by his presence, by his unnerving life force, by the onslaught of regret and sorrow that came with each new topic, and by the inescapable realization that our paths had diverged years ago and that we no longer shared anything in common except old memories, hurt, and disappointment.

Tanner rose as well, carrying his cup to the sink, the two of us gingerly slipping past one another.

I was about to offer him a ride downtown, when Tanner asked, "Do you have time to show me your house?"

EIGHT

What?

My knee-jerk reaction was *No*. Or, more precisely, *Hell, no*. Certain design aspects of my house might look a tad too familiar to Tanner. On the other hand, I loved my place. It made me happy when

I was home and cheerful when I was on my way home. Maybe he'd forgotten about that house we'd talked about building so long ago.

Pride overcame misgivings and architecture overcame exhaustion.

"Actually, this place was a carriage house."

One eyebrow shot up. "Really?"

"I'll show you." I retrieved my laptop from the coffee table in the living room and settled back at the counter. This time, though, I sat farther away, the computer between us on the counter. I might be prideful, but I wasn't stupid. I didn't want his energy worming its way into my cells and doing who knows what.

I pulled up some pictures of the original structure. The carriage house had been small, a mere two-and-a-half bays wide and two-stories high, and had been sold off from the original estate decades before. It wasn't much to look at, except as an oddity. The lot it sat on, though, while narrow, was deep.

"I bought the place three years ago. The house hadn't been lived in for two years and, as you can see, was in terrible shape. Burst pipes, broken windows, water-damaged floors. I considered razing it but the wood exterior was basically intact and I liked the idea of giving new life to a unique neighborhood structure."

He studied the photos. "It's amazing. I can see those original bones in the exterior."

My heart fluttered, surprised by how much those simple words meant. "I gutted the interior, added a third floor, and extended the back of the building." I had also enclosed the rear with floor-to-ceiling glass (which was obvious, of course) but didn't mention it because a window wall had been a primary element of the house

Tanner and I had once dreamt of building.

He looked up from the laptop, his eyes meeting mine. "Did you enjoy renovating the house?"

"Do you enjoy playing the guitar?"

Those new laugh lines around his eyes crinkled. For a moment, we shared a pleasure, an understanding of what made the other person happy.

"Still want a tour?" I asked.

"Of course!"

As we stood up, I explained, "Although the house is three levels, the square footage is twenty-five percent less than an average new house. To make it feel larger, I've used a variety of strategies to create the 'illusion of space.'"

We headed back downstairs. Standing next to Tanner in the foyer, I was overcome by a sense of déjà vu, wrapping me in memories of time together in our old apartment. The feeling was so sudden, so unnerving, that I felt dizzy. Inhaling sharply, I glanced over at Tanner but he seemed unfazed, merely glancing around curiously.

I, though, felt caught between the past and the present, a dream and reality. Maybe Tanner, with all his energy, was a black hole warping time and space.

I quickly put on my architect's hat before he could sense something was off. "I started here at the front door with my tricks. This hallway could have felt tight with the staircase on the left. But the floor-to-ceiling windows at the rear open the space up, making the passageway brighter and more expansive. And by making guests walk to the rear of the house to access the staircase, the view into the garden enhances the sense of depth.

Tanner nodded and turned his head as I pointed out more details.

"I also recessed the guest bathroom and the coat closet here to make the foyer feel more spacious, as if belonging in a larger house."

Tanner chuckled. "You're like a magician."

I escorted him down the hallway and he wandered into the guest room on the right while I stayed in the hall. Unlike the animated, pulsating atomic particles that Tanner and his bandmates mimicked on stage, our movements felt stilted, as if we were trying to maintain a neutral distance, moving in prescribed orbits to make sure we didn't collide—because how awkward would that be?

Stepping back into the hall, Tanner stopped at the windows to gaze out. "Great yard. From out front I thought it would be pocket-sized."

"One of the reasons I bought this place."

We took the stairs back up to the second floor, me in front. Suddenly I realized that my butt had to be about even with Tanner's gaze. Why had I put on these tight lycra yoga pants this morning? I hastened up the remaining steps.

At the landing, I sneaked a peek at Tanner and was mortified at the sly smile on his face.

Damn him. This man knew me intimately—from my body to my soul and all the places in between. But that had been when we were a couple, lovers; it was disconcerting that someone could still know me at that level when we no longer shared any part of our lives. That knowledge, that familiarity, made him dangerous, made it too easy to slip into old habits.

Twelve years ago there had been everything between us; now there was nothing. There could be no fling, no one-night stand with

Tanner. He had been my forever man, not a dalliance.

I averted my face and started talking about safe things. "As you'll notice, the living room is completely open to the staircase. By eliminating walls and hallways on the second and third floors, the rooms appear larger."

"Smart."

We moved onto the kitchen-dining room area. "I would have liked an island here but the room was too narrow. Islands are great additions to kitchen spaces because they have heft to them. They anchor kitchens the way fireplaces anchor living rooms.

"I solved the problem by using this two-level peninsula with extra deep cabinets on the kitchen side for prep work and a taller, shallower counter on the dining room side for eating at." I can talk with guests hanging out at the counter or the dining table if I'm entertaining or have a view of the backyard when I'm alone.

We skirted on past the dining table to the rear windows. "As on the first floor, I've used the outdoors to visually extend the living space on each of the upper levels." I pointed to the deck just outside, used for grilling, with steps leading down to a patio off the guest bedroom for dining and entertaining. "On the third floor, I've tucked a balcony under the eaves at the rear of my office for rainy days."

"It's like being in a tree house," Tanner remarked.

While the words sounded pleasant enough, his tone had shifted—almost accusatory. Having lived together for two years plus, I could still read Tanner's body language and inflection, elements too personal to have changed much over time.

Shoot. Had he recalled more than I thought he would about the house we had talked about building? He no longer seemed amused by my spatial wizardry.

I shot him a look, but he wouldn't meet my eyes.

To defuse the situation, I ignored his tone. "That was the idea. And the view is even better from the third floor."

I let Tanner go up the stairs first this time. The view of his rangy body, though, didn't make me feel better. The atmosphere in the house had changed.

The last room on the tour was my office. We walked over to the glass sliding doors that led to the balcony. To the right of the door was an old-fashioned drafting table. I always felt more creative working on its sloped wooded surface than sketching at the worktop in my office. I'd perch on the swivel stool and look out on the backyard for inspiration. I'd bought this table for our apartment in L.A. so I could work at home and spend more time with Tanner when he was in town.

I didn't mention the table. I also didn't point out any more of the tricks I had incorporated on this level, such as the vaulted ceiling.

Tanner had become quiet, withdrawn. A deep "V" lodged between his eyebrows. My breathing faltered. For the first time, I had no idea what he was feeling. I only knew it had to do with my house.

I needed air. I opened the doors quickly and stepped out onto the balcony. Tanner followed more slowly.

I stood clutching the rail, the spring air bracing. Tanner remained silent, his gaze directed inward, not outward to the lime-green garden waking from winter. A blank mask stretched across his face, his body stiff.

After an uncomfortable pause, Tanner finally turned to me, his knowing eyes drilling into mine. "It's a wonderful house, Jessie. Open, unexpected, light-filled, innovative, comfortable yet elegant."

But the delight that should have been behind those words wasn't there. The tone was more grudging than pleased, and his usually generous mouth was pinched as though spitting out soured words.

I stiffened, anger pricking at the back of my neck. The attributes he mentioned reflected many of the characteristics we had talked about for our home. But, as far as I knew, he didn't have a copyright on those adjectives.

I coolly replied, "Tell me about where you live." I wasn't going to apologize for what I'd built or feel sorry for him. No doubt he lived in some fabulous abode.

When he finally replied, the tension in his shoulders and torso remained, but there was less bitterness in his voice. "My place was built in the late 1930s. It had more room than I needed but also had the privacy I wanted. Plus, the site could accommodate a lap pool."

I nodded. Growing up in Seattle, Tanner felt recharged near water—whether he was on it, in it, or just around it. That was why our dream house had needed a view of water. When I'd asked him once whether he preferred the ocean or a lake, he had surprised me by favoring the lake; he said there was too much power in the ocean to contend with every day. I'd almost laughed. I knew exactly how exhausting that was, given his pounding life force.

Distracted by my thoughts, I said the first thing that popped into my head. "I'm surprised you live in an older home. Somehow I imagined you in a contemporary residence."

His pupils shrank to mere pin points. "I didn't think I could be happy in one you hadn't designed."

His words struck astonishingly fast and hard.

I punched back. "You could have had any architect you wanted.

Any house you desired."

"I didn't want just any house." Then, with a voice as cold and hard as steel, he said, "And I can't believe you built ours."

There were many things I'd done wrong during our time together, but how could he fault me for what I had done after we separated?

"This is not our house. Besides, you know my aesthetic. Why would you think this house would be different?" Then another thought struck me. "Or, when you asked for a tour, were you trying to confirm your suspicions?" I was hoping my words would wound.

"And since when do I need your permission to build a house? You didn't need my permission when you got married." And he certainly hadn't asked permission before using drugs or having a child.

Tanner widened his stance in response. He reminded me of a porcupine. I wouldn't have been surprised if the hackles on his back were up, ready to let loose their quills.

"You were the one who left," he growled, as if that explained everything.

"Then why care about this house?" I narrowed my eyes at him.

Instead of firing quills at me, however, Tanner deflated, shaking his head in confusion. "Maybe because I wanted our house as much as you did?"

I understood. My house was important to me, not only as refuge and comfort, but also as a physical reminder of our one-time dream. It was all a bit ironic, though. I felt he had "moved on" in his relationships and he seemed to feel that I had "moved on" from one of our shared dreams.

We stood in silence for a moment on the balcony. From the pain carved into his face, I expected that he, too, was trying to bind his wounds, still raw after all this time.

My heart ached. I would never have imagined a time when words would become weapons between us. We'd been able to talk about my brother without antagonism, but now our history, the ever-present hurt, and the mutual accusations—both spoken and unspoken—kept intruding. I guessed there would always be friction between the ways things had once been and what they were now.

But enough was enough.

"This was a bad idea," I said. "I can drop you back at your hotel if you want, as I need to stop by my office anyway. Give me a minute to change. You can stay here or I'll meet you downstairs."

Tanner remained, wordless, on the balcony.

I hurried into my bedroom, grabbed some clothes from the closet, and scooted directly from the closet into the bathroom, shutting the door to the landing.

I washed my face and then changed quickly—jeans, silk lilac blouse, and navy blazer. I didn't want Tanner wandering around my office and stumbling on old photo albums. I also put on some lip gloss and a little mascara—plus some dangly earrings. Tanner had always kidded me about the gypsy-like earrings I wore, but they were the spice to my otherwise classic clothing preferences.

Finished, I crossed the landing back to the office.

Tanner wasn't there.

As I started down the steps, I heard rustling in my bedroom.

Damn. He had clearly not been invited there.

Fury battled with mortification as I edged into my own room.

Tanner was standing in front of my dresser, staring. Perched atop the dresser were the remaining ten teddy bears he had brought back from his road trips. In addition to watching over me while he was on tour and proclaiming his safe return home, the bears had also symbolized . . . celebratory homecoming sex. And those bears were still the last thing I looked at every night before I went to bed.

I wanted to yell at Tanner not to touch them. I didn't want my adored companions tainted with resentment or memories of how different things were now. The bears had always been a comfort, never a sorrow, reminding me only of the good times.

He picked one up. "Chicago." He went through the same routine with each one. As he touched them, I clutched the stair railing behind my back to steady myself, gnawing at the inside of my lower lip until I thought it would bleed. Placing the last bear back down, he scanned the room.

I knew what he was looking for but said nothing. He would have to ask.

"Where's Teddy Seattle?"

Warily, I replied, "Teddy Seattle resides in my office—along with other mementos."

The air in the room sparked with tension. Those damn bears manifested too much of our past. It was like walking in a field of high-power transmission towers; I felt the electricity buzzing along the back of my neck, the hairs standing on end. Were I to touch anything metal, I'd be fried.

And, dammit, it was my *bedroom*. I needed to get him out.

Instead, he walked over to the windows, his back to me. Once again I couldn't breathe. His larger-than-life personality monopolized the space and there simply wasn't room for air. He and my small house—vaulted ceilings notwithstanding—were not suited to one another.

Suddenly turning, he covered the distance between us in three strides and broke the unspoken rules of engagement we had established earlier. He was now so close I could feel the warmth of his breath on my skin and could almost taste his mouth. His brown eyes challenged me.

"Are you happy, Jessie?"

What did he want to hear? That I couldn't live without him? Obviously, I could. Or would he rather hear the opposite—that I never thought of him—so he could rid himself of guilt?

"I . . . I'm grateful for everything in my life, Tanner."

He stared hard at me. My breathing faltered. His eyes were dark, hooded. I sensed the intensity in his body, just as I had sensed it that first day we had coffee, when I had willingly let it ensnare me. Now, however, I felt like a small animal caught in the glare of a hawk, afraid to move.

After what seemed an eternity, I stepped away.

"C'mon, Tanner. I'm sure you've got things to do."

NINE

I grabbed my purse off the console at the top of the staircase on the second floor while Tanner, regrettably, remembered his jacket in the dining room. I descended the steps quickly, Tanner in my wake.

What a relief to be outside. The tension that had been ready to ignite in my bedroom started to ease out of my body.

On the way to my car, Tanner stopped, turned, and took a last look at my house. Maybe in apology he said, "I like how you incorporated the third level into the existing building. It seems part of the carriage house, yet distinct."

"Good. That's how it's supposed to read."

Now that we were out of that lightning rod of a house we could be civil again. Turning back to my car, I saw my neighbor across the street leaving his house. He had his workout bag with him. I hoped he was in a hurry.

Spotting me, he waved and I waved back. When he noticed Tanner, however, he dropped the bag by his car and crossed the street, not even bothering to look at traffic. His face registered recognition—and surprise.

As the man approached, Tanner stepped in closer to my side.

Great.

The two men couldn't have looked more different physically. Nick was a couple of inches shorter than Tanner and had an athlete's build, while Tanner's long-limbed build disguised his strength. And in contrast to Tanner's dark brown hair, Nick's was Southern California blond, appropriate since he'd grown up there.

As the two men sized each other up, I mentally rolled my eyes at the schoolyard demonstration.

"Nick," I said, jumping in, "this is Teddie Daulton, a college friend. Teddie, this is Nick Parris."

They shook hands, more aggressively than necessary.

Nick flashed a smile. "Nice to meet you, Teddie. I'm a big fan." Then he had to add, "I'm surprised Jessie hasn't mentioned you."

Tanner's eyes narrowed. "If you know Jessie at all, you know how private she is."

The score was tied.

"What brings you to town?" Nick asked.

"I was meeting with members of Congress. What do you do?"

"I work at a think tank. Socio-economic issues."

"Impressive," Tanner conceded.

That searing heat was creeping up my neck yet again. The exchange had the potential for getting testy—which was rather funny, given my history with both men. "Well, I don't want to keep you, Nick. You're obviously on the way to the gym."

Then Nick just had to say it. "Are we still on for next Sunday night?"

"Yes," I said tersely.

"Indian or Chinese?"

"Chinese's fine." I didn't need a reminder of last night's disaster at an Indian restaurant.

"And are we good for this Monday morning as usual?"

"Sure." By now I could hardly speak around my clenched jaw.

"Great to meet you." Nick shook Tanner's hand again. Something about Nick's smile suggested he was the victor.

In the car, I glanced over at Tanner's flushed face. He took the brunt of his frustration out on the seat belt, trying three times to latch it with more force than required. But how could he have expected to claim victory when everything he and I had was in the past and whatever he thought Nick and I had was in the present?

When we'd lived together Tanner had never been jealous. He trusted me as completely as I trusted him when he was on the road. It had to feel unsettling to consider the possibility that my loyalties lay with someone else now.

Too bad. I had been forced to get over that hurdle after the many tabloid stories and his first marriage.

As I pulled out of the driveway, Tanner asked, a little calmer after finally winning the bout with the inanimate object, "How well do you know him?"

"He's my neighbor—and jogging partner."

"You run with him?"

I glanced over. "Don't sound so surprised. Three mornings a week before work. It's my workout for the day, but for Nick it's just a warm-up. He's an Ironman competitor." I didn't mind fanning the flames of jealousy a bit.

"Ironman?" He frowned.

I couldn't resist adding, "Yep, and smart to boot. He's just written a book on the generational effects of inequality of access to opportunity."

"Are you seeing him?"

This from the man who had been linked with nearly every starlet in Hollywood after his first marriage dissolved. Perhaps what he'd said about not yet finding a Significant Other to introduce to Jason was true—but it sure wasn't for lack of auditioning.

"He's a friend."

"A friend with benefits?"

Biting back my ire, I replied, "Mineral. And bigger than a shoe box."

He paused. "What?"

"Oh. I thought we were playing Twenty Questions." I turned right at the next light and picked up speed.

"I'm interested in your friends," he replied.

"Yet you haven't asked about my friend Charlene from last night.

After all, I was out to dinner with her—maybe I play for both teams now."

I looked over to see him glaring at me, but there was a hint of laughter at the corners of his mouth and eyes.

After that we drove in silence.

But I couldn't stop thinking of him sitting next to me: his woodsy scent; the wave in his hair; the calluses on the fingers of his left hand settled on the arm rest, inches from me; his familiar profile in my peripheral vision; that all-too-familiar mouth with its sly grin; and, of course, the ever-present pressure on my lungs and heart that his closeness induced. Only the manicured beard was unfamiliar.

By the time we neared his hotel, however, I was back thinking of the earlier conversation about Alex. Tanner had given me a present. Already I felt more at peace with my brother's death.

When I pulled up to the entrance, I didn't get out of the car. I didn't need my knees buckling or the heat from his touch racing through my body, wreaking more havoc. It was upsetting enough to know that I still reacted to him physically after all this time apart.

But I was beyond relieved to know that he was healthy. That was another gift he had given me this day—one that meant the world to me.

As he opened the car door, I whispered, barely able to get the words out, "It . . . it's good to see you healthy, Tanner. For you it probably seems like a long time since rehab. But for me, it's like just finding out you're in recovery. I can't tell you how grateful I am that you're safe. And I can't tell you what it means to me that you remember Alex. I should have known better. I'm sorry."

Looking as sad as I felt, Tanner placed his left fingers lightly on the side of my face. Then he let them slide down to the side of my throat, leaving them there for a moment. My body ached at his touch and at the memory of a thousand such touches. A tear escaped down my cheek.

"I'm sorry, too. For everything."

Then he got out of the car and walked into the hotel—without looking back.

TEN

My office was a sanctuary from the tempest Tanner had set loose in my house. No one was in; the bullpen unlit. I could hide in my burrow in peace and quiet—no unexpected questions, no physical disorientation, no dark memories.

Stephanie was at the top of my to-do list. I wanted to get the radon information to her by the time she finished the condo walk-through with the inspector.

I pulled some articles together and wrote a cover note pointing out that the condo association would probably want to retest her unit and then test adjacent units as well. Remediation was more effective if nearby affected units were treated simultaneously. Which was a good thing but might take longer since other unit owners would have to be notified and their units tested.

I almost wished Stephanie and Joe would decide against this property. Not because they couldn't handle the repairs—they could. But I wanted them to be excited about moving into their first place, not bogged down with workmen, schedules, and time delays. Given the known problems—having to contact the condo association to determine responsibility for the remediation and cost, waiting for the remediation to be performed, and the cosmetic repairs that had to be done—much less anything the home inspector found, it was all becoming a bit much. Getting a first home together should be fun.

But it was their decision. And it might still be a good enough deal to make it worth the hassle.

At the end of the note, I reminded Stephanie to call me any time with questions.

With that email sent, I could finally do what I'd been wanting to do since talking with Evan yesterday: check out the Ideas Competition.

Washington, D.C. has been fertile ground for design competitions since its founding. The Washington National Monument, the World War II Monument, and the Vietnam Veterans Memorial, among many other memorials, are all results of competitions, as was the original Smithsonian Museum building and several of its newer museums. Plus, both the White House and the U.S. Capitol Building were products of design competitions—two hundred years ago.

The more well-known form of design competition is the "Project Competition" in which a sponsor, such as a government entity or a corporation, seeks design proposals with the intent of building the winning submission selected by a professional jury. Designs are submitted by participants for free; the payoff is construction of one's project if it is selected. Winning can be a very big deal, even career-changing. But if the competition is popular, meaning hundreds of submissions, a person would probably have a better chance winning against the house in Las Vegas.

In an "Ideas Competition," though, which is what Evan had

mentioned, there is never any intent on the part of the sponsor to build one of the designs submitted, and therefore no chance of a significant payoff. There is only a small monetary prize awarded to the top finishers—more of an honorarium. The primary purpose is to continue the dialogue between architects and the public about what the role of architecture should be in shaping the environment and people's lives.

Only a synopsis of the competition was available online; the full program wouldn't be available until after the city's press conference launching the contest. That way, all competitors begin the challenge at the same time, with the same information, and subject to the same time frame.

The competition was entitled "The Future in a Small Box" and sought innovative proposals for a small downtown site, not yet identified, currently being used for surface parking. The city was looking for innovative building ideas that would bring value to downtown and diversify city amenities. The small site just happened to be the platform for the debate.

It sounded wide open. The perfect challenge.

After work I went home and headed straight to the kitchen, it suddenly occurring to me that I hadn't eaten lunch. As I nibbled a chunk of *asiago pressato*, I checked my home answering machine.

Several friends had called and left messages, including Charlene. "Hey, Jess. How are you doing—this day after the epic performance? Thought you could use some company. Care to join us for supper?"

"Us" was Charlene's seventeen-year-old daughter, Isabelle,

and her mother, Ida Louise. When I first met Charlene, she was a divorced mother, a little younger than I am now, with a nine-year-old. I couldn't believe that Isabelle had only one more year of high school before heading off to college. During the summer, she and Charlene planned to make the grand tour of college campuses.

About three years ago, Charlene's mother had moved in as well. Ida Louise had suffered a stroke and had needed help initially for everyday activities. It was easier for Charlene to keep an eye on her recovering mother and teen daughter with the family consolidated. The arrangement had worked so well that they'd continued it, even though Ida Louise had regained her health and independence.

I called her back. "Thanks for the invitation, Charlene. But lack of company hasn't been a problem." I left a dramatic pause.

Charlene waited.

"Tanner was over here this morning."

"What!" Her voice crackled with surprise.

"He got my address from a mutual friend. And he was a heck of a lot madder today than he was last night." I swallowed another bite of cheese.

"Teddie Daulton was at your house?" she asked accusingly.

"Gee. I'm sorry I didn't call and invite you to join us. Maybe you'd like the cup he drank coffee from as a souvenir?" I enjoyed pressing her buttons as much as she did mine.

But she didn't laugh. "Are you okay? Why did he come to see you?"

"I'm fine. A little tired from the confrontation, but fine." Then I explained briefly why he'd shown up.

"He says he left a letter for you." Charlene's voice was skeptical.

"Do you believe him?"

"I do. And I feel stupid. I should have known he wouldn't have ignored my brother's passing." But I didn't tell her about Tanner's other revelations—that Alex had stayed in touch with him, offering continued friendship and support, and that Tanner was now paying Alex's kindness forward. That was between Tanner and me, at least for a while.

To divert her, I added, "And he wasn't happy when he saw my house. A few things struck him as too like the place we had talked about. Then he had the nerve to try to guilt me into feeling sorry for him because he lives in a sprawling 1930s property and not a contemporary house—like it was my fault."

"Is it?"

"Charlene! He can hire any architect in the world to design a house for him. Nothing's stopping him."

"Hmmm. Apparently, something is. In fact, it sounds like maybe he was as much invested in your one-time dream as you."

I stared out at the garden. Could that be true? I mean, Tanner had said this morning that he had wanted that house, but I'd assumed he was talking in the past tense.

Almost from the start, Tanner and I had talked about a future together. It had seemed inevitable. By the time we moved to California, we knew we'd get married, have kids, and live in a house that I'd design. Our daily reality, though, centered on our careers. While our future was not uncertain, it was without time lines or details.

When Tanner hit the road with mPulse, those dreams became more important to him—at least initially. After his second road trip, this time to the Midwest, we'd lain in bed his first night back, catching up. We were on our sides, facing each other, still basking in the warmth of his homecoming, his left arm under my head and his other hand on my abdomen.

Out of the blue, he asked, "How many children should we have, Jess?"

My body thrilled to the question, the words sending shivers down my spine and goose bumps up my arms.

We had talked about children before but from the intensity of his voice, rumbling from deep within his body—or maybe his heart—I knew this was a commitment.

"Two?" Just like my brother and I. "What are you thinking?"

"Three. But you know me, I'm an only child and I like the idea of a house filled with rug rats."

Overwhelmed by the image, I grabbed his hand and kissed those long, beautiful fingers. "Three it is."

He gathered me closer. "I love you, Honey. I've always loved you."

It was a call-and-response ritual—a shorthand we had developed to express our love, trust, and respect for each other as simply as possible.

"I love you, Tanner. I'll always love you."

The future had begun to take on reality and form.

My heart ached, thinking of that evening.

Tanner had managed to obtain all those things—marriage, a home, a child—without me. He didn't need my house as well.

"It was just a dream, Charlene. Not reality. And he's always had the option of building something on his own."

"Then maybe it wasn't just the house stopping him."

Good grief, I was not going to feel sorry for Tanner. "Look, I apologized for throwing water on him. I don't feel the need to apologize for anything else."

But even as I said it, I knew it wasn't true.

"Anyway, thanks for the offer of dinner but I'm going to pass. It's been a long day. Tell Isabelle and your mom hi."

After we hung up, I sat at the counter for a couple of minutes. I was physically exhausted from the conversation with Tanner, and my body felt bruised from the clashing words and emotions.

But it was the silence that had been most devastating.

There should have been so much to say, to ask, to understand, even to apologize for, about the disaster that had been our relationship, yet neither of us had said a word. Did that mean that a relationship that had once been of such importance no longer had any impact on our present lives? Or had we simply been cowards—afraid of examining our actions, afraid of choking on curdled words, afraid of exposing our scars to fresh truths? Was it better to leave things unexamined for fear of what we'd find?

No wonder my house had become the flash point for our anger and hurt. And maybe that wasn't so bad.

Perhaps it was better to leave unexamined what had happened so long ago.

ELEVEN

Sunday afternoon I worked at home on the façade of the library expansion. I wanted the exterior to look as innovative as the new tech center inside, but also to be a welcoming and integral part of the surrounding neighborhood.

Many libraries seem to turn inward, despite being community buildings. While the original library building I was expanding had been constructed of brick, my addition would be composed of glass, metal, and wood to project a more open and texturally exciting appearance.

And as part of the welcome, there would be ample seating outside, including two curved concrete tiers—like a mini-amphitheater—for teenagers to congregate on and connect to the library's Wi-Fi.

But my eyes kept wandering to the backyard, unable to focus on the library façade. All those storage boxes with memories of Tanner that I had so carefully packed away had been dislodged and torn apart yesterday, their memories tumbling out in disarray. All open for reexamination, remorse, and regret.

Well, if I was just going to think about Tanner, I might as well go outside and tackle some spring cleanup. I could brood in the garden equally well.

As I drained the last of my coffee, the doorbell rang. I crossed over to the front window and peered down at the street. I wasn't going to repeat yesterday's mistake.

Parked at the curb was a red BMW. Charlene.

When I opened the door, my friend held out a paper bag.

"Truce?"

I took the bag and peeked inside. A container of Ben and Jerry's Phish Food Ice Cream—my favorite.

I looked up at her. "I'll think about it. Maybe after the ice cream."

We headed up to the kitchen.

As I scooped the ice cream into two bowls, I asked disingenuously, "So are you here for your consolation gift—the mug Tanner used?"

Charlene gave me a dirty look, then thought better of it. "Do you know which it is?"

"Of course." I didn't, having washed both mugs last night. But she had a chance of getting the right one. I picked out one of two mugs at the front of the cabinet and handed it to her.

Grinning, she touched the rim with her fingers. I rolled my eyes. Then she filled the cup with a little water and drank it.

"God, water never tasted so good," she declared, her eyes gleaming with mischief.

"It's probably the lingering flavor of coffee that has you so excited."

"This isn't the cup, is it?" She handed it back to me.

I laughed. "There's a fifty-percent chance it's the right one."

"No, you probably packed Tanner's mug away in a safe place, never to use again."

She was just trying to get a rise from me, but I answered her seriously. "No, it's memories I've tried to repack today. But after yesterday I can't seem to stick them neatly back into a cabinet, like this mug. Nothing quite fits. I was so sure I knew what had happened."

I handed her one of the bowls of ice cream and took the other. As we sat down at the counter I asked, "So why are you really here, Charlene?"

She grinned. "I know how mortified you were after the restaurant incident. I wanted to make sure your apology to Teddie D yesterday didn't include any promises of compensation for physical pain or mental anguish he might have suffered, or that he hasn't extracted any other promises for reparations because of your remorse and guilt. Like deeding your house over to him or making breakfasts for him for a month."

Heat colored my face.

By nature, Charlene was a truth seeker and truth sayer. She would make a great judge—Solomonic, even. Sometimes, though, she'd get uncomfortably close to the truth. If Tanner had asked for something, like an apology to his companions, I probably would have given it to him. Particularly after his disclosures about my brother.

But I could play along.

"If I were Tanner, I would stay as far away as possible from me and liquids. And believe me, there's a better chance of me marrying him than deeding my house over to him."

Charlene chuckled. "Walking his dog and cleaning up poop?"

"There's no dog, at least not that he mentioned. And thank goodness for the three thousand miles between us. That eliminates a lot of possible favors. I suppose he could ask me to give him a tour of Washington the next time he's in town, but I'd make it all boringly architectural and he'd beg me to stop within ten minutes. I think I'm safe."

I felt better. Charlene and the ice cream, swimming with delicious little catchable chocolate fish, had helped.

That sentiment lasted all of a few seconds.

"I was thinking last night"—my friend appeared strangely

hesitant yet unable to contain her curiosity—"that you're the 'green-eyed girl,' aren't you?"

After we broke up, Tanner had started writing songs about an ex-girlfriend with green eyes. Initially the songs had been raw and personal—and a big hit with fans. After he got out of rehab, they'd become more ironic and droller—and an even bigger hit. I'd reconciled myself to the songs by acknowledging that anything was fodder for Tanner, while assuring myself that he had taken poetic license.

I loathed those songs.

I shrugged as if the topic were of no interest and dipped my spoon back into the chocolate ocean of ice cream, with its marshmallow foam and caramel eddies, to snag more fish.

"Probably. He frequently commented on the color of my eyes. But those songs aren't real, Charlene. They're fabrications, breakup stories steeped in emotion, designed to entertain the audience and suggest that his fans can relate to him as he too, the big rock star, has been screwed and spat on by love. The image took on its own persona. I don't understand half the references."

She mulled it over for a minute while I continued to cast for fishies rather than meet her eyes.

"Well, the image of the green-eyed girl certainly has staying power for him. It's a long time to hold onto a conceit that doesn't have import."

"I'm not saying that the image isn't important to him, only that it has no relevancy to me—or very little."

"Are you sure?" Her blue eyes searched my face.

"Twelve years of no contact speak for themselves."

"Maybe, but the clock has reset, hasn't it? You've talked."

"Only because I threw water on him. It didn't reset by mutual intent." Besides, Tanner and I had our chance and it hadn't worked out. Who in their right mind would want to revisit a relationship that had gone so wrong?

She opened her mouth to argue the point further but, glancing at my expression, she stopped. We scooped up the last fishies with our spoon-nets.

"So, what went wrong with the relationship?" Charlene was nothing if not direct.

But there were things no one else ever needed to know about Tanner's and my relationship, things I could never explain.

Like what it was like to see your lover and best friend, the person you admired most in the world, disappear into addiction; to watch the person with whom you were physically and emotionally intimate move beyond your reach; to see the dreams you had shared evaporate; and, to realize that you were only second-best when it came to the drugs.

Or what it was like to live in the chaos he created. The mood swings. The manipulation. The sudden disappearances, from which he would come back high. The self-victimization. The drug-induced self-doubt. The ever-present pressure of a gathering storm about to blow. Those bright highs that made him happy and confident—until they didn't. And underlying it all, my constant fear for his health.

Or sex—going from what Tanner had described as "knock-your-socks-off-soul-affirming" to anything but. Intercourse becoming just another way for Tanner to keep the demons at bay.

Or how it felt when I finally came to understand that I couldn't "fix" Tanner, no matter how much I wanted. Only he could find his way back from his mad wanderings. But that understanding had come with a profound sense of failure and guilt on my part. Shouldn't I have been there for him "in sickness and in health" given our commitment?

But what I personally regretted most was the loss of Tanner's emotional strength. He had been so steadfast in our early relationship. His constancy and support making it possible for us to pursue our personal goals, whether together or apart.

Without him, I felt as if my underpinnings had been kicked out from beneath me—the world no longer solid, no longer comprehensible. I went from enjoying challenges and taking risks to retreating from life's unexpected twists and turns.

"It was the drugs, Charlene," I said. That was the easy answer—blaming the breakup on Tanner and the drugs.

But it takes two to tango, right?

Often, I'd wondered what would have happened if the relationship had run its natural course—if Tanner's addiction hadn't prematurely ended it. I wanted to believe that we would have stayed together, but maybe the reality was that the drugs were a symptom of an underlying problem.

If our relationship had simply died of natural causes, I could have moved on. If our dynamic together simply hadn't worked, lesson learned. But with the relationship ending so abruptly, with no sense of resolution, I had felt stranded in limbo, always wondering what might have been or worrying that there was something else I should have done.

Charlene nodded. "I'm so sorry. I get why it's hard for you to talk about it. I remember reading about the band's alleged drug problems."

"Hardly 'alleged.' But it is a relief to see how healthy he is now. I've always worried about him, even after rehab. But I feel guilty even on that score. Why couldn't I convince him to go into rehab earlier?"

Charlene reached out her hand and rested it comfortingly on my arm. "Love can't always save another person, Jessie."

My skin broke out in a cold sweat at the truth of her words. She had lost her father to cancer when she was sixteen.

"You're right. Thank you."

"So how did you leave things?"

"Tanner asked for my email address and other contact information, but I can't imagine him using it."

We were going to become pen pals? Friend each other on Facebook? I didn't believe our relationship could be normalized through social media.

Yet, I'd given him the information.

TWELVE

It was a relief to be back at the office Monday. A sense of normalcy after a weekend embedded in the past. Sunshine after the storm.

Yikes.

Maybe I had retreated a little too far into routine and structure. When had I decided to settle for safe?

Oh, yeah, about the time I'd split from Tanner.

But it wasn't fair to blame him. He hadn't coerced me into taking fewer risks. Instead I had opted for safe harbor from the chaos that had been my life that last year with him, forging a career path that was more secure.

But Tanner's comments this weekend about my dream of having my own firm had chafed. And, the worst thing was, he was right.

I was happy at Pearce & Associates, but perhaps I could incorporate more of my earlier goals, like sustainable design, into my current work.

And there were always the competitions.

Someday maybe I'd even thank Tanner for reminding me of those early passions . . . career passions, that is.

"Morning, Stephanie."

"Jessie!"

Stephanie was bouncing in her seat. I didn't think it was from caffeine this early in the morning.

"You look happy. Were you able to resolve things on the condo?"

"Yes! But not like we expected?"

"What happened?"

"When we did the walk-through with the inspector he pointed out that the HVAC unit needed to be replaced? It was eighteen years old?"

"I'm confused. You decided to go ahead on the place?"

"No, no! Joe and I decided that was the last straw?"

"But you're okay with it?" I asked, still puzzled.

"Well, not initially. But yesterday, our agent called to tell us that another unit had come on the market in the same building but on the fifth floor? Within thirty minutes we had toured the place."

A smile started working its way onto my lips.

"The condo is at the top of our budget but it's been fully upgraded?

In a way we like. We could just move in?"

"Stephanie, that's great. It's funny how things work out."

"There shouldn't be a problem with radon, right?"

"No, by the fifth floor, any gas should have dissipated. You still should have a test done, but it would be unlikely."

She beamed. "That's what we thought. I hate to ask you this again, but could you walk through the house with us this weekend? You see more issues than we do?"

"We could do it sooner if you'd like. Any night this week—except Wednesday." Charlene and I didn't play volleyball on the Mall any more, but we did play in a league in Northwest on Wednesdays. It helped maintain our sanity for the rest of the workweek.

"Can you? I didn't want to ask?"

"If you really want this place, you and Joe should get it under contract as soon as possible. You don't want anyone else discovering it."

"Can you do it tonight?"

"Absolutely."

Stephanie picked up the phone. "I'll call our agent right now."

When I hadn't heard from Stephanie yesterday, I figured the couple was having second thoughts about the first-floor unit. But this option was great news. Stephanie was excited, the way it should be with a couple's first house.

After I'd checked in with everyone on their projects I headed for Evan's office.

In his late forties, Evan looked the quintessential architect, meticulously dressed and wearing wire-rimmed glasses. Occasionally he wore bow ties—a wry nod to a professional quirk—but today he was sporting a fabulous tie of deep purple, blue, green, and gray overlapping blocks, their edges blurred as if streaked with rain, inspired by the art of the late Jerry Garcia of the Grateful Dead. Evan had at least twenty Garcia ties, any one of which could brighten up the office on the gloomiest winter day.

Evan was at his desk and waved me in.

I sat down on one of the visitor chairs, and said, "I looked at the website for the Ideas Competition."

"What do you think?" he asked.

"The competition has potential. The proposals are to focus less on what-is and more on what-can-be. From the day of the press conference we'd have four weeks to complete our submission, for a due date of June 3." That was a suitable timeframe; the office couldn't spend a lot of time on a project with no immediate return.

Evan leaned back in his chair. "Who would you want on the team?"

"I'd like Eliot and Sharon."

Eliot Cooper was a third-year intern with a keen interest in technology. He had worked with me on an Ideas Competition the previous year seeking prototypes for temporary pavilions that could be set up on the National Mall in the hot summers to provide shade for tourists. We submitted a design that mirrored the natural environment: pavilions mimicking a cluster of shade trees. We didn't win, but we received an honorable mention.

The other staff member, Sharon Malone, had joined our company in the fall, right out of graduate school. This competition would be an intense, hands-on training course for Sharon. I'd be able to assess her strengths and weaknesses and help her better understand the design process.

Evan nodded. "Go ahead then. Talk with Eliot and Sharon."

I nodded. Competitions are very fast-paced. Not everyone has the time or energy to spare. I would be living on coffee during the competition—but then, I love coffee.

THIRTEEN

Showing tremendous restraint, Trish Dumont didn't phone from L.A. until Tuesday, four days after Tanner had called her for my address.

She had left a message on my home answering machine. Because of the three-hour time difference, I fixed dinner first—well, reheated a lemon chicken rice dish from the night before.

It had been a good day.

Both Eliot and Sharon were gung-ho about participating in the competition. At least Eliot knew what he was getting into. I hoped Sharon would feel as positive at the end of the grueling experience as she did now.

Plus, last night's tour of the condo with Stephanie and Joe had gone well. The kitchen and two bathrooms had been renovated tastefully. The only thing they might have to do before moving in was paint the master bedroom—unless eggplant was their color.

Now the happy couple had a contract on the unit, subject to radon testing and a home inspection. Probably time to think about a housewarming gift.

"Hi, Trish. What's new?" I asked disingenuously.

Silence. I could almost hear her mind whirring away, deciding how candid to be. Redhead that she is, Trish finally opted for bluntness.

"Teddie called last Friday. For your address. I just wanted to see if he had gotten in touch with you." Then she added, "Remember, you said if he ever asked for your address or number after going through rehab, I could give it to him."

"Yes, I remember. And yes, he did pay a visit."

"How did things go?"

"As well as could be expected, considering I'd poured water on him the evening before at a restaurant."

"What?" This was followed by a thud and then a muted "damn." Trish tended to talk with her hands. When she got excited, the phone would go flying.

"Why in the world would you do that?" she asked, after recapturing the phone.

"Well, I always was a little crazy around the man."

She wasn't deterred.

"I don't understand."

Time to put her out of her misery. "It turned out to be a misunderstanding—about my brother. Which I apologized for." I gave Trish a few more details than I had Charlene since she knew all the parties involved, including my brother.

"I'm sorry, Jessie. I did tell Teddie about Alex's death."

"I know. I should have realized that he would have responded but I wasn't thinking clearly. Not hearing from him hurt, and over the years it's increasingly galled me. But what was so odd was that

I didn't even know I was going to throw the water on him when I walked over. I actually beamed at him right before drowning him."

Trish giggled. "I shouldn't laugh. But it is kind of funny. I'm sure it was the last thing Teddie expected."

"I hope so. It was certainly the last thing I expected."

"He asked for your address once before so I didn't think anything about it. I thought maybe he had contacted you earlier."

"What?" It was my turn to be surprised. "He never contacted me."

"Oh."

"When was this?"

With an audible sigh, she replied, "It . . . it was about a year after rehab."

No wonder Tanner thought I lived in Virginia, because at that point I had.

Why had he asked Trish for the information? And why had he never acted on it? That was worse than never asking for the information in the first place.

"I'm sorry, Jessie. You never said anything, so I didn't ask."

I tried to rebound. "No, it's okay. Surprised, that's all."

Normally I would have chatted longer, or at least asked about Alan, but I was desperate to get off the phone. I said goodbye hurriedly, telling her I'd call on the weekend.

Then I sat there, staring at the phone in my hand.

FOURTEEN

From: T. E. Daulton
Subject: Postscript
Thursday, 4/25/13

My breath stalled in my throat.

I was home, checking emails before conducting research on lighting fixtures for the library expansion. As messages downloaded, Tanner's name had popped up.

I hesitated, my finger hovering over the touchpad. If I clicked on it, would I get more entangled in the past?

I pressed the pad.

Jessie,

I'm sorry you never received my condolences. I was not uncaring, but I was careless in not making sure you had received the letter.

On the plane back to L.A., it occurred to me that you may not have realized that I had written a song for Alex. A phrase from the letter I wrote you had stayed in my mind for years, eventually becoming the song "Too Soon." I hope you're familiar with it.

I'm glad I finally had the chance to tell you what your brother meant to me—even if the price was getting drenched.

Tanner

Familiar with the song? It was from the first album Tanner had recorded after going through rehab—his only solo album to date. When I'd listened to that album, I knew something huge had happened to him, though I didn't learn about his detox till later.

Fueled by drugs, mPulse's music had become increasingly complex. But in that solo CD was a lightness I hadn't heard in a long time. Every note was vital, every word essential to the message, and every silent void crucial for catching one's breath before being swept forward. The songs were lean but brimming with rock-and-roll energy. Tanner had received a Grammy for Album of the Year.

"Too Soon" honored a man who had died young but had lived a full life. Tanner's voice was raw with emotion as he sang, the lyrics obviously personal.

I had assumed the song was about a musician friend who had died of an overdose. But in recalling the lyrics now, I couldn't remember any overt references to drugs, only to how much the man had inspired others and how much he would be missed. I had probably leaped to the idea of drugs because of my own long-standing fears for Tanner.

I wrapped my arms around my chest, rocking back and forth.

Tanner had written a song for Alex—a song that had touched countless people and would touch countless more.

Without thinking, I typed back.

Tanner,

I've always been moved by "Too Soon" but never imagined it had been written for Alex. Thank you for letting me know. It was already a beautiful song but now it means everything to me.

Jessie

After sending the email, I Googled "Too Soon" on my laptop. I read and reread the lyrics until I could have quoted them backwards.

Tanner's email underscored how mistaken I had been about him and my brother all these years, not only regarding the condolence letter, but also their continued friendship, his song in memory of

Alex, and his admiration for my brother and desire for his respect.

What else had I gotten wrong?

FIFTEEN

"So, you and Teddie D?"

Nick was at my house for dinner. He was wearing khakis and a navy Polo shirt that highlighted his dark blue eyes. He had three looks: gym rat, preppy, and business. I'd never seen him in blue jeans.

I was setting the table while he emptied cartons of chicken with broccoli, moo shi shrimp, and stir-fried string beans into serving bowls and placed vegetable spring rolls onto a small plate.

My face burned and I turned away. Nick and I had gone jogging three mornings that week without him expressing any curiosity about Tanner. I'd finally relaxed, thinking I had escaped more embarrassing questions.

"It was a long time ago, Nick."

"How long?"

I went into the kitchen to pour us some tea.

"At least a millennium."

"No, really."

"Well then, how about a decade? We met our last year in college. He had formed mPulse that summer and the band was playing clubs around Chicago."

"What happened?"

Having tried evasive maneuvers with Charlene, I tried honesty with Nick

"I don't know." I said, handing him a cup.

His eyes widened. "What do you mean? The breakup came as a surprise?"

"No. I know what happened. I just don't know why it happened."

We sat down. I ladled the chicken onto some rice and then slathered a spring roll in duck sauce. Nick had the shrimp.

"After college, we moved to L.A. so I could attend graduate school and Tanner could launch his music career. We were committed and making plans for the future. He'd even met my brother and parents."

As I ate the chicken, I painted the relationship with the broadest of strokes. Then I added, "It was when the band started touring that the problems began."

Nick frowned. "Was he unfaithful?"

I shook my head. "I don't think so. But even the first road trip took a toll on him. When he got home, he was restless and tired. By the end of the second tour he had lost weight.

"Tanner has this innate ability to touch his fans, but as his natural energy reserves dried up on the road he resorted to drugs. The band thought of amphetamines as fuel to get them through the next performance, just like the gas needed for the van to get to the next gig."

I wasn't hungry anymore. But I didn't want Nick to feel uncomfortable, so I reached for the shrimp, put some on my plate without the pancake, and pushed it around with my fork. Nick started on the chicken.

"Unfortunately, what Tanner thought would be a temporary assist became the bigger problem. The situation deteriorated with each trip. Eventually I begged him to go to rehab." I had even considered deferring my graduate program to help him, to go on the road with him, but quickly realized the situation was past that gesture.

"I left him over Christmas break my second year in school. I could no longer deal with the addiction, watch his health worsen, or stand by helplessly waiting for word of him overdosing while on the road."

When Tanner was touring, I barely ate or slept. Anxiety was my constant companion along with an ever-present tightness in my chest, like a noose constricting both my heart and lungs.

Nick reached over and patted my shoulder. "I'm sorry."

I shrugged. I had replayed all this so many times over the last week, trying to figure out if another outcome had been possible, that I was numb.

"The good news is that he got clean, though he didn't enter rehab until five years after I'd left. That's one of the things I regret most—that I couldn't get him into treatment sooner."

"Does he usually call when he's in town?" Nick was staring at me with his inquisitive eyes. I could almost see the gears working, filling in a couple more pieces of my life.

Again, the heat slithered up my throat. His question couldn't be farther from the truth, and I was ashamed: that Tanner and I hadn't talked since I'd left; that I had been angry at him for years about something he hadn't done; that I had not been able to help him; that I had never apologized for leaving, even knowing I had taken the easy way out. And if there was one thing I should never have done to Tanner, it was to have taken the easy way out. It was no better than him taking the easy way out with the drugs.

"No. I ran into him at a restaurant last Friday." I described the encounter and when I got to the part about tossing water on Tanner, Nick burst out laughing.

"Oh, my god, I wish I had been there, Jess. Please, please, the next time he is in town, can I be your dinner date? He must have been stunned. And you of all people. You're so self-controlled."

Nick had me laughing as well. "He was as surprised as you are, but by the next morning I can tell you he was madder than a wet hen." Tanner would have liked my joke. He loved wordplay—the cornier, the better.

"Do you still like him?"

Good grief. Nick was as bad as Charlene. "I'll always love Tanner. But reality got in the way." I hoped it sounded reasonable.

"You know, when you introduced us, he seemed quite . . . uh, possessive."

"It was probably more a reaction to you than anything to do with me. You know, two alpha males." I manufactured a smile to let him know that however Tanner had acted, it had little to do with me.

Nick studied me for a minute. I waited, picking at the shrimp. I noticed it had gone dark outside.

Putting down his fork, he pushed himself slightly away from the table, as if the polite dinner conversation were over. If I were a child I'd be worried about what was coming next.

But I wasn't a child and I wasn't worried about what he had to say—at least, not too much. I put down my fork as well.

"You'll probably say that this is hindsight, but there are times when I look at you, Jessie, and you seem to hold yourself as if you're hurt—like you've taken a body blow and are protecting the wound. I've always wondered what—or who—had hurt you so deeply."

I stared at him, feeling faint. Sometimes it had felt like a truck had smashed into me. But it had been a blow to my heart, not my body.

And I was still protecting it.

"Definitely hindsight," I responded lightly.

Nick shook his head, the set of his jaw rejecting my quip. "Nope. You took a serious hit." He eyed me thoughtfully. "I think I could take Teddie in a fight, even though he's taller. You know I go out to California all the time to visit my parents. I could make a detour and bloody up that obnoxiously handsome nose of his."

Alex had made that same offer. At the image of my brother and Nick vying for the privilege of blooding Tanner's nose, I started laughing.

I almost believed he was semi-serious. It was sweet, but years too late. Besides, I could defend myself well enough.

Once I started laughing, Nick conceded, "Well, maybe your cold shower was as effective as a punch, especially given that it was served in public."

When I finally regained my voice, I stammered, "The fact is, yo-you're not the first person to offer. That was my brother." Nick knew I'd lost my brother years ago. Alex's death was something that connected us, as we had both experienced the loss of a loved one. "But I happen to like Tanner's nose."

"Another body part?"

That set us off again.

When I'd finished dabbing at my eyes with napkins, Nick said, more seriously, "Really, if he ever hurts you again, just let me know."

I couldn't imagine that happening, but I nodded. "Thank you.

But I doubt we'll have much interaction. And to be fair, he was very hurt when I left . . . although I will say he moved on rather quickly."

"Yes. I can relate to that."

I knew he could.

I took the opportunity to refresh our tea so we could finish dinner more normally.

Over the fortune cookies, Nick started to speak, faltered, and then started again. "I . . . I have a favor to ask. Would you join me for dinner on Saturday, June eighth? It's an office dinner."

I was surprised. We never mixed our friendship with our business lives.

"What's the occasion?"

"It's a dinner recognizing several associates for their work. I'll be one of them."

"Nick, that's great. Congratulations!" What an honor to be chosen from an organization known for quality. Hey, if he was willing to defend my honor, I could attend a business dinner.

"I'd love to join you."

Nick dated occasionally—more than I did—but his girlfriends lasted for a shorter period than my more sporadic companions. After we met, we dated twice (without benefits, Mr. Nosey Daulton) but had fallen instead into a friendship that felt comfortable and safe.

"If at some point you'd rather invite someone else, I'll understand," I added.

"No. Anyone else might attach too much significance to the occasion. You won't do that."

I got it. The evening wouldn't change our relationship. Of course, people at the party might think we were intimate, which could make things slightly awkward for him. But Nick deserved to enjoy the night and if he wanted my company, I'd be there.

After clearing up and packing the leftovers in their cartons so Nick could take them home, we walked downstairs.

"Are we still on for tomorrow morning?"

"Argh." I hated running on Mondays and he knew it. The rest of the week was fine, but Mondays were a psychological speed bump.

"It's good for you, Jess. Builds character."

"My muscles happen to prefer indolence. But in the event it's not too late for them to develop character, I'll join you."

He placed his hand on the back of my neck as he leaned forward and kissed me on the forehead.

"Goodnight, kiddo. Sweet dreams." "Kiddo" was a running joke. He was all of a year older.

"Goodnight, Nick."

But I never returned the sentiment of sweet dreams. Something told me his dreams weren't so sweet.

I really liked Nick. He was smart, kind-hearted, an all-around great guy. I had also become quickly aware of his intensity, a quality that works like pheromones on me. Unfortunately, whereas Tanner's energy and drive had originated from a good place—music—much of Nick's intensity was forged from pain. Dating Nick, after living with Tanner, would have been the proverbial "jumping out of the frying pan and into the fire."

And if there was one thing I had learned from Tanner, it was that I couldn't fix someone, no matter how much I might want to. Like Tanner, Nick would have to find his own way home. In the meantime,

I could be a friend, supporting and encouraging him, a calm haven in his sometimes-unbearable world.

I no longer trusted love, but Nick no longer trusted life.

SIXTEEN

From: T. E. Daulton
Subject: Lawsuit
Saturday, 5/4/13

Nausea swept over me. Lawsuit? Had Charlene been right? Was Tanner such a diva that he was going to sue me for throwing water on him?

Hands sweaty, dread eating at my stomach, I clicked on the message.

Jessie,

I could tell from our recent visit that you've worried about my health over the years. I didn't think you'd be concerned once you'd left but I should have at least asked Trish to let you know I'd entered rehab.

I was suddenly overwhelmed by sadness. How could Tanner think I wouldn't have worried about his health, whether I was with him or not?

If he didn't understand that, then he was as mistaken about me as I had been about him and my brother.

In case you'd still worry, I wanted you to know that I'm suing a tabloid for a story alleging I was back on drugs. There's no truth to the article and my lawyers and I are confident we'll win, but I don't want you worrying that I'd fallen off the wagon in case you heard the story.

I'm used to these fictitious claims, but I filed the suit for Jason's sake. Taking your advice, the two of us have started a more adult discussion about drugs—and alcohol. I was afraid that if I didn't respond to the assertions, he might believe the story (it's in print—it must be true), consider me a hypocrite, and tune me out. I've told him that the publisher is selling sensationalism with the hope that no one will take the trouble and expense to hold the paper accountable. They miscalculated.

Whew. At least the case wasn't against me. But I still felt shaky. Why do we like to see our heroes toppled? Why not a positive story about someone fighting their addiction? Don't we want to see people succeed? Or are we so small we prefer to read about people who fail so we feel bigger?

Tanner had every right to do what he needed to ensure his reputation and guard his son's innocence and trust.

On a happier note, I took Jason to an exhibit at the Getty Museum. It's entitled "OverDrive." The theme is how cars, infrastructure, the entertainment industry, and housing shaped the development of L.A. You would have enjoyed it. The photos from the era of big cars and the buildings designed for those cars reminded me of your school design project for highway rest stops.

Of course, I then had to take Jason someplace fun afterwards. LOL. Actually he enjoyed the exhibit, particularly the display on cars.

What is it about boys and cars? I don't remember going through that phase but as Jason would say, that was probably because they didn't have cars back when I was a lad. . . .

By the way, I really like your house even though it probably didn't seem that way. I was disconcerted by how familiar it felt and how much it reminded me of you—elegant, surprising, smart. It was an odd déjà vu experience. Even though our house had never been a physical reality, it had apparently taken on form and substance in my mind.

Tanner

"OverDrive" sounded like a good event for a history major and his son. I could almost hear Tanner chuckle at his LOL joke.

But I couldn't believe he remembered that studio project from my first term at UCLA. The highway rest stop prototype was a deceptively simple little project. Yet it involved all the design basics—siting, orientation, access and egress, multiple structures, mechanical systems, diverse materials, and imagery.

I had decided to go retro, building on car and drive-in restaurant motifs from the mid-twentieth century to conjure up the heyday of long cars with mammoth tail fins but employing modern materials to lower building and maintenance costs. I'd ended up using a butterfly roof for the picnic table pavilions. They looked futuristic, but as imagined in the 1950s. I wanted tourists to see even everyday rest stops as part of the fantasy that is California.

At the time, Tanner had commented that he could envision Buck Rogers pulling in—which is exactly what I'd been aiming for.

I hadn't planned to respond to the email, but I was grateful for the warning about the story.

The add-on about the Getty exhibit was Tanner's way of lightening the main message. But the exhibit reminded me of another event taking place in L.A. later in the—

Damn, what was wrong with me? I didn't need to play tour guide for Tanner and his son. But it was second nature for me to suggest something Tanner might appreciate. Besides, responding wouldn't entail entering a long-term contract with him for an email relationship.

Tanner,

Thanks for the heads-up about the lawsuit. Occasionally the tales of Hollywood do make the long trek east. . . . Plus, you were right to set the record straight for Jason.

And since we're speaking of truths, I worried constantly about your health until I heard that solo album. Just as I should have known better about you and my brother, you should have expected better of me. When I heard that album I could finally breathe. You might want to consider an apology for thinking I no longer cared.

The exhibit you saw with your son sounds like a lot of fun. It reminded me of the biennial Solar Decathlon that will be held in L.A. in October in which teams of college students design and build small houses utilizing solar power. The students' work is amazing. Jason might be impressed by houses designed by kids not much older than he. Of course, afterwards you'll have to take him someplace fun.

As to not remembering a fixation on cars at his age, I'm sure that was because you were lusting after guitars. . . .

Jessie

As to liking my house? It was too late for compliments. Tanner had been angered by my place, déjà vu or not.

Rereading my message, the tone in the second paragraph sounded a bit churlish but I hoped Tanner still got my humor. At this point, the two of us had gotten so many things wrong I couldn't tell who owed whom what apologies.

SEVENTEEN

Tuesday morning, Evan, my two team members, and I attended the press conference for the "Small Box" Ideas Competition. At least two hundred people were in attendance and the conference was being streamed for competitors located outside the D.C. area as well. In wrapping up, Mayor Gray stressed the charge of exploring new uses and technologies for the site.

All the property information, including the location and the full competition brief and rules, was now available on the Internet. After the conference we visited the nearby site, which bordered D.C.'s central business district, not far from our office. The immediate neighborhood was pretty evenly divided between mid-rise residential and office use. The lot was small, as promised, but it was a corner site and within walking distance of several subway stations and the many restaurants located in Chinatown and along the Seventh Street Corridor. It was a pretty sweet property.

When we got back to the office, Eliot, Sharon, and I settled ourselves in the conference room. First, we talked about the purpose of participating in the competition and how to respond to the challenges of addressing innovation and bringing value to the city. Eliot manned the dry-erase board as we identified elements that we wanted to be part of our proposal. Some of the factors highlighted were: affordability, energy-saving technologies, diversity of use and users, and sustainable materials.

Once we had our overarching priorities, we started brainstorming uses for the site. We had set up three dry-erase boards: one for residential uses, one for office uses, and a third board for "other." Ideas were coming so quickly that Eliot had to keep nudging his black-rimmed glasses back up on his nose as he switched from board to board. Ideas ran the gamut from conventional to more specialized uses, such as hotel, retail, museum, education, or community- or health-related functions. Initially, no idea was discarded.

By close of business, though, we had winnowed the ideas down to two so we could develop the ideas more fully the following day. One thing about any design competition is that you need to come up with the concept quickly. If you're a quarter way through the submission timeframe with no viable idea, it's already too late.

That night I had plenty of research to do on our two contenders. The ideas we had chosen to explore were not the most imaginative of our brainstorming suggestions, but both could bring diversity to the city; innovation could come in the execution of the design.

When I powered up the laptop, I wasn't surprised to find an email from Tanner.

Jessie,

Yes, I do owe you an apology. (Nothing like having to ask for one is there?)

I assumed when you left that you'd had enough of the drama.

Not that I blamed you—it wasn't pretty. I thought you had given up on me, the physical distance between us a metaphor for how you felt.

Damn it. I hadn't engineered the separation well and was aware of it at the time. But the separation had never been a metaphor for escape. Well, not until after his second marriage, when I had moved east, deliberately distancing myself from Tanner's world and carving out my own creative life.

I went online to check out that Solar Decathlon. The competition sounds fun so I've added it to the list of things to do with Jason. Thanks for the suggestion.

Also wanted to let you know I'm working with Alan. I wrote a couple of songs for a friend and I'm sitting in on the recording sessions, providing back-up vocals and guitar. Alan is producing the record. I can't tell you how busy that man is and how much in demand. But you and I always knew how gifted he is.

And, you're right—I was thinking about guitars at Jason's age. . . .

Tanner

Forget the Solar Decathlon, forget Alan. I kept rereading that second paragraph. Not that it mattered anymore, and I could understand why he might find it easier to interpret the separation that way. But maybe it was time for him to understand that my leaving was supposed to be something more than a facile metaphor.

Tanner,

I no longer want your apology as you couldn't be more wrong about why I left. The separation wasn't some sort of "metaphor." Of course, I still cared. But in leaving I intended to disabuse you of any notion that I supported your drug use or was willing to profit from it in any way. As it was I had condoned it far too long and I could no longer stand what it was doing to your health.

    J

I pressed Send, hurtling the message on its way before I could rethink it.

I went into the kitchen and heated water for tea. As I waited for the water to boil, I paced my small kitchen.

It was true that I couldn't watch what the drugs were doing to Tanner . . . but what was even more terrible was that my presence seemed to exacerbate his problems.

EIGHTEEN

When I arrived at the office in the morning, a vase of flowers dominated the counter of the reception desk: a dazzling array of lilacs and lime-green hydrangeas with white roses, peonies, and lilies in a champagne-colored, cut glass vase. I inhaled the mingled perfumed scents deeply, relishing the early extravagance of summer.

"What a beautiful arrangement, Stephanie. Is it a special occasion?"

"I don't know? They're for you?"

Were they or weren't they for me?

I glanced at the attached envelope. Yes, it clearly stated Jessie Hartley. My lips pressed together. Was this an apology, or was it meant to impress me with how quickly Tanner could get flowers to me?

"Who are they from?" Stephanie asked.

Definitely a question, and not one I wanted to answer.

"Don't know. I'll take them back to my office and find out."

"They sure are lovely?"

"That they are."

In my office I placed the arrangement in the center of my work table and opened the envelope.

Jessie,

My apologies. I seem to have been wrong about many things from those troubled days.

TD

No joke. But then I had gotten just as many things wrong and I didn't even have the excuse of mind-altering drugs.

Part of me wanted to put the flowers back in the lobby. That way I wouldn't have to look at them and be reminded of those mistakes.

But I'd never stopped listening to Tanner's music because of our past. I suppose I could treat the flowers the same way and appreciate them simply for their beauty. I picked up the vase and put it on my desk—the better to indulge in their exuberance.

After morning rounds, I joined Eliot and Sharon in the conference room.

As soon as I settled in a chair, Sharon asked, "Jessie, did you know that by living in a micro-apartment, one's carbon footprint can be reduced by over a third?"

"And, if you make other adjustments in your lifestyle, like accumulating less stuff, it can be reduced even more?" added Eliot.

It appeared we had all done our homework. The team's favorite idea for residential use had been micro-apartments. I was familiar with the concept (after all, our firm designs college residence halls) but had wanted to get a better idea of the philosophy—and realities—of this emerging housing type.

As I discovered the previous night, micro-housing is generally defined as dwelling units with an area of between 250 and 350 square feet. Even in the upper range, the square footage is at least thirty percent less than a newly built studio apartment in downtown D.C. Below 250 square feet of space, the size becomes more appropriate for communal housing with shared kitchens, bathrooms, or living spaces, though it is possible to build a fully-contained abode in less than 250 square feet. A nano-house, perhaps?

Many international high-density locations, like Hong Kong, Japan, and several European cities, already embrace this housing typology. The U.S. has been slower to adopt it, with San Francisco and Seattle on the leading edge of the movement and New York and Boston dipping their toes in. District of Columbia regulations allow construction of micro-units, but so far, no building permits had been issued.

There are many features to commend these mini-units. Because they're substantially smaller, rents should be lower, meaning that some entry level workers might be able to live in downtowns rather than commute long distances (along with the associated costs). But it wasn't just about cost. As Sharon had mentioned, a resident's environmental footprint should be smaller both because of the unit's size and because of the use of smaller and more efficient appliances.

And that's where the concept of micro-housing becomes especially interesting. Other environmental, technological, and sustainability issues could likewise be addressed at this scale, all coalescing nicely into a philosophy of building small, reducing the impact on the environment, and creating a more thoughtful, intentional lifestyle. My own house espoused many elements of this philosophy.

But in the hands of the wrong developer, one intent only on cramming as many units as possible into a building without attention to the details, micro-units could devolve into something cramped and unlivable—like flop houses of old.

Sharon commanded the dry-erase boards this morning (but with less athleticism required as we were debating only one option at a time). We started with identifying potential residents for tiny apartments.

"Graduate students," suggested Eliot.

Millennials! wrote Sharon,

It didn't take long to create a substantial list of people who might take advantage of this more minimalist lifestyle: from individuals (recent college graduates entering the workforce to internationals used to smaller apartment to retirees wanting to take advantage of the city's many amenities) to businesses and organizations (such as corporations needing temporary housing for employees from out of town or the many museums that had artist-in-residence programs). Plus, there are many workers in D.C., such as members of Congress, who are here for only part of the week. If the units and building were designed well there could be a healthy demand for the micro-units.

Now the question was whether you could design a residence at this diminutive scale that not only functioned as a self-contained apartment, but was rentable, livable, and even inspirational. Would someone coming home to their micro-apartment at the end of the day feel as happy as I did?

The other option we were considering for the site was incubator office space. Business incubators provide both rental space and practical business advice to start-up companies. But incubators weren't new to D.C.; high-tech and bioscience start-ups were already the focus of several such efforts.

Buried in the ideas we had slung at Sharon, though, was an unconventional user for the space, antithetical to the typical science- or tech-oriented start-ups. Washington, D.C., isn't known as a fashion mecca, yet it has a small but active community of diverse designers. Providing flexible work space and basic business management services to entrepreneurs involved in apparel, jewelry and home décor design could help get them established. Why shouldn't D.C. be a supporter and patron of fashion and, even better, grow this sector of the economy?

As we debated the pros and cons of the two options, Eliot and Sharon evinced a personal interest in the micro-apartments.

From my research, millennials seem to have a natural affinity for this housing type. Eliot and Sharon both lived in the suburbs and had long commutes. They were excited by an opportunity to design something that could (theoretically) make living in D.C. a possibility.

"I'd be willing to downsize to a smaller unit for an urban social life," Eliot explained.

"Exactly!" Sharon seconded. "With D.C. as part of your living room, you don't need as much indoor space."

"Plus, no roommates, if the price was right. We could finally be adults," added Eliot, all ready to move in.

I was leaning toward micro-housing, too. At the start of the project yesterday, when we had been tossing out ideas for potential uses for the site, Sharon had been quiet, shy. But the more we'd discussed micro-housing, the more she participated. This could be a project that captured her imagination and inspired her to express herself more confidently.

Plus, micro-housing had more applicability to our work as a firm.

When I presented Evan at the end of the day with our recommendation to pursue the micro-apartments proposal, he beamed.

"Sounds great," he said. "I can't wait to see what your team comes up with."

Looking at the beautiful flowers on my desk on the way out that evening, I thought of Tanner. I was in a much better mood. We had our "hook." Now my team just needed to write the song.

When I got home, I emailed Tanner.

Tanner,

Thank you for the flowers. They're stunning.

I assume they're an apology for making me throw water on you when you were here in D.C. If you ever make me throw anything at you again, I will expect double the number of flowers—or jewelry.

Apology accepted.

Jessie

I snickered. Tanner would get my humor, but man, I bet the Rock Star would be annoyed.

NINETEEN

The next evening, I received Tanner's reply:

Jessie,

Has anyone ever called you exasperating? Impossible? At least you liked the flowers . . . although I'm confused now as to why I sent them.

Tanner

Ha. Tanner had called me impossible countless times.

Tanner,

Nope. No one has ever called me impossible or exasperating. Wonderful, kind, smart, of course, but definitely not exasperating.

By the way, I'm glad to hear you're in the studio even if it's to work on someone else's album. Any plans to head back yourself?

I've got a new project. I shanghaied my two youngest staff members (innocents that they are) for an architectural Ideas Competition. We have 4 weeks to submit our proposal. The long hours remind me of graduate school—and I still drink too much coffee.

Jessie

After reading and replying to a couple other emails, I was about to turn off the laptop when I got a reply from Tanner.

Jessie,

I'm curious about your competition. It was your passion for architecture that convinced me to pursue music when I doubted myself. As you said, how could one not at least try to pursue one's passion?

I've thought about that conversation many times. On those

seemingly too frequent days when writing doesn't come easily, and particularly in that dark time right after rehab when I feared I had lost my ability to create.

Maybe that's what the flowers are for? In which case I should send you more.

And, yes, I am heading back into the studio with the band. Just waiting for Alan's schedule to open.

Tanner

I recalled that earlier conversation. It was the day after Tanner and I were first introduced. He had called me mid-morning the next day and we met up at a nearby coffee shop and had talked non-stop. Ideas and words tumbled out faster than we could speak them. It had been heady, exciting—and a little scary. Who was this man? I didn't want to miss a word he said, a gesture he made, his energy already working its way into my body.

For much of the conversation we talked about our passions—music and architecture. His grandfather had been his mentor, teaching Tanner to play piano at six and giving him his first guitar at ten. By thirteen, Tanner was writing songs. His recounting of some of those early love songs had cracked me up.

"Do you plan on continuing the band after graduation?" I asked, certain of the answer.

His eyes sought his coffee cup as if he could find the answer there. "The three of us have talked about the possibility, but it's a tough business. There's no guarantee of success. I'm not sure I can rationalize trying to make a go of it."

I gave him an incredulous stare. "You're kidding, right? There's never certainty in any career when you start out. I have no idea whether I'll make a good architect or not, but it's what I love, what I'm passionate about. I can't imagine not pursuing it. Could you really pass up the opportunity to do what you obviously love?"

I anxiously started shredding a paper napkin beneath the table into smaller and smaller pieces.

"Music is what I want. More than anything." He took a sip of coffee while considering his next words. "I believe my bandmates have the talent. But with friends talking about nine-to-five jobs or graduate school, I feel like I'm not being serious about the future."

He took a deep breath, then set his forearms on the table, one fist wrapped in the other, as he leaned toward me.

"Music is my passion, like architecture is yours. You're right. I don't think I could be satisfied if I hadn't at least tried to live a musical life."

Slowly a smile emerged, his expression transforming from resignation to relief. "So, no plan B?"

"No plan B." I touched his arm lightly in support and delight, the first of thousands of such gestures. Meanwhile, the pieces of napkin fell to the floor like celebratory confetti descending on a parade. "Besides, do you even have a choice? I know I don't."

"When you put it that way, no. Music is a faucet I can't turn off. I even dream about it." He grinned.

I almost melted from the wattage. "Thank god. I'm glad I'm not the only one with weird dreams." We burst out laughing, not only relieved at knowing we shared the same excitement about our futures, but also because we recognized something fundamental and familiar about the other person.

Damn it. Tears slithered down my face as I sat at the computer. I hadn't known that he had lost his music after rehab. For a creative person like Tanner, that period must have been terrifying. And how tempting must it have been to fall back on drugs to keep the fear at bay? Yet, he hadn't.

I was grateful he'd found solace in our talk from that day so long ago. Life would have been desolate if I had lost both him and his music.

Tanner,

I'm glad that first conversation resonated with you when you came out of rehab. So many people have found such pleasure, comfort, and community in your music, including me. I'm glad you'll be making more soon.

I believe that memories are not just remembrances from the past but still hold for us in the present a spark of life from that moment they happened—like that first conversation. Do you?

Then, to lighten the message, I briefly described my vision for the Ideas Competition and signed off.

It had been a long week. Between the demands of the competition, keeping my project teams on track, and juggling my own projects, I was stretched thin. But I loved competitions, I loved the synergy that a good collaboration can generate like the interaction I had with Sharon and Eliot, and I especially liked exploring this housing typology.

There was much about micro-housing and the ethos of the movement that could be translated into other social issues, such as emergency housing and shelter for the homeless.

For a while, a classmate at UCLA and I had talked about working together after graduation to address these issues. Russ and I had it all worked out: I would bring the design skills and he would bring his knowledge of materials, technology, and production methods to the collaboration. But the realities of getting my architect's license had sent me down the more conventional path of working at a large firm. And I had loved the work, just as I loved the work at Pearce & Associates.

Because of our common interests, though, Russ and I had stayed in touch. Currently he was involved in utilizing sustainable technologies, such as green roofs and solar power, to reduce operating costs for commercial and government office buildings. I wondered if he was satisfied with how things had turned out.

Not that I was thinking of making changes. I mean, I had a great thing with Evan.

I was merely curious.

TWENTY

Friday night, at a nearby bar, I met up with a few classmates from UCLA, all of us now working in D.C.

Every few months we'd get together. It was always fun to hear what was going on—new firms, new job titles, new projects, new babies, new spouses. Life definitely isn't static. Normally I looked forward to the reunions, but tonight I was anxious, my stomach sloshing like a washing machine with too light a load.

Fifteen minutes after I joined the group, my stomach finally started to calm. Maybe the final person wouldn't show.

I was sitting next to Mark, who was good friends with Russ. They had even been each other's best man at their respective weddings.

"Have you heard from Russ lately?"

"Yeah. He's doing okay," Mark replied.

Hmmm. *Doing okay?*

Before I could quiz him further, a petite, black-haired, ethereal sprite of a girl (complete with pixie haircut—in case anyone missed the reference), flounced into the bar and plopped down on the empty seat next to me: Dana Reardon.

I had not wanted to encounter her tonight. I was still too livid about the letter from Tanner she'd intercepted. Another time, when the wound wasn't so fresh, maybe I'd confront her.

Not that receiving the condolence letter would have changed anything between Tanner and me. He had already met his first wife and they were having a child. But what the letter would have provided me was comfort, some kind words, and warm memories about my brother when I had desperately needed them.

I braced myself for her usual greeting.

"Hey, Jessie. What's up? Heard from Teddie D?"

This was always Dana's greeting; she still found the question amusing after all these years. But maybe the fact that she'd asked it for so long reflected some sort of perverse remorse on her part, like she couldn't let go of what she had done.

Wait. What was I thinking? This was Dana. She just liked pushing buttons.

Dana's and my relationship hadn't always been so prickly. During our first year at UCLA we'd been decent friends. But as school went on and the design problems became more complex, the friendship had deteriorated. The gap between Dana's ideas and actual designs kept widening, her projects workaday solutions without a creative spark.

I nodded at her, ignoring the question as I always did. Then I deliberately turned my back on her—which I never did—and continued my conversation with Mark, although I asked nothing more about Russ.

But Dana was as oblivious to my turning away as she was blind to so many other social nuances and kept right on talking to my back in her breathy, child-like way.

"Did you know Teddie Daulton was in town recently? And some woman threw water on him? In the middle of a restaurant. Can you believe it?"

I spun around, staring at her. She bubbled over with the joy of having this dirt, jouncing on her seat like a six-year-old child. You'd think she was sharing awesome news—like getting a gold star in kindergarten.

My blood boiled at the fact that she had learned of the story and that she was so eager to spread it.

She gasped audibly in her excitement. "I bet it was one of his bimbos. Someone he'd jilted."

Excusing myself to Mark, I got up and went to the bar to get another club soda. When I came back, I pulled up a chair between two other colleagues.

"Anyone participating in the 'Small Box' competition?" I asked.

Two of the guys answered yes. Dana moved her chair closer. When there was a local architectural competition, she was always fishing for ideas, her pointy little elfin ears a-twitching.

Knowing the score, we all started throwing out the silliest ideas for the site we could think of. My favorite suggestion was to use the property for vertical farming, which entails building high-rise glass-curtained structures that are essentially greenhouses. Actually, the idea wasn't as whacky as it might sound. Vertical farming was already being utilized in large, urban centers, particularly in Asia. But what would be whacky would be to build such a low-revenue producing project on expensive downtown land.

Under different circumstance I might have felt sorry for Dana, having to rely on others for ideas. But this evening, my blood continued to simmer.

When I got home, I grabbed my laptop and started typing.

Tanner,

I failed to mention that Dana Reardon moved to D.C. a couple of years ago. Her husband is on the staff of a congressman from California. Tonight, I got together with some colleagues from UCLA who work in D.C., hoping Dana wouldn't be there. But, of course, she showed up.

In case you can't hear me out there in L.A., I'm screaming in frustration. She related the story of "some bimbo" drenching you with water when you were last here.

I resent being called a bimbo. At the time, I was an avenging Valkyrie . . .

Why does she know this stuff? More importantly, why does she still care?

Sorry, I'm venting, but I was too furious to confront her.

Jessie

The next morning Tanner responded:

Jessie,

Yes, you did fail to mention that little tidbit.

Innocent as I mostly was regarding the letter about your brother, it was me you poured water on. Certainly, there had to be a pitcher of beer close by with her name on it? And I personally know how good your aim is.

The next time you meet with your friends, give me advance notice. I'll be happy to fly out and confront her. I'd have no compunction tossing beer on her—just as she had no compunction withholding my letter from you.

Tanner

Damn. The guy always could make me laugh.

TWENTY-ONE

Eliot, Sharon, and I were in high gear.

My two teammates were working on the design for the micro-apartment unit. Their charge was to create a place that might be small in square footage but would allow its occupants to live large. No insignificant task!

To achieve this, they had to maximize the open space so that the room could multi-task—one flexible area in which residents could cook, dine, work, entertain, sleep, create, and thrive. The space would transform throughout the day—with an assist from technology. The concept seemed fitting since millennials, who are prime targets for the units, had grown up with Transformer toys and high-tech gadgets.

And, if that wasn't enough for my two mentees to contend with, I also wanted the units standardized so they could be built off-site!

Meanwhile, I focused on the apartment building. The first thing I did was eliminate the traditional but usually underutilized ground floor lobby and place a more compact foyer to one side of the building. A ground floor is prime revenue space; a restaurant or retail store in place of an unused lobby would mean additional income to the owner.

The entrance foyer would include a reception desk and an adjacent management office as well as a small waiting alcove across from reception.

While this gateway into the building might be modest in size, its impact would be big. We decided the walls on the right, as one entered the entrance hall, would incorporate different electronic displays: streaming news feeds in the alcove and a Twitter Wall as one moved to the elevators. Also, a continuously-updating weather report would be displayed near the elevators on each floor. These vibrant, ever-changing electronic displays would make an exciting statement about this new type of residence and the people who lived there.

Communal space for residents would be located on the top floor. This lounge would multi-task just like the apartments. Residents working remotely would have tables with charging panels for phones and tablets as well as several treadmills with desktops. Coffee would be available 24/7.

Outside would be a small roof-top patio with seating and tables; potted plants would soften the surrounding urban hardscape. Then we'd bring a bit of that outdoors back inside by installing a "bio" wall of living plants in the lounge to keep the indoor air clean and oxygen-rich.

The three of us also researched technologies applicable to the project. Eliot chose photovoltaic energy and Wi-Fi, Sharon picked LED lighting, and I opted for green materials and modular construction.

Modular construction, which involves assembling the individual apartment units off-site, could mean a reduction in building costs, although I didn't think the approach had been tried in D.C. before. But while I didn't know much about pre-fab construction, I knew someone who did.

"Russ, I'd like to pick your brain about a local Ideas Competition. Do you have a few minutes?"

Russ Howard had remained in L.A. after graduation.

"Sure. How can I help?"

I explained the competition and our proposal to build micro-housing on the downtown site. "Since all the units will be identical, I wondered if building each unit off-site and then lifting them into place by crane would be feasible. Also, could it be more cost-effective?"

"It's certainly possible. Can you email me a copy of the briefing materials as well as any apartment and building plans you've sketched so far? That would give me a better idea of possible cost savings."

"I appreciate your help, Russ, but don't spend too much time on the project. It's just an Ideas Competition. But if you do notice other ways to make the project more environmentally friendly, let me know."

"Sounds like fun. I'll enjoy working on the puzzle."

Then, my mouth kept right on talking while my stomach vigorously questioned my sanity. "By the way,"—was that phrase ever really casual, or merely an attempt to sound casual?—"do you ever think about the firm we once talked about? I'm really intrigued with this housing typology and its smaller carbon footprint. I feel it has the potential to serve as a template for many public housing issues that remain neglected."

Russ hesitated. "Sometimes. To compensate, I work with Habitat for Humanity in my spare time. It's not the same, of course. My influence on what we do and how we do it is limited. But it's a start."

At least Russ was trying to live the principled life we had once talked about, whereas I seemed to live it only when time and opportunity intersected.

"It's more than a start, Russ. That's good work."

"Thanks. I'll email you my ideas about the project."

"Great."

What in the world was I thinking, trying to gauge Russ's satisfaction with his work? I needed to determine my own path before dragging someone else down that path with me. Yes, I was enjoying this competition—it called to me. But to change career paths now would mean giving up much of what I had worked so hard for.

Yet, to my ears, Russ had sounded . . . dissatisfied.

But I didn't spend much time that evening contemplating my future. Instead, as I ate dinner and finished reading *The Washington Post*, I ran across the story of Tanner's suit against the tabloid.

Tanner had won and the tabloid was instructed to pay several million dollars in damages. The article quoted Tanner as saying that the suit had not been about compensation, but about making this publishing outfit, and others like it, accountable for their journalism. The financial award would go directly to the charity Doctors Without Borders.

Which struck me forcibly. I pulled out my laptop.

Tanner,

I just read about the lawsuit. Congratulations on the outcome.

I'm sorry Jason had to be told about it. It must have been difficult for him, even knowing you were okay. Take him someplace fun to celebrate your win over exploitive journalism—no place in the least bit educational!

Also, Doctors Without Borders was the charity my family designated for friends wishing to make donations at the time of Alex's death. It was an organization he admired and hoped to be associated with. Good choice.

Jessie

I didn't know when these emails between Tanner and me had gone from sporadic communiqués of accusations and apologies to notes sharing pieces of our lives.

Was it wise? Probably not. But I wasn't prepared to give them up. Maybe we could have a bit of that intellectual companionship he and I had once shared, within the safety of the Internet. No talk of our relationship, no talk of our past—just a sharing of work and ideas.

TWENTY-TWO

"We've talked about this before, Jessie, but if you're serious about having children you need to make some decisions soon."

I was at the gynecologist's office for my annual checkup. And yes, we'd had this conversation before. For several years running. And Dr. Bening was right.

But I couldn't commit. I kept waiting for the perfect time to be a single mother. But as they say, apparently there is no perfect time to have a child.

"One thing in your favor is that you've used a diaphragm for birth control, as opposed to the pill. A recent study suggests that that method doesn't age eggs the way birth control pills may. Plus, of course, you don't have to wait for the hormones to get out of your system, so you can get pregnant faster."

That was good news, but it didn't help me with the most basic decision: biological child or adopted? If I wanted a biological child, time wasn't on my side. I was already on the down side of fertility at this point. Dr. Bening and I had talked about freezing my eggs as a way of keeping that option open. Adoption, on the other hand, would take some of that time pressure off. But there wasn't any guarantee that either approach would produce a child.

And it didn't help that my folks desperately wanted grandchildren to dote on, especially after Alex died. And frankly, I resented Alex a bit for leaving me to deal with them on the subject.

Damn Tanner. He had gotten a child out of his addiction and all I'd gotten was an STD test. Not that I thought he'd been unfaithful.

But I had to take control of my own health, so as soon as I left him, I had an STD panel performed. Everything was fine, but it had been an unimaginable action to have taken after believing that Tanner and I would be together for a lifetime.

"If you decide to conceive," the doctor continued, "I read a study, maybe ten years ago, in which women given musk to smell every day became pregnant quicker. The musk acts as a pheromone and results in shorter menstrual cycles, which means the women ovulate more frequently, giving them a better chance of getting pregnant."

I almost laughed. I was already familiar with that technique—"Eau de Tanner." I wondered if I could recreate his scent for that purpose. A bottom note of musk and a middle note of cedar were obvious. But what about the top note? Definitely not citrusy or floral. And not something spicy; he didn't smell like food. No, it had to be something light and fresh. Possibly green—like fresh-cut grass or a crushed herb?

No. Tanner loved the water, needed to be around water. Sometimes he even tasted of salt. That top note had to be aquatic. I wondered if they made a scent that evoked salt water and that sense of well-being at the release of ions as ocean waves crested and frothed.

I bet Tanner had been approached many times about developing a men's fragrance. I could create the scent and he could sell it: "Teddie D." No, he'd never go for an eponymous fragrance. Maybe something more archetypal—like "VIR", the Latin word for man and the source for words like virile and virtue. Yes, that would be fitting.

Or, maybe I'd keep the elixir all to myself.

"That sure sounds like more fun than fertility drugs," I squeaked, still immersed in my musings.

Dr. Bening laughed. "Well, don't wait until the decision is out of your hands."

I'd add it to my growing list of next-to-impossible-to-make decisions. But at least the checkup had been normal.

On the drive back to the office I couldn't stop thinking about Tanner's son. Before Tanner had shown me his pictures, Jason had been a shadow in the background; just one more factor confirming that our relationship was over. Now he was flesh and blood.

Yet Tanner had once committed to having children with me. I idly fantasized about taking him to court. Hadn't they done that in days past? What was it called? Oh, yes, breach of promise. I don't think he'd deny that he had agreed to children. I'd hire Charlene; she would eat him up and spit him out. But what would be my compensation? A sperm donation? No, then I'd be no better than his first wife.

Plus, I suppose he could countersue, arguing I'd dumped him before the terms of that promise could be realized.

Rats. I was back to the real world of having to make an imperfect decision in an imperfect world—a world even less perfect now that I was contemplating careening madly off a safe and promising career path. Financial stability could be a real concern in the short-term, possibly even long-term. I'd probably have to sell my house to generate the funds needed to get a new business up and running. Worse, I might have to leave D.C. for a town more sympathetic to micro-housing.

Was I prepared to do any of that, much less abandon the chance of having a child?

Okay, I'd give myself until the end of the year to make a

decision about having children. By then, if I were serious about a new practice—and hadn't developed cold feet, severe panic attacks, or terrifying night sweats—I should have some initial plans in place and a better understanding of the potential financial and lifestyle ramifications.

And if I still couldn't decide about having a child at that point? Then, by default, the decision would be made.

TWENTY-THREE

It was controlled chaos in the office.

Our submission was due Monday—only five more days, including the weekend.

And we were a man down.

That morning, Eliot, Sharon, and I had been in the conference room trying to finalize the various pieces of our presentation.

In the competition brief, the sponsor identifies what presentation materials he wants, e.g., presentation boards, 3-D model, PowerPoint presentation. Only the items specified will be reviewed. For this competition, teams were required to submit two boards, each thirty-six by thirty-six inches. Everything we designed, every explanation needed, and every feature we wanted to highlight, had to fit on those two boards.

In a way, the presentation boards served as our outline and kept us focused on the relevant material. At the start of the competition, I had pinned two regulation-size pieces of paper on the wall near the work tables in the bullpen. A grid was laid out on each sheet. Initially we'd filled the grids with just the name of each critical piece (floor plan, introductory statement, etc.) but quickly started filling the grids in with work product—both text and visual.

The rest of the office staff provided us steady feedback on the boards: how they read from a distance, whether the ratio of text to drawings was appropriate; whether the size and font used for the text was readable. The office's input was particularly important because they saw the boards as a judge would—without intimate knowledge of the project's details. The two boards were in constant flux.

At the last moment, we had decided to flip the pocket for the pocket-door to the bathroom to the other side of the entrance. Sharon had raced out to make the change on her computer so we could update the presentation board.

She never made it. In her rush, she'd swung her wheeled desk chair a little too energetically on its plastic protective mat and had ended up on the floor. Grabbing for the desk as she fell, she'd brought the keyboard down on top of her, as well as several reference books.

At the racket, everyone's head popped up.

But Sharon hadn't. When Eliot and I got to the bullpen she was still sitting on the floor, gasping for air, her right ankle already puffy. I asked Eliot to get a cold wet towel from the kitchenette while I examined the ankle. I'm no doctor, but I've seen my share of sprained ankles on the volleyball court.

A sprain wasn't fun, but one got used to accidents in architecture school. Sleepless nights and very sharp—and very pointy—X-ACTO blades, used for building 3-D models, made for mayhem. I'd seen worse. At least she wouldn't need stitches.

Eliot and I lifted Sharon to the chair, wrapped the cool towel around her ankle, and elevated her foot on a storage box.

Sharon looked stricken. I wasn't sure whether it was from pain or shock. I shooed everyone else away so she could steady herself without onlookers.

"Got your breath back yet?" I asked.

Sharon nodded, but she clenched her arms tightly across her chest, muscles straining.

"A doctor should check your ankle. Can I call one for you?"

She shook her head, even though the first tears were seeping through the wall of willpower she had erected.

"The sooner they look at your foot, Sharon, the better."

"But . . . but . . . I can't leave now. We've got too much to do." Her voice and body were shaking with frustration.

I gave her a big hug for her dedication as she sat propped up in her chair . . . and then I lectured her. "I shouldn't admit this, but it's only a competition."

I glanced around the office. "No one heard that, right?"

"What did you say?" ricocheted around the space, followed by heads shaking in mock disbelief.

"Taking care of your ankle, Sharon, is more important than a perfect presentation."

Sharon frowned, as if to argue.

"And, if you go to the doctor today, you might be back in time to finish the project. Besides, I'm not going to have you limping around the office the rest of today, with your ankle swelling to the size of a melon and a tea towel flapping in the breeze."

A slight smile emerged, although her forehead was still furrowed and her eyes scrunched up. Pain was setting in now that the initial shock had passed. After more half-hearted debate, Sharon allowed me to call the doctor.

Stephanie and I helped Sharon down the elevator and into a taxi. Stephanie would accompany her to the doctor and our office administrator, Karen, would take over the reception desk. One of Sharon's roommates would see that she got home.

Poor Sharon. She had invested so much time and effort in this project and she wanted to see it through. But if she stayed off her foot for a day or two, maybe she'd be back in time to put the final presentation package together.

It was time to pick a name for our proposal.

Open competitions are anonymous; there is no presentation before a panel of judges. Each submission is assigned a number as it's received. That way judges are not influenced—either positively or negatively—by the big names in architecture. Even Thomas Jefferson had to submit his proposals anonymously for the Capitol Building and the President's House (later to be known as the White House only because of the design selected)—and lost.

After a day and a half of staying off her feet, Sharon was back at the office, hobbling on one crutch and wearing hiking boots to accommodate the compression bandage and swelling. Although I didn't want her on the swollen ankle too soon, I was glad she was in the office for this debate; a conference call wouldn't have been as cathartic after a month of designing, researching, and probably staring at the bedroom ceiling late into the night as she thought about everything still needing to be done. No, this step was like putting the bow on the package.

For we couldn't just label our proposal "Micro-apartments" as there could be twenty other submissions for micro-housing. The judges need an easy way to identify each anonymous submission, something memorable as they moved quickly through hundreds of proposals to make that first cut.

For better or worse, I usually resorted to wordplay for competition titles. Even if the title made the judges groan, they might at least remember it.

I had two potential titles. "I know these two phrases don't exactly trip off the tongue, but they seem fitting. They're referential and play on the transforming nature of the units. Ready?"

Eliot, Sharon, and I were in my office, sitting at my worktable with the inevitable cups of coffee. They nodded.

"The first possibility is 'More than Meets the Eye: Transforming Micro-Apartments.' This title combines the common idiom with the tagline for the Transformer toys many of you grew up with and captures the idea of the apartments being organic, flexible, and multi-functional."

Two sets of eyeballs rolled noisily in their sockets, like pool balls colliding. I sighed.

"The second possibility modifies the phrase 'Go Figure' to 'Go ReconFigure: Transformative Micro-Apartments.' This name conveys both the idea that tenants can reconfigure the open plan units as they desire and that the apartments may have a transformative impact on those who live in them as well. You have to admit that the judges might at least remember 'Go Figure.'"

"Um," Eliot grunted, obviously not convinced.

"Hey. I like it. The title's fun and expresses what we're aiming at," Sharon offered, after considering it for a moment.

"Well, think about it overnight. Or see if you can come up with something better that is both concise yet indicative of the potential of this housing type."

That night I emailed Tanner, setting out the two titles. After all, he was the high priest of playful one-liners and puns.

Over the last several weeks, Tanner and I had exchanged messages on a regular basis—me informing him about the progress of the competition and him letting me know how things were going in the studio with his band.

Tanner voted for "Go ReconFigure." He liked the sense of action and self-discovery the title conveyed.

Either Eliot and Sharon had found out how hard it was to come up with a meaningful and catchy phrase or the second option had grown on them overnight. (No doubt the latter.) So, in full agreement Saturday morning we settled on "Go ReconFigure: Transformative Micro-Apartments" as the title of our proposal.

Let's hope the judges would feel that the apartments lived up to the title.

TWENTY-FOUR

Monday, mid-morning, Eliot and Sharon (still hobbling on one crutch) taxied our entry to the submissions office. Sharon wouldn't let go of that presentation until she made sure it reached its destination. For all their hard work, Evan was giving the two the rest of the day off.

I was proud of my team. The micro-unit designed by Eliot and Sharon had turned out great—efficient, well-organized, and livable. To maximize the open space, floor-to-ceiling built-ins lined one entire side of the unit, shifting from closets and storage nearest the entry and bathroom, to pantry and mini-kitchen midway, to living room storage, and finally to a desk and entertainment area nearest the windows with wall space for a flat screen TV and docking stations for electronics.

A wall unit located between the bathroom and the living space provided a dining table directly opposite the kitchen for day use which could be folded back into the unit at night when a bed was pulled down. But the open space was also designed so residents need not use the wall unit at all but could fashion the studio space to fit their individual needs.

Moreover, Russ had confirmed that the units could be built off-site at a lower cost. We had included information on the cost savings along with suggestions for sustainable building materials.

Truly a viable housing option offering something new for both D.C. and the residents.

And, just maybe, micro-housing could become a new niche for Pearce & Associates.

The following Tuesday the winners would be announced online. Then, for two months, the submissions would be exhibited at the National Building Museum. I'd take my team to study the entries later. That's where the real value lay at this point—not in some trifling award.

Around noon, Sharon knocked on my door jamb. On her way out of the office for some well-earned rest, she had her messenger bag strapped over her chest so she could handle the crutch more easily.

Her oval face was flushed, partially camouflaging the smattering of delicate freckles on her light caramel skin. "Do you have a minute?"

"Sure. Come in."

Sharon settled into a chair. Several thin braids, decorated with beads and worked into her naturally-curly, shoulder-length dark brown hair, got caught under the bag's strap and she spent a minute pulling them out.

"Thanks for participating in the competition, Sharon. These contests aren't easy. They requite immense amounts of commitment, stamina, and hard work." Then I chortled. "And I always conveniently forget just how much hard work before starting the next one."

"That's what I wanted to talk about, Jessie. I really appreciate being included on the team. I learned so much about design. It was an amazing month. I felt so connected."

A month ago, Sharon would have been fiddling with her hands out of shyness and discomfort; now she sat confidently in the chair, leaning towards me, actively engaged. She finally understood she was part of a team. She had always been free to ask questions and voice her opinions, but now she understood that we wanted her input. And now that she'd found her voice, I knew we would be hearing a lot more from her.

I beamed at her. "Good. You'll always need to find a way to connect to a project's purpose and own it. It doesn't matter whether you're twenty-four, working on a retirement complex, or like me, a Gen-Xer, working on an apartment complex for millennials. And that commitment and inspiration can come from many places. Watching you and Eliot tackle the apartment design with such energy was one of my entryways into the project."

Sharon was all smiles, pleased to know that not only had she been inspired but that she had inspired as well.

"Don't ever lose that passion for your work, even though some times will be harder than other. Maybe it's not the project you wanted to work on, maybe you're not happy with your team, maybe you feel you're doing too much grunt work, maybe you have too much going on in your personal life. But finding the excitement and purpose in each project will give you immense satisfaction—regardless of whether you win the competition or the commission. And by the way, you may want to keep reading up on

LED lighting—you're now our in-house expert."

When Sharon had taken on LED lights to research, I had treated her investigation as a master class, quizzing her, making her recommend the best approaches.

Sharon nodded. "I'd also like to learn more about the next generation of computer-assisted-design software."

Taking the initiative. Boy, she had come a long way. "Perfect. You and Eliot can be the co-leads on exploring the newest technology and report back to Evan and me."

"Thank you." Sunlight was beaming through the window onto Sharon's face. Puffy half-circles temporarily underlined her eyes, but a new inner light shone determinedly in them.

"You're welcome. Now it's back to the real world. You won't have adrenaline fueling you any more so you're going to have to find other ways into your projects, but I know you can do it. And if in doubt, come talk to me."

Sharon stood up and tottered over. I stood up, too, and we gave each other a warm hug.

When I got home that evening, I had an email from Tanner.

Jess,

You must be relieved that the competition is over after all the long nights. I can't believe how much time you put into something that will not be built.

Also, can you explain to me why architects are willing to give away their ideas for free? Of course, not everything an artist creates will be a commercial or critical success so we need to find joy and satisfaction in the act of creation itself. But it seems like architecture competitions take advantage of people's willingness to share and exchange ideas a little too much. I mean, don't other people take your ideas and use them themselves? Or am I being cynical?

I liked your idea about memories retaining a spark of life from the moment an event occurs. Some memories feel so real—the colors, sounds, and smells from an earlier time startlingly alive and clear. Maybe there's a song there. Can I share songwriting credit with you?

Tanner

I snorted.

Tanner,

You're not the first person to suggest that architects are a gullible and too trusting species—even some major architects argue that point, refusing to participate in open competitions. But competitions are one of the best ways to get a point of view out there for consideration, especially for those with new voices.

Besides, architecture is like any art form—building on past traditions but striving for a new expression to reflect the present. Your music references the blues but with your own spin. The collective spirit benefits all artists.

But then again, maybe we architects are gullible . . .

If you can find a song in the idea of memories, it's all yours.

Jess

TWENTY-FIVE

Two days later I had a meeting with our structural engineer about the library extension site. His office was on my way to work so I stopped by. I was beginning construction drawings and needed to resolve a couple of foundation details.

Early for the meeting, I checked phone messages. One from Evan said that he'd just set up a meeting at eleven with a potential new client.

When I arrived at the office slightly before the appointment, Stephanie nearly leaped out of her chair.

"You won't believe who's in the office! With Evan! Guess who?"

I didn't think she meant the rock group, The Guess Who. They were before her time.

"Mies van de Rohe?" I responded.

Her face scrunched up, all quizzical. "Huh?"

I wanted to laugh. Well, she'd said I wouldn't believe who it was, and since the architect who had coined "less is more" died in the '60s, I would have been very surprised indeed had Mies been in our office.

"I have no clue, Stephanie. Who's here?"

Her eyes opened wide. "Teddie Daulton! Teddie D is in our office!"

My heart stopped beating. Really. From shock. Where was a defibrillator when you needed one? I gripped the reception counter.

What in the world was Tanner doing here? Had he just stopped by the office to visit while in town? This couldn't possibly have anything to do with Evan's message, could it?

Despite the heat crawling up my neck, I forced myself to ask calmly, "What about Evan's eleven o'clock appointment?"

Stephanie's chair had become a trampoline. Each time she spoke, she bounced, and the chair rebounded her higher. The bounces became exclamation marks. "That's what I'm trying to tell you, Jessie!" *Boing.* "Mr. Daulton is the appointment?" *Boing, boing.* "And he's here! In the office!" *Boing, boing, boing.*

Finding it difficult to breathe, I unbuttoned my suit jacket. Only two nights ago, Tanner had sent me an email. He had said nothing about coming to D.C.—not for advocacy work, not for a visit to Walter Reed Hospital, and certainly not for AN APPOINTMENT WITH MY BOSS.

My legs wouldn't work. Or maybe it was my brain. With three thousand miles between us, Tanner and I had achieved a certain cordiality. But in the flesh? In our last encounter our reactions to each other had been visceral, the result of long-held emotions, hurt, and habit—our responses instinctive, not rational. None of those feelings had suddenly disappeared, so why would he think things would be better today?

Stephanie was still talking. "God, you are so lucky. You get to be in a meeting with him? You've got to tell me afterwards what he's like?"

A jerk? Swallowing that response, I said, "Guess I better find out what's going on."

Then I pleaded with my legs to move.

Turning the corner from the lobby into the bullpen, I saw Tanner, through the floor-to-ceiling glass, already settled in Evan's office. Every head at every desk in the office was swiveled in his direction, not one person even pretending to work.

Could I blame them? The man was larger than life—even though he was in disguise today, dressed in charcoal slacks, a medium blue shirt (bound to set off those damnable dark brown eyes), and a navy sports coat. But try as he might, he was no Everyman. It wasn't the clothes that made him but the charisma that seeped from every pore. Even I couldn't resist looking at him. And although the door to Evan's office was closed, I could feel Tanner's energy crackling through the glass. It was a miracle it hadn't shattered.

Evan caught sight of me and waved for me to join them. Tanner turned my direction, a mischievous grin on his lips. I nodded back at Evan and ignored Tanner. Until I found out why he was here, there would be no smiles for the Rock Star. He had invaded my territory without a heads-up—or my permission.

I stopped at my office along the way to stash my bag. I didn't delay, though. I wanted to get to Evan's office quickly for damage control.

When I entered Evan's office, Tanner stood up, all smiles and goodwill.

"I understand you two know each other," Evan said.

"Yes. We met in college." I didn't know what else Tanner had said so I left it at that. I certainly wasn't going to make our past relationship public knowledge.

"It's good to see you again, Jessie," Tanner said, moving in for a hug.

I swiftly stuck out my hand. My office, my rules.

He was taken aback only for a second and then the smile returned as he shook my hand.

"This is a surprise, Teddie. I didn't think we'd run into each other so soon. What brings you to Pearce & Associates?" I deliberately used his common name to put distance between us. I would have said "Mr. Daulton" if Evan hadn't already known we were acquainted.

Evan's eyes gleamed. He was a huge fan of rock music, which explained the Jerry Garcia ties. But his demeanor suggested this occasion was about more than meeting a guitar hero.

"Have a seat, Jessie. I think you'll be pleased to find out why Teddie is here." Oh, great. They were already on a first-name basis.

Evan motioned for me to sit on the sofa, where Tanner was already ensconced as if in ownership. I wanted to take one of the chairs but, like an obedient child, I sat on the sofa, tucking myself against the arm rest, as far from Tanner as possible.

Tanner's dratted life force pummeled me anyway.

Meanwhile, he rested comfortably on the sofa, his right arm perched on the back of the couch, almost touching my shoulder, and let Evan bring me up to speed on what had already been discussed. It was surreal to see these two men—who came from different decades and opposite sides of the country—converge in the present in front of me. The two should never have met—one was from the past, the other from the present. They represented opposing elements in my life and should have canceled each other out.

"Teddie is offering us a wonderful opportunity."

I glanced at Tanner. He was gazing innocently at Evan, but a smile played about his mouth. Heck, he could barely keep it from bursting into a gallop. Whatever the deal, it must be good.

I switched my attention back to Evan.

"Apparently he saw your house recently?"

I nodded, still not sure where this was heading.

"Well, Teddie would like you to design him a second home."

What? I clamped my lips together before my jaw dropped. Tanner wanted me to design a house for him? Since Evan had referred specifically to my house, was it to be similar to the one Tanner and I had talked about building together? The one to be filled with three children? Was Tanner hiring me to build him our house?

Evan knew I loved designing one-of-a-kind homes. He expected me to be pleased about this "opportunity."

I wasn't. For Tanner had realized I would say No, so he'd done an end run on me by going to my boss first. He could then sit back disingenuously as Evan explained—and who would expect me to be delighted. What firm wouldn't want to build a home for Teddie Daulton? Perhaps Evan already had visions of *Architectural Record* or *Architectural Digest* in his head.

And I'd have to be a team player, wouldn't I? Especially with a partnership on the line—or could Tanner possibly think he was helping me secure the partnership? But I didn't need—nor want—his help. Yet any way you looked at it, I was screwed.

Tanner joined in. "It would be a lake house. Since I was last here, Jess,"—the use of my nickname in the office was jarring—"I've been looking for and finally found the perfect lot. Closed on it Friday. Flew here last night and called Evan this morning to set up this meeting. I'm looking forward to getting the project started now that I have the site. You're going to love the view."

Somehow, I doubted it—particularly if it was the lake view we had once talked about.

Obviously, I was expected to say something but I wasn't swallowing the Kool-Aid. "I'm surprised. You never mentioned anything about building a new home when you visited." I narrowed my eyes at him. Initially he'd been angered by my house, not charmed by it.

Tanner raised an eyebrow at me. For the first time, I saw uncertainty in his expression. "I . . . had plenty of time on the flight back to California to think about the possibility."

So, in his fantasy, once he had decided to build, I was to embrace his proposal with open arms. Didn't he realize what he was asking? My blood pressure started rising.

With excellent timing, Evan jumped in. "Then it sounds as if your recent encounter was fortuitous. Tanner made reservations for lunch, so we'll continue this discussion over lunch. Till then, Jessie, would you show Teddie around the office and introduce him to the staff? And don't forget to work out the details for visiting the site." Evan smiled benevolently.

"I hope you'll enjoy the restaurant, Jess. It's Rasika." Tanner grinned wickedly, back in control.

Damn the man. I gave him the evil eye.

He smirked.

"That's one of Jessie's favorite restaurants," Evan observed helpfully, oblivious to our childish mugging.

Everything was going exactly as Tanner had planned.

But how could we work together? I could barely be in the same room with him without some malfunction of my body. Plus, there was that constant undercurrent of anger and hurt between us, no matter how hard we tried to ignore it.

And more importantly, how could I design Tanner something wonderful without all those past emotions and expectations getting in the way?

But I would put on my game face, show Tanner around the office, and make him think I was buying into the idea. Then, when I had the opportunity, I would appeal to his better nature, and convince him that this . . . collaboration . . . was truly a horrendous idea.

TWENTY-SIX

I escorted Tanner to the nearest desk and began introductions. Tanner was charming—inquisitive about what everyone was working on and how long they had been with the company. If this had been a normal situation, I would have been pleased at how comfortable he made each person feel—as if they were the most interesting thing in his life at the moment. Affability is one of Tanner's super powers.

But walking through the office with Tanner wasn't normal and I felt blindsided and bruised at the way he had approached this. His lack of respect for me in showing up unannounced and in talking to Evan first crawled disturbingly around my belly.

Halfway through the greetings we arrived at Eliot's desk. As soon as I mentioned Eliot's name, Tanner's face lit up.

"The Ideas Competition! Jessie has written so much about the great work you and Sharon did."

That creature crawling around my stomach started sprinting and I felt sweat on my back. I had been introducing Tanner as an acquaintance and a possible new client. Now it was exposed that I had been updating Tanner on a regular basis about the competition. I had unwisely trusted in his discretion.

I turned away from Tanner and called Sharon over. I didn't want him to see how betrayed I felt.

"Teddie, this is Sharon Malone, who also worked on the competition."

"Of course! It's very nice to meet you." He proffered his hand.

Both kids were beside themselves when they realized that Teddie D was familiar with their micro-housing project.

"Eliot, Sharon, why don't you set up the PowerPoint presentation for our proposal in the conference room?" The show hadn't been part of the submission requirements but we had prepared it for occasions like this. "When I've finished introducing Teddie to everyone, you can give him a ten-minute run-through."

"Hey, that's a great idea," Tanner said. I almost expected him to break into song.

My two young colleagues scurried off, though Sharon was sidling a bit like a crab now that she wasn't using the crutch. Thank god, I hadn't written Tanner about Sharon's injury. No doubt he would have asked about her ankle out of concern—which would have been far too personal.

Our last stop was the lobby. Turns out Stephanie was a huge fan of In This Together. In her excitement, her voice went up an octave. At least exclamation marks punctuated her comments, rather than question marks. But now I regretted the blue-glazed pots I had given her as a house-warming gift for the flowers she wanted to grow on her balcony. She would probably have been happier with one of Tanner's CDs.

Before joining Sharon and Eliot, I asked Tanner if he'd like some coffee. I was merely being polite as I was the one in desperate need of the caffeine to reboot my brain now that the shock of his presence was wearing off.

Like most architects' offices, the walls of the hallway and work spaces were lined with photographs of buildings we had designed. Once we'd poured our coffees, Tanner wanted to know which ones I had been involved with. I pointed them out as we walked back to the conference room, me in the lead to speed things along.

Suddenly, not hearing footsteps behind me, I turned to see him staring at one of the photos. It was a shot of a small residential complex located in rural Maryland that I had designed for retired clergy. The firm had received a design award for the project from the local chapter of the American Institute of Architects.

He turned to me, his brown eyes thoughtful. "It's wonderful to see your projects built, Jessie. It must feel incredible to have something you've designed take on physical form."

"Probably a little like you recording an album," I sidestepped lightly.

He nodded. "But you leave an imprint on the environment."

"True. But you leave an imprint on the people who listen to your music. And your impact is far more immediate and personal."

Ignoring my comments, Tanner continued, "You know, I miss hearing you talk about buildings. You probably won't believe this, but when a lecture or special exhibit on architecture is announced in L.A., I try to go."

Time slowed for a moment. I'd assumed he would come to hate the topic once I left. Perhaps it was like me with his music—despite everything, I could appreciate it as distinct from our relationship. Well, except for the green-eyed girl songs. I guess our heady, early days together had predisposed us to appreciate each other's chosen field even after the breakup.

Tanner lingered a minute longer in front of the picture, tracing part of the building lightly with his fingertip.

His gesture almost broke my heart. The tenderness in it unexpectedly reminded me of the touch of his fingers on my face six weeks earlier, when he had said goodbye in front of the hotel. I longed to change places with that damn photo.

Once Tanner and I were settled in the conference room (me in my own chair finally), Sharon and Eliot ran the PowerPoint presentation. My team enjoyed sharing their proposal with Tanner and he was equally engrossed, asking insightful questions and complimenting them. His comments even suggested he might have done a little research himself.

God, it sucked. At one time this was what I had wanted; this is what I had imagined our life would be—sharing in each other's work and creations.

At the end of the presentation, Tanner commented that he found the project "compelling and relevant to today's social issues."

He couldn't have made Eliot and Sharon happier.

Time to find out what was really going on.

As I closed the door to my office, Tanner spotted Teddy Seattle in the middle of my bookshelves. In a flash he was across the room, picking up the bruin.

"You really do have Teddy Seattle. I'm not sure I believed you." His eyes sparkled at the reunion.

I sat down at my work table with my back to the bullpen. He would have to sit opposite me, which meant he'd have to maintain a positive face for the audience—but then he was used to that.

"Is that why you stopped by? To check on the bear? See if I really had him?" My voice was calm and I had widened my eyes as if in wonder. Heck, I was batting my eyelashes to highlight the innocence of the question.

Tanner wasn't fooled. He set my bear back down like it was radioactive. "I told you why I'm here, Jessie. I want you to design a lake house." He strode over and sat down.

"Then why didn't you talk to me first?" My voice had dropped half an octave. "Now it's nearly impossible for me to say no to Evan. Is that really how we should begin a collaborative project?"

He tilted back in the chair casually, as if to counterbalance my intensity. "I checked the company's website. It says Evan handles new business."

Was he being deliberately obtuse?

"Don't patronize me. Why couldn't you and I have discussed this first?"

He slowly settled the chair back on the floor and then leaned into me, pushing back, compressing the air between us. "Because you'd have said no. I figured going through Evan might give you time to realize that this could work."

Aha! He had been determined to have his own way—even if it meant sucker-punching me. My hands started shaking and I placed them on my lap, out of sight.

Yet it didn't make sense. He had been angry when he saw my house, not comforted by it . . . although, admittedly, he had later apologized.

"Why, all of a sudden, do you want this house?"

Tanner picked up a rigid, vinyl paperweight in the shape of a wadded-up blueprint from the table, studying it. His eyes remained on the paperweight as he replied. "Maybe it's not sudden. You know I've always wanted a house near the water. Plus, you know what I want. Maybe I just saw this as the opportunity to finally build it."

"Don't kid yourself. Anything we talked about twelve years ago for a house is hardly relevant to your life today. I'm sure your tastes and expectations are now quite different from when I knew you."

Tanner's eyes met mine. "They may have changed some, but probably not as much as you'd expect."

I leaned forward, my hands now clasped tightly together on the table, and said softly, "When you left my house, Tanner, you were furious that I had built a place similar to the one we had talked about. Maybe you were even angry that the house makes me so happy." His eyes narrowed.

"So why would you want a house anything like mine? There are architects in California who could give you something fresh, something that reflects you now."

Tanner ran his hand roughly through his hair.

I wasn't trying to hurt him, but this house might, if he built it for the wrong reasons.

I pushed harder. "Or would hiring me to design this house be penance in some perverse way for you? Or, perhaps the opposite—punishment for me?"

That got him.

The compressed air between us crackled.

"You're right." His expression was grim. "When I saw your house, I was angry. I couldn't believe you'd built something that was ours."

Then his eyes softened. "On the flight back to L.A., however, I realized how happy the house made you. I thought maybe something good from those early days might bring me the same solace." He looked down blindly at the paperweight still wrapped in his hands.

He, too, was still caught in the past? My throat constricted. Those irreparable mistakes we had made so many years ago kept us perpetually chained to those days.

More gently, I asked, "But what if it doesn't, Tanner? What if the house brings you sadness?"

Without looking up, he replied, "Then I won't be any worse off, will I?"

My body, which had always sided with Tanner, melted at the misery bared in his words, though my brain was still angry at him for not talking to me first.

I considered the two of us—estranged for twelve years, never achieving closure, scarred with wounds as fresh as if they had just happened, anger lurking seconds away and guilt just as constant a companion, our history distorted by who-knows-what misconceptions, and unable to trust one another in our hurt. As I tried to imagine us working together on this project, my mind imploded at the impossibility.

I burst out laughing, my body shaking in unison . . . and couldn't stop. The whole idea of Tanner and me collaborating was so absurd, so crazy, so ridiculous, that it seemed madness to consider it. Tears streamed down my face as laughter rolled up my throat. The tension I'd felt since discovering him in the office drained out of my tightly wound body.

Tanner stared at me.

Over my tears, I stammered, "You . . . you realize this is a terrible, quite insane, absolutely mad idea, don't you?"

Tanner's face broke into sunshine. "Probably. No, definitely the worst idea ever."

"And it's going to hurt like hell?"

"Undoubtedly."

"Well, at least we agree on something. I suppose it's a start." I wiped the tears from my face with the backs of my hands.

So, I would try to work with him because I could see how badly Tanner wanted this, how much he needed this to work. And I understood because I found solace in my house.

But it didn't mean I was happy. He had done an end run on me and hadn't been honest. And while he acknowledged that the process might be painful, I didn't think he had a clue about how difficult it would be for me, being demoted from his partner to the hired help.

I wouldn't be designing *our* house; I would be designing *his* house. But maybe I owed him this—for abandoning him while he was addicted, for making things worse for him when I left, and for the gift he had given me regarding my brother.

So, despite the jumble of clashing emotions stuck in my chest, I said, "Okay, I'll come out. But this will be an exploratory meeting only. I'm not committing to taking the job until I see how we work together. We'll develop a program for the house and look at the lot. After that, we can decide whether to move forward—and either one of us gets to say no."

With what sounded like relief, he agreed.

"Can you fly out Friday for the weekend?"

I almost agreed, then remembered Nick's company dinner. "Um, I can't. I've got . . . something scheduled."

"Can you get out of it?"

"No. I committed weeks ago."

"Something with Nick?" he asked a bit sourly.

"Yes." Who was he to expect me to be available now that he was ready to push forward on his project? "He's being honored at a dinner."

"Definitely wouldn't want you to miss that."

His tone implied anything but. I innocently agreed which raised the ghost of a smile from him.

I suggested instead flying out the following Friday. We could develop a program for the house on Friday, visit the property Saturday, and finish with some preliminary sketches on Sunday.

"Why don't you stay at my place?" he offered. "I've got plenty of room. That way you'll get a better sense of how I live."

Stay at his place? I didn't know anything about his personal life. Would Jason be there? Was Tanner seeing someone? Did a girlfriend live with him? Might she even be part of the discussions?

"You could have the guesthouse," he added, when I didn't answer immediately. "You'd have privacy but be close enough that we could work late and you wouldn't have to worry about driving back to a hotel."

Well, I was curious to see his home and how he lived. And curiosity always won out when it came to architecture. As long as I could disappear when I'd had too much of him or this proposed project, the guesthouse should work.

I nodded. "Fine." But he didn't get to dictate everything.

"While I'm in L.A., I need to meet a colleague for dinner. Let's assume I can set it up for Friday night though I'll have to confirm. I'll rent a car at the airport so I can make the dinner meeting."

"Business dinner?"

I wanted to answer "bigger than a shoe box" as I had when he'd asked about Nick in April. But Tanner was now a possible client, so I politely replied, "Potential business."

"You're welcome to use one of my cars while you're in L.A. or call Uber if you'd rather not drive. That way I could pick you up at the airport."

I considered the offer. "Uber would probably work." It was only a semblance of independence, but it would do.

He smiled. "Then it's settled. I'll meet you at the airport next Friday and you'll stay at the guesthouse. You can email me your flight information when you have it."

Then Tanner's eyes darted in the direction of Evan's office as if detecting movement. "Uh, would you prefer a restaurant other than Rasika?" he asked hesitatingly, almost as if in apology.

It was a nice gesture now that he'd won the battle. And the truth was that I would prefer an unlicensed food truck right now to Rasika. But I wasn't about to show weakness.

"No. Rasika's fine."

TWENTY-SEVEN

Our office was only four blocks from the restaurant but Evan would never let a client, much less a rock star, walk that distance. He hailed a cab and took the seat up front, leaving me with Tanner in the back.

I know it seems gentlemanly to let a woman get into a cab first. But entering a cab should be one of the exceptions, like going through a revolving door. There is no way a woman can gracefully slide across a backseat in a pencil skirt without having it hike up. A total impossibility under any laws of physics.

Although maybe that's why men don't offer to get in first as Tanner didn't seem to mind the view in the least. His eyes gravitated to my exposed thigh and the corners of his mouth turned up. When I jerked the skirt down, his mouth exploded into a full-blown grin at my modesty—an unspoken reminder that he had seen far more, once upon a time.

But that was in another lifetime.

Evan, half-turned in his seat, was unaware of our backseat skirmishing, like a clueless father. "Have you been to Rasika before, Teddie?"

I threw a threatening glance at Tanner. He started to laugh, but smartly turned it into a cough. "Uh, yes, though I have to admit that my last visit was the most memorable."

He was in too good a mood, now that he had gotten his way. I moved my foot sideways and "accidently" kicked the great man.

"But I'm sure today will be just as unforgettable," he added, glancing my direction, his eyes laughing.

Getting out of the taxi was no easier than getting in—maybe worse. As I started to slide across the seat, Tanner turned to offer me a hand. I whispered darkly, "Turn around and let me get out." He remained planted, those damnable eyes still twinkling.

It wasn't that I was self-conscious about my body—but Tanner had had his chance. With what dignity I had left, I stepped out of the cab, hoping there would be no near Britney Spears moment. Then I brushed past Tanner and headed to the front door of the restaurant.

Not that I was anxious to enter. Would anyone recognize me? Did they have a wanted poster of me in the kitchen in case I showed up?

The maître d' welcomed Tanner. "Ah, Mr. Daulton, it is good to see you again. I am so sorry about what happened when you were here last. Our apologies, sir."

Tanner smiled nonchalantly. "These things happen. I'm just sorry for the inconvenience."

Heat pricked at my neck, but I held my ground. He could have his fun but I would have the final say as to whether we moved ahead on his project.

Putting his hand on the curve of my back, Tanner indicated I should follow the hostess. A charge of electricity coursed through me from his touch.

And he wondered why I had never married.

Once we were seated, a server came to the table with bottled water. Tanner, after his glass was filled, moved it away from me and made a point of moving his knife to a safer place as well.

I thought of reminding him that I still had mine, but instead I smiled pleasantly at him—like a Stepford Wife—then raised my glass of water to him, before taking a sip.

Meanwhile, Evan was asking Tanner what the maître d' had been referring to.

At his question, water spurted out my nose and I started coughing.

Stifling a laugh, Tanner leaned over and thumped me—hard—on the back.

"Are you all right?" he asked, handing me his napkin to dry my face. "Should I ask for some towels?"

Still coughing, I shook my head. Tanner was enjoying this far too much. He had been wise to relocate his glass . . . and knife.

With unbridled enthusiasm, Tanner told Evan the story—in detail, if not exactly truthfully: an unhappy fan, not liking his rhymes, had thrown water on him. Evan's mouth was agape.

I wondered what Evan would do if he discovered that "fan" was me?

Chills suddenly swept my body. Could Tanner be setting me up in front of my boss? Dangling the carrot of a job in front of Evan and then exposing me as the perpetrator of the offense? Project gone. Partnership gone. Would Tanner do that to me? He certainly had no allegiance to me anymore. We were at the scene of the crime. Was this a case of revenge being a dish best served cold?

I took a deep breath. No. That was impossible. Tanner didn't have a mean bone in his body. He was a generous person. It was my guilt coloring the situation, not his desire for revenge. If anything, he probably thought he was helping me get that partnership—not that I needed his help.

"Does that happen often—that someone assaults you?"

Tanner could barely keep from laughing at Evan's disbelief and immediate sympathy. "Thank goodness, no. But everyone's a critic, right?"

"Oh, yes. We get that in our field as well. Probably more, since our output is physical as well as artistic."

Tanner nodded, the two bonded in solidarity against critics.

I was off the hook. Tanner seemed to find the whole disaster amusing—at least in retrospect.

I sat back, relaxed a little, and let the two men get acquainted, these two men who were both such an important part of my life.

Halfway through the meal, Tanner asked how I was enjoying the food. Softly, so Evan couldn't hear, I replied, "It's a lot better than the crow I ate after my last visit."

He choked back another laugh.

If only he'd been drinking water.

TWENTY-EIGHT

That night after work I called Russ Howard at home. This wasn't a conversation to be had in our offices.

My stomach was in shreds as I waited for someone to pick up the ringing phone. I hadn't planned making the call this soon, but Tanner's visit had triggered this conversation.

Russ's wife, Sally, answered. She was a special needs teacher with a huge heart, completely devoted to her students.

"Hi, Sally. It's Jessie Hartley."

We spent a couple minutes catching up. When my heart rate had settled back to normal, I asked, "Is Russ around?"

She handed the phone off to Russ.

"Hi, Jessie. Have you heard back on the competition?"

"Uh, no. Won't hear back until next week."

Then, in a weird way propelled by my own fear, I took the leap—a terrifying, gut-wrenching, chill-producing jump into the unknown.

"This competition has really made me think about the issues we used to talk about, Russ. It's reminded me of the type of architecture I had intended to do. Projects directly affecting people's well-being."

Russ was silent.

That was okay. This conversation was all on me. My dream, my gamble.

"I've been very happy at my firm. But suddenly, it isn't as . . . fulfilling. I've been more engaged working on this competition than anything I've done in a while. It made me realize how far from my heart's work I've strayed."

I kept rubbing the back of my neck as I talked, trying to ease the tension. But it wasn't helping my knotted stomach.

"Anyway, I'm wondering if you have any interest in revisiting those ideas and working together. I know this probably sounds like a crazy proposal. You're settled, I'm settled. It would be a huge risk—probably bigger than huge. Gargantuan. But I want to be more in control of the work I do. And your talents and mine have always meshed well.

"To let you know how serious I am, I'm pretty certain to get partner in the next year or two if I stay at my firm. But partner feels more like a negative than a positive right now."

At a distance of three thousand miles, I sensed Russ gathering his thoughts—or maybe his confusion.

"Jeez, Jessie. I assumed you were happy at your firm. I'm not sure what to say. I'm shocked."

"I get it. Sometimes I feel like that when I run the idea through my own head. But I'm going to be in L.A. at the end of next week and thought maybe you and Sally and I could talk over the possibility at a restaurant Friday night. Maybe by then you'll know whether the idea holds any interest or simply terrifies you."

He paused, then chuckled. "Probably both."

Well, at least it wasn't a flat-out no.

We arranged where and when to meet and I hung up the phone with a shaking hand.

Wow. I couldn't believe I'd done that. My heart was racing. This idea of an alternative future that I had been toying with, poking at, and testing in the privacy of my brain for the last month was now suddenly alive out there in the world.

I might be panicking, but I was also elated.

TWENTY-NINE

I was double-checking everything. No runs in the black stockings. My small, sequined black clutch in hand. Jewelry on. Little black dress—which even I had to confess looked hot. It had been a long time since I had been out on a formal date . . . well, in this case, a formal non-date. I looked like that put-together person inhabiting the fantasies in which I encounter Tanner—not that I had that fantasy anymore. Reality had been too demoralizing.

Damn, I was nervous about this outing. No matter what Nick had said, it sure felt like a date. To make it feel more casual I walked over to his house.

Nick opened the door before I knocked. "Jessie. You look amazing."

The compliment was heady.

He looked good as well, exuding athleticism and masculinity, his light blond hair slicked back, a beautiful peacock-blue and black tie accessorizing his well-tailored black suit, which did nothing to disguise his muscularity.

"Thanks."

"Got everything you need?"

"Yep, I'm set."

Cocktails preceded dinner. The large hotel conference room, set up for dining, was crowded and noisy, the mood sparkling. The din of conversations sounded silvery, like the clinking of champagne glasses. It was festive—even with club soda in my glass.

With his hand at my elbow, Nick guided me through the crowd, selectively introducing me to people. Being Washington, D.C., the first question after the greeting was usually "What do you do?" followed by "How do you know Nick?" Women, especially, were curious. If anyone got too curious about the relationship, Nick moved us along.

As he escorted me around the room, I almost felt we were dancing—albeit some newfangled business waltz. It felt sexy to be on this man's arm and the focus of his attention. No wonder someone else might believe the relationship to be escalating.

But it was a relief to finally sit down for dinner with no more questions about how Nick and I had met.

Our companions at the table seemed to be primarily economists and their Significant Others—or maybe everyone at the Institute sounded like a quant.

When people at the table found out I was an architect, I was besieged with questions. What impact was the global economy having on my industry? What are the barriers to entry that might discourage competition? How significant is technology to architecture? How do architecture firms respond to changes in the marketplace and economy?

I felt like a rare, endangered species. Had these people never met an architect before? Or, maybe it was a hazing rite, as Nick seemed to be chortling behind his napkin.

But I didn't mind. These were either issues that Evan and I talked about periodically as we assessed operations or questions that Russ and I would be talking about soon.

In return, I picked their brains: Could architecture ever become a commodity where cost was the only criteria? Could small architecture firms withstand the creation of larger and larger global architecture firms? Could a company differentiate itself in an industry in which large firms were becoming generalists, covering almost every conceivable building type, and in which small firms were becoming increasingly specialized?

But midway through dinner I was just moving the food around my plate. Listening to everyone's opinions about the economy and architecture was giving me indigestion.

Nick seemed to sense my uneasiness and patted my hand reassuringly. "The economy's not collapsing any time soon," he whispered.

But he didn't know about my fantasy. The economy collapsing wouldn't be the problem if the business plan I created wasn't sound to begin with.

But the economists' responses to my queries had highlighted two factors for success: find a distinct niche and then design the business so it could respond quickly to changes in the market. That was something I could take to dinner with me on Friday.

Nick didn't leave my side except for the few minutes when he had to speak about the policy implications of his research. Peers had overwhelmingly deemed his book required reading for politicians and others invested in creating a strong future for our youth and the economy. Several state governments had already approached him about how to implement his ideas. MacArthur Genius Award, anybody?

When we got home, Nick walked me to my house.

As we stood at the doorway I said, "Thanks for inviting me. Oddly enough, I enjoyed it."

"That's good. Most people would have wilted under all the questioning."

"It's good to reflect on these issues occasionally. You never know when it might come in handy. And it was even better to see you honored for your work. Congratulations."

"Thanks. And thanks for joining me."

He leaned in.

The night had been intoxicating. Nick's hand on my arm, his unwavering attention to my well-being at the party, being part of the group recognizing his success, feeling his breath on my neck as he whispered to me over dinner—had all been incredibly intimate. My pulse quickened and my blood stirred unaccustomedly.

I almost tasted his lips pressing mine.

He kissed me on the forehead.

"Good night, kiddo. Any chance you want to run tomorrow?"

Damn. I should have known better but resented the yearning. To give myself time to regain my composure I went for the laugh, as usual. "No. Someone kept me up too late this evening. You can talk to him if you have a complaint."

"I shall have a serious talk with that guy. But thanks for coming tonight, Jessie. I appreciate it. Sweet dreams."

"I'm glad you asked. 'Night, Dr. Nick."

As I got ready for bed, I thought about that kiss that wasn't. There was no doubt I'd been high on intimacy. But I didn't think the yearning had necessarily been about Nick. I think it was more about the lack of intimacy in my life.

On the other hand, maybe it was a bit about Nick.

Only two men hovered on the periphery of my life—both unavailable. One unattainable man might have been a learning experience. But two? That was a pattern. And I was the common denominator—which made me the problem.

THIRTY

People who knew of my upcoming trip to L.A. all had different takes on the project.

Evan was ecstatic about the potential job, of course, while the rest of the staff wanted "details" on Tanner.

Charlene, who was still cross with me for not having told her about Tanner in the first place, thought it hysterical—and very karmic—that my pouring water on Tanner had led to me possibly designing a house for him by the water.

And Nick (who was picking up my mail and newspaper while I was away) was concerned.

He had come over to pick up my house key. "Are you sure you should do this, Jessie?" he asked, his eyes troubled.

We were standing on my front porch, enjoying the last splashes of color from the sunset as evening overtook us.

I shrugged. "Not my first choice. But this weekend is only to see whether we can work together. Besides, I've got other business in L.A."

Nick raised his eyebrows. "What would that be?"

I hesitated. Except for Russ, I hadn't mentioned a word to anyone about the possibility of a U-turn in my career. But after weeks of pondering the idea, I was interested in Nick's reaction; he had good instincts.

"It's about my work."

Saying it aloud to an objective third party might let me gauge how insane it sounded.

"You know how much I enjoyed working on this last competition?"

Nick nodded.

My toe in the water, I took the plunge and explained about Russ and reviving old dreams. "I'm having dinner with him and his wife tomorrow night. We'll bat around the idea, see how it feels. I don't have a clue what Russ's reaction will be. Heck, even I'm torn and it's my idea. When I consider the potential upheaval to my life I'm terrified, but when I think of the work I could be doing, I'm excited."

Nick's expression was thoughtful. "I know how much you like your job, Jessie. If you're thinking about a change, it must be important to you. Would you be able to stay in D.C.?"

"I'd probably have to relocate."

"To California?"

"Most likely. The West Coast is a better fit, at least initially. Both the small house and green movements are more accepted there. And Russ lives in L.A."

"Does Teddie D know about this?"

I grimaced. "Heavens, no. And, please don't say anything to anyone. Not even Charlene."

"Of course. But if you want to talk when you get back, I'm here. It might help you decide whether the move feels right. Discomfort or fear isn't a legitimate reason not to pursue your vision."

Man, that sounded a whole lot like the advice I'd given Tanner in that coffee shop so many years ago. Now I was on the receiving end. "Thanks. In some ways I'm more nervous about the dinner with Russ than I am about the weekend with Tanner. Talking about the future is much more nerve-racking than rehashing the past."

Nick laughed—I wasn't sure whether it was with me or at me. "Let me know how that strategy plays out."

THIRTY-ONE

As the plane lifted off from Dulles Airport, I glanced out the window, watching the beautiful, green rolling hills of Virginia pass beneath the plane as we headed west to L.A.

It was a relief to be away from the office. I couldn't bear one more question or comment about Tanner from my staff. Yes, he was an icon but that wasn't how I knew him.

It was rather ironic, though, that I was happily fleeing my office to not have to listen to another question about Tanner while on my way to the icon itself.

Tanner was at the curb when I exited the terminal.

He grinned at me, the warmth of his smile echoing in his eyes. Another of his super powers. Resistance was futile. I smiled back.

Once he'd stashed my bag, he stepped back up onto the curb and gave me a quick hug I wasn't prepared for. It was a tease of an embrace—perhaps passing for a handshake in Los Angeles. It left me wanting more.

I latched onto the nearest thing to divert my attention. "Is this a Tesla?" The car was a metallic-silver sedan.

"Yes. Got it a couple of months ago."

He opened the door for me and I got in. Once I was seated my head cleared, the world around me normalized, and, by the time Tanner got in, I was stifling a laugh.

"What was it you emailed me about boys and cars? I believe I know exactly where Jason gets his interest in cars."

Tanner rolled his eyes. "Why in the world did I write that? I should have known those words would come back to bite me."

We both laughed and some of my nervousness dissipated.

As we left the airport, Tanner asked, "Weren't you supposed to hear about the winners of the competition this week?"

"Yes, they were announced Tuesday."

"And you didn't let me know?" He eyeballed me accusingly as his right hand shifted gears.

I laughed. "One, I've been busy getting things in order so I could come out here. Two, I thought it better to tell you in person."

"Sorry. What happened?" he asked, his eyes back on the road.

On Tuesday the staff had gathered in the conference room to watch the livestreaming of the results. Over three hundred teams had entered! The fourth-place winner was announced first. Even knowing the odds are against you, you still eagerly wait to hear your project announced next.

"We didn't win," I said.

He flashed me a look of disbelief. "Are you kidding me? It was a great project. We need housing like that." He swiped his right hand through his hair.

"Too bad you weren't on the jury. We obviously thought so, too." I waited a beat. He was getting worked up over our loss. It was cute. He seemed to have become invested in the project over the month I'd emailed him, topped off by meeting the team.

"We did take second place," I finally admitted.

In the office everyone had whooped and hollered, with Evan leading the cheers. Sharon had looked shocked—first time out and her project had taken second place. But we'd quieted down quickly to hear why the jury had selected it. "'Go ReconFigure' is a bold micro-housing proposal, taking the traditional twentieth-century passive apartment building and transforming it into an electronically-responsive building fit for twenty-first-century lifestyles, as well as addressing social and sustainability issues."

Evan had ordered pizza for the office to continue the celebration over lunch.

When the food was delivered, Eliot, Sharon and I toasted each other with our pizza slices. It was a bittersweet moment for me, though. I loved all these people, our camaraderie, our synergy. If Russ and I moved forward, it would be only the two of us initially. No Sharons, no Eliots. No mentoring.

"That's great!" Tanner said, unaware of my ambivalence. "Was the effort worth it?"

"Well, not financially. But placing second out of three hundred submissions in a well-run and highly contested competition looks good in a company's portfolio. And who knows? It may generate business down the road."

"What entry could possibly have beaten yours?" Tanner was taking this very personally.

"Remember the other option we'd considered—incubator space for fashion designers? The winning submission proposed using the site as incubator space for high-tech businesses—which isn't innovative in the least. But fashion designers? Clearly novel. We were so close." I pinched my thumb and forefinger together until they almost touched. "But I'm glad we pursued the micro-apartment option. It's more relevant to our company."

What I didn't tell Tanner was that it also had me rethinking my career.

THIRTY-TWO

Our first year together in California, Tanner and I would sometimes drive through the hills of L.A.—along roads like Mulholland Drive or Laurel Canyon Boulevard—and gawk at the houses, a curious mix ranging from traditional to ultra-modern in style, and from modest to sprawling in size. We had laughed at the extravagance of many of them.

Now Tanner lived there.

He slowed the car alongside a tall stone wall fronted by an equally tall, dense hedge. A metal gate slid open.

In front of us was a two-story house, loosely based on a Mediterranean villa. It had been built in the first half of the twentieth century, when "revivalist" residential styles, such as Spanish Colonial, Mission, and Mediterranean, were popular. These temperate-climate designs, incorporating outdoor features like courtyards, covered arcades, terraces, balconies, and covered outdoor living rooms, are perfect for the Southern California clime and lifestyle.

I stared at the house. It was beautiful, warm, and welcoming. The center portion of the house had a large, arched wooden door with glass sidelights. That entry was flanked by a large room to each side. Beyond this central core, the two original wings were asymmetrical, giving the house a more casual feel. The exterior stone was a pale pinkish-yellow, and the woodwork around the arched door and windows was a polished, high-sheen dark brown. The two tones imparted a lovely glow to the house, as if lit from within.

On the far left, a recent addition angled away from the front garden, perhaps to gain a better view of the back yard.

My eyes returned to the wing on the right: a one-and-a-half-story room set back slightly from the main façade and topped with the most beautiful leaded glass dome—a sparkling diaphanous crown. It was gorgeous. During the 1930s, the space had probably been a conservatory.

Goose bumps exploded on my arms, making me shiver. I was glad I had on a jacket or Tanner might have made fun of my physical reaction to a mere building. I wasn't ready to be teased yet. My emotions were a little raw—the structure was extraordinary, a wonderful piece of architectural history . . . and Tanner's home.

Tanner parked by the garage near a small white van. We stepped onto white gravel and Tanner took my bag out of the trunk.

"So, what do you think?" he asked, sounding both anxious and excited. He stood stiffly, soldier-straight, awaiting my verdict.

I sighed. "It's beautiful, Tanner. The proportions are elegant and the understated Italian details lovely. The place feels timeless—as fashionable now as it would have been seventy years ago."

Tanner's shoulders relaxed. "I feel that too—although I wouldn't have been able to say why. Thanks for explaining."

He opened the front door and ushered me in. Unexpectedly, a vision of being carried across the threshold flashed through my mind. Dammit. That wasn't good. I didn't even like that tradition. I'd rather walk over the threshold hand in hand. Wait, why was I even debating the two approaches?

Just being in Tanner's house was making me loopy. No wonder he had been hypersensitive walking through my place. Our two houses were summoning up past dreams and overlaying them on the present. What memories had ambushed him? At least I'd be smart enough to stay out of his bedroom—even if it were on the tour.

Or I could just yell uncle and go home right now. I didn't relish a weekend of battling ghosts.

Shoot. I couldn't. I had the dinner with Russ tonight, my reward for coping with Tanner and this house.

We walked past the staircase to the rear of the hall, which opened onto a terrace. Stepping outside, I breathed deeply and admired the setting. The fabulous backyard sloped steeply until it reached a flat expanse.

Two levels of formal terraces, the one we were on and a lower level (suggesting a third and lower floor), connected the house with the lawn. And smack-dab in the middle of the garden was a lap pool. A true seaside villa. At pool level, trees enclosed the yard, but from this terrace I could see over them to the city. Tanner had the best of both worlds—a view and privacy.

"It's lovely," I murmured.

Tanner turned to me, smiling, and said, "We'll go to the guesthouse first. When you've freshened up, we can have lunch."

I nodded. The clothes I had on reeked of too many people packed in too small a cabin for too long. Plus, some time by myself would give me time to reflect on why I was here: to conclude one chapter and begin another.

We descended the steps to the lower terrace. "It's funny, but I feel our two backyards are similar, although your yard isn't sloped," Tanner observed.

"That's because my deck and balcony provide the same sense of verticality." Now I understood why he had been so attracted to the views from my house: they had reminded him of home.

We followed a path off the lower terrace, past the recent addition, to the detached guesthouse. The small retreat resembled even more a cliffside Italian villa, built as it was into the hill. Discovering this miniature treasure hidden on the backside of the hill was like unexpectedly coming across a Fabergé egg.

"This is fabulous, Tanner."

"High praise, coming from an architect." From his grin, I knew he was pleased.

He slid open the glass door into the living room. I'd been expecting a studio unit but it was a stunning one-bedroom, complete with living room and contemporary kitchen, three times the size of the micro-apartment my team had designed. Floor-to-ceiling telescoping glass doors ran the length of the dwelling and accessed a wide, parallel stone terrace, edged by a low, stone seating wall. Outside the bedroom, an arbor, laden with fragrant, pendulous lilac and white flowers, shaded the terrace. A sanctuary.

Tanner put my bag on the couch. "When you're ready, I'll be in the sunroom, which is the second room to the left of the staircase coming in through the back."

"I may be a while. I'm grimy from the flight."

He was already heading for the door. "Take your time."

As I showered, I thought of this sparkling little guesthouse. If I moved to California, something this size would be perfect as I got the business up and running. I noted that it had its own path to the driveway. I could put on blinders as I walked to and from my car every day so I could ignore Tanner and any girlfriends. I'd almost be willing to do that for this little gem. I wondered if he ever rented the place out.

Good grief! Was I delusional?

Living in a place next door to Tanner, much less owned by him?

Okay, not this place, but another guesthouse. L.A. had thousands. I didn't have a problem living in a smaller place—as long as the price was right.

Having spent too much time in the shower, I quickly dried my hair and put on black slacks with a teal tunic and a narrow black and silver belt to wear over it. It was more casual than the suit I had worn on the plane but still professional for this afternoon's work. Then I replaced my small gold hoop earrings with a dangly, medium length pair made of silver with iridescent bluish-green opal pendants.

I studied myself in the mirror. Did I look twelve years older? I didn't think so, although maybe the lighting in here was forgiving. My body, though, felt the full weight of these last twelve years, crammed as it was with unfulfilled dreams, regret, and unanswered questions.

But maybe I could turn things around. Create something wonderful for Tanner. Get some answers. See Tanner for who he was now—not some lingering figment of my imagination—so I could move on. One foot was still anchored in the past with Tanner but the toes of the other foot were now dipped into the future with Russ. Maybe I could start shifting my weight forward with this trip.

THIRTY-THREE

I stepped into Tanner's living room. What would it reveal about him?

Glancing around at the generous room, which spanned the depth of the house, I almost laughed aloud.

Tanner had said his "tastes" hadn't changed, but this room strongly suggested otherwise. The walls were painted a light camel color, with undertones of yellow and red providing depth—a sophisticated take on standard beige. Thick vertical brush strokes added texture and drama.

In the center of the room were two oversized contemporary leather sofas in a dark Bordeaux color, along with several chairs upholstered in a mushroom-colored print with just a hint of rose, all focused on a large fireplace. It was a bold color scheme. Above the mantel hung a vibrant landscape of Tuscany that I recognized as one of Trish's.

When Tanner and I had been together, he'd had little concern for color, much less décor. The black tees and shirts he performed in hadn't been a deliberate fashion choice. The basic wardrobe and monochrome color palette were simply two less distractions from his music. Plus, after days on the road, he didn't care what he put on as long as it was reasonably fresh.

But if the color choice and décor in this room were any indication, he had come to appreciate the details and subtleties of design.

Near the back terrace, the room was set up as a library with dark, built-in shelving and cabinets for books and audio equipment as well as a simple table desk. Photos, books, CDs, and magazines were scattered atop the desk and on the shelves. That portion of the room looked lived-in, but I doubted he conducted much business there, given its ready access by visitors.

The entire room radiated a masculine ambience but it was warm, casual, and unpretentious rather than overpowering—an aesthetic I could integrate into the lake home.

The framed pictures on Tanner's desk beckoned me, but the sounds of a guitar wafting from the next room were more compelling. The guitar reminded me of all the times our apartment had been similarly awash in Tanner's music. The notes plucked at my heart, warming my blood but saddening me as well. More of these conflicting moments were probably hiding in ambush for me over the next two days. But this weekend wasn't about replaying emotions. It was about architecture—present and future.

I edged into the garden room, not wanting to disturb Tanner at work. Perched on a stool, his eyes partly closed, he was focused on a song he heard playing in his imagination. The sight was so achingly familiar that I grabbed the door jamb.

Architecture, Jessie. Focus on the room, not Tanner. I forced my glance away from Tanner and followed the source of the sunlight upward. The room was a delight. The amazing oval glass dome set into the ceiling was like a multi-faceted jewel, the beveled glass sending rainbows of sunlight dancing around the room as if the dome were composed of stained glass. The spirit of the room hovered somewhere between the nave of a gothic church with a rose window and a carnival carousel with its colorful bright lights.

A grand piano stood to my left. Like many musicians, Tanner plays multiple instruments. When we'd moved to California we bought a cheap upright piano for our apartment so I know how well he plays. During a concert, Tanner will often perform a song or two on piano. Standing at the keyboard, playing with the entirety of his body, he brings fresh energy to the performance, propelling everyone to their feet—if they weren't there already.

But if Tanner wanted to compose, his choice had always been an acoustic guitar. The music seemed to flow directly from his heart though his hands to the strings. From the number in the room, I'd guess a guitar was still his first choice.

This setting couldn't be more unlike the cramped apartment we had lived in, where between my drafting table, the piano, and Tanner's guitars, we barely had room to navigate. Did he ever think back fondly to that apartment? I hoped he did.

Or, perhaps, what he remembered was how empty the place had felt when he came home that day in January.

Tanner opened his eyes. He must have heard my mind droning on.

He set the guitar aside.

"Are you feeling better? You look beautiful."

The blood rushed from my face at his words. There was always something so naked in Tanner's voice when he called me beautiful that it affected me deeply. It made him vulnerable somehow—like I was his Achilles' heel, perhaps. Even today.

"Much better, thanks."

"Ready for lunch?"

"I can wait, if you're working."

"No, I'm at a good stopping point. Have you been standing there long?"

I didn't want him to think I'd been spying. "No. Just long enough to admire the room. It's a wonderful space."

"It is, right?" He stood up and stretched, twisting his neck to release the strain. "This room is one of the reasons I bought the house. I felt there was music to be made here. I love to come into this space with its crystalline light in the mornings and write."

As I followed him back into the living room, I asked, "How long have you lived here?" Suddenly I was thrown off-balance by my own question, my breath catching in my throat and my knees wobbling in an attempt to betray me.

When I had been in this room just minutes before, I had experienced it architecturally, for what it said about Tanner's aesthetic. But how could I not know when he'd bought this house? How he lived now? What things made him happy?

I grabbed a chair next to me, steadying myself as I had that night at Rasika. But now I understood part of the reason Tanner had been so angry about my house—it represented something unfamiliar, when the expectation was that it should have felt familiar, like a second skin.

Tanner, two steps in front of me, stopped and turned to answer my question. He appeared unaware of my distress. "After my stint in rehab, Ron and Mike wanted to hit the road touring. The rehab counselors, however, suggested I keep life simple that first year. So I ended up staying in L.A., concentrating on recovery and going to as many NA or AA meetings as I could.

"But the penthouse I'd been living in before rehab became a depressing reminder of my addiction. And it wasn't ideal for Jason who was four. So, I started looking for a house. When I found this place, I knew it would work for both of us. I could start writing again in the sunroom. I had room to put in a lap pool. Jason would have plenty of outdoor space to run around in when he came over. And I would have quiet for the first time in a long while, to figure out what I wanted. I felt I could get control of my life again here."

"A creative refuge?"

Tanner nodded emphatically, a lock of hair dropping down onto his forehead—like a hook. "Exactly. So, that first year out of rehab, I bought this place, made renovations and moved in. Because I couldn't tour with mPulse—and had no idea when I would be ready—we dissolved the group so that Mike and Ron could move on. That was hard—I had always felt such an obligation to the band."

His voice had gone flat and his eyes stared off in the distance. Yes, his recovery had broken up the band. But I remembered all too clearly the burden of responsibility he had carried for the trio for so many years—and the consequences. I touched his arm lightly. "You did the right thing, Tanner."

His eyes focused back on the present. Touch had always been an essential form of communication between us. It felt no less vital now, the physical contact reassuring me as well as him that things were okay. But now it was a false familiarity.

"When I returned to the penthouse from rehab, I went through the motions of recovery but had no real idea of how to restart my life. The creative well had dried up. No music flowed. It was a tough time—left to my thoughts without the companionship of music."

Yes, he had emailed me about that period. I couldn't imagine not being able to sketch, the white paper remaining blank in front of me.

"When I moved here, I made myself go to the sunroom every morning. Whether I wanted to or not. Slowly, tunes emerged. What a relief to feel music again. I would compose and play until lunch, and then go to a twelve-step meeting. Once the pool was completed, I swam every day. I kept to a very structured schedule. Still do. Eventually I added a personal trainer and a chef as part of my commitment to staying healthy."

He had taken his hard-won sobriety seriously. These actions he took every day weren't an afterthought but an integral part of his life. I hadn't considered the insight Tanner would gain during rehab. I sagged against the chair, my relief heavy as I absorbed his words.

I'd known emotions from long ago would be conjured up this weekend; however, I thought the sorrow from the past, as well as the fresh resentment of being hijacked into this job, would protect me. I was no longer, however, facing my one-sided remembrances of the man, long warped by time and heartbreak, but rather the flesh-and-blood man who had his own pain and heartache.

"As I started to find solid footing with my life and music, I decided to make the solo album. Melodies were flooding my brain. It was exciting but scary as hell—so recently out of rehab and on my own without a band."

He had found light in the darkness, maybe even exorcised many of his demons through that solo album, using music to reach acceptance about his addiction.

"It's an amazing album," I said. "It was obvious that something life-changing had happened."

Listening to the songs on that recording had reminded me of when I had first heard him—when he sang from his heart. His music had always been personal, but in that solo album he exposed his soul in the singing of every word, in the playing of every chord. There was no filter, his own pain transformed as something to be shared and recognized as universal. A positive message for others still in the darkness.

"Thanks." His tone had lightened. He was back in the present. "But my preference is still for a band. There's something inspiring about playing with others."

I nodded. It was like the Ideas Competition. We create something better when challenged and inspired by others. Maybe he and I could achieve that with this lake house.

But the pain reappeared in his eyes again. "I wish I'd been able to take your advice earlier about entering rehab, Jessie."

God, I didn't want us both falling down that bottomless rabbit hole of the past. "I'd never say 'I told you so,'" I replied, batting my eyelashes and suggesting precisely the opposite.

Tanner snorted.

We crossed the foyer to the room on the other side of the entrance hall.

Aha! The first signs that an eleven-year-old boy lived in the house. And another of those stomach-churning, mixed-emotion, roller-coaster moments—admiration for the relationship Tanner had developed with his son even during his addiction, but also a reminder of the family we had once anticipated.

Ostensibly this was the dining room, a mirror image of the living room, with glass doors on the far end accessing the terrace. There was even a long formal dining table centered on the fireplace. With seating for eight.

But that was all a front. The room was devoted to Jason. A comfortable couch and several colorful bean bag chairs competed with the table. Cabinets held board games, books, and all manner of electronic gadgets. Over by the terrace was a foosball table and opposite us was a pinball machine. Were the dining room table ever used, it was probably as a fort or tent.

"Excuse the mess. Jason's stuff mysteriously migrates here from his bedroom."

"Well, that's weird. I thought some of this stuff might be yours. Like the pinball machine?" Tanner had always loved pinball arcades. The manual dexterity he'd honed playing instruments gave him a competitive advantage. "Maybe a board game or two?"

His face went blank. "I plead the fifth."

I laughed. "That's your right, but it might be more helpful to include a TV and game room in the lake house to accommodate these essentials."

I spread my arms to underscore the evidence.

He laughed. "Fine, just make it soundproof. Please."

"Done."

I noticed what looked like a survey and some documents lying on the dining table. "Is this the information on the lake property?"

"Yep. After lunch, I thought we could spread everything out and take a look. I really don't know what to do with this room. If I have company for dinner I prefer using the breakfast room."

I smirked. The problems of a large house.

"I know what you're thinking, Jessie." Tanner smiled a bit self-consciously.

"I'm sorry. I find it amusing—from our cramped little apartment to this wonderful place. It's impressive."

He gave me a searching look, but I was serious.

We turned left into a hallway. I peeked into the breakfast room on the right and understood why Tanner preferred to entertain here. The room was more intimate, had perfect proportions, and provided a better view of the city from the table.

"As you know, Tanner, my place gives me great comfort. I sense this house makes you happy as well, even if you have more space than you know what to do with. I can imagine you rambling quite contentedly through it at night."

He nodded. "I usually am happy here, though sometimes it doesn't feel quite right. But I don't know if it's the house that's off then, or me."

THIRTY-FOUR

I was half a hallway behind Tanner as he entered the kitchen, having lingered in the breakfast room.

"Is lunch ready, Pamela?"

I froze. Well, my body froze. My heart frantically tried to leap out of my body and flee to safety.

A girlfriend? My throat knotted up like a fist and my mouth went dry. Wouldn't Tanner have mentioned his girlfriend was here? Was she to be part of the conversation this afternoon?

I stepped tentatively out from behind Tanner into the kitchen. A cute, youngish woman stood at a kitchen island, chopping vegetables next to a small prep sink. Short, curly blond hair peeked out from under a cornflower blue, flower-printed kerchief. She had on a white apron.

"Yes, Mr. Daulton. I've got it set up on the lower terrace like you wanted. I've also started on the meals for the next couple of days. Oh, and I've restocked the refrigerator."

Okay, not a girlfriend. My heartbeat resumed its normal rate, though I was still shaky.

Not, of course, that Tanner couldn't have a girlfriend. Just that it would be nice to have a heads-up if she were here.

"Thank you. I'd like you to meet an old friend of mine. Pamela, this is Jessie Hartley. Jessie, this is Pamela Lange, my chef."

I said hello and Pamela gave me a wave, the knife still in her hand.

"Pamela is a lifesaver," Tanner said. "She fixes most of my meals when I'm not traveling and keeps my refrigerator and freezer stocked. You probably remember I was never very good at cooking."

I pulled myself together. "Yes, but you were very, very good at picking out music to accompany a meal."

"True," he replied with mock pride. "But if it weren't for Pamela, I would be eating tuna out of a can for dinner. She keeps me healthy."

Pamela smiled shyly.

Meanwhile, curious as ever, I'd glanced around the large, recently renovated kitchen with its white cabinets and mid-tone cerulean blue island. Another reference to the Mediterranean?

A discrepancy caught my eye. Pamela was right-handed. I looked back at the refrigerator and freezer behind her.

"It's very nice to meet you, Pamela. I'm glad you're keeping Tanner healthy."

She looked at me, confused.

Tanner intervened. "For some crazy reason, Jessie calls me Tanner."

I rolled my eyes. "Because it's your name?"

I could tell the chef wasn't sure whom to believe.

"Pamela, you should have told Teddie that it would be easier for you if the refrigerator door opened the other direction."

She knew immediately what I meant. "It-it-it's really not a bother."

Tanner looked at us. "What are you talking about?"

The refrigerator and freezer were both large stand-alone units, with the refrigerator on the right. The doors for the two units had been set up so that they opened from the center, like a set of doors. I explained to Tanner that because the counter was to the right of the refrigerator it would be easier for his chef, when taking food out of the refrigerator to place on the counter or stowing groceries in the fridge from bags on the counter, if the door opened from the counter side. And, given that Pamela was right-handed, it would be more efficient as well.

Tanner laughed. "I should point out that Jessie's an architect. If it helps, I'll get it fixed."

A rose-pink flush rose charmingly to Pamela's cheeks. Hesitantly, she replied, "There's no hurry, but it would be easier."

"Consider it done. Let's have lunch before Jessie decides something else needs to be changed."

THIRTY-FIVE

The warmth of the sun on my face. Jewel-toned hummingbirds darting in and out of the lush magenta bougainvillea overhead. Song sparrows, wrens, and finches calling out to friends. A dog barking faintly, several houses down. The strong, spicy scent of lilies wafting up from the garden bed below. Crows proclaiming dominion.

Being surrounded by nature—instead of cooped up in the house surrounded by all things Tanner—was a welcomed balm for body and heart.

Tanner and I were relaxing at a table under a trellis on the lower terrace, the counterpart to the one at the guesthouse at the other end of the garden.

We sat in comfortable silence, sipping our drinks, enjoying nature's performance. Too soon—despite my grumbling stomach—Chef Lange appeared with Caesar chicken salad wraps and cold peach soup. But the light sandwich and nectar-like soup were perfect accompaniments to the setting.

I refilled my glass of tea and squeezed a freshly cut lime wedge into it. The juice squirted everywhere except into the glass.

"Ow." Tanner rubbed one eye and gave me a dirty look with the other.

I couldn't help but laugh. "Sorry. I didn't do it on purpose."

"So you say. Maybe you have some sort of passive-aggressive disorder?"

"Why? Do you think anything in our past would warrant such a thing?" I was kidding . . . sort of.

"No comment." He reached out and took the dish of lime slices away from me.

"What's the recent addition?" I tilted my head toward the building.

"A recording studio. Built it a couple of years after moving in. I'll show it to you later this weekend."

From the glint in his eyes, I knew it had pride of place.

"I'd like to see it. I've never designed a personal recording studio before."

"I'm just making sure we start on the lake house today. Knowing you, you'll want a detailed explanation of every piece of equipment."

I arched my eyebrows. I had no idea what he was talking about.

Tanner chortled—which made me even warmer than the sun had.

"By the way, I want to include Jason in our discussion about the new house."

What? My heart went racing. His son? Seeing the photos of him had been difficult. Seeing his toys had been almost as difficult. What bodily impairment might befall me when I actually met him?

"You and I will visit the site tomorrow by ourselves," Tanner continued. "He'd be too much of a distraction—running around and asking a bajillion questions. But he'll join us tomorrow night for a cookout. You can tell him more about the process than I can." Hastily he added, "It'll just be the three of us."

This was all becoming so uncomfortable and awkward that it was almost funny. The universe seems to possess a wicked sense of humor at times—and Tanner seemed oblivious of his complicity.

I must have paused too long.

"Is that okay?" he asked, his voice betraying concern—and a little hurt.

But it wasn't his son's fault. And he was right that Jason should be included. And since he had specified "three" there shouldn't be an ex-wife or girlfriend joining us.

"Of course." My voice cracked like a teenage boy's but Tanner didn't seem to notice. He was smiling again.

At least I had twenty-four hours to acclimate to the idea. I should be grateful. That was twenty-four hours more warning than when Tanner had shown up on my doorstep or at my office.

As I gazed back out on the garden, I recalled my earlier thoughts about those past Sunday drives through these hills. "Did you ever imagine you would succeed like this?"

Tanner stopped eating and slowly put the chicken wrap down on the plate. In the ensuing silence, the chirping of the birds seemed amplified. I even heard a bee buzzing in the arbor above.

His eyesight seemed to turn inward for a moment. When he finally spoke, his voice was low, wounded. "This is never what I thought of when I envisioned success. You of all people should know that."

His reaction startled me. But I understood. Our past disappointments hadn't left us much trust in the other person's good intentions. We questioned everything the other person said, looking for censure or blame, while we were really stewing in our own guilt. I was constantly off-balance around him—wanting his trust, but certain of having lost it long ago. How in the world were we to find firm footing to make this project work?

I shook my head. "The question wasn't intended to be disparaging. I was thinking of this place as a physical representation of what you've achieved, not as an end in itself."

He stared at the table, still in the past. "All I wanted was to make music, Jessie. Good music."

I wanted to reach out and reassure him, but I didn't trust myself. I had to rely on words. "You've made great music, Tanner. I know how hard you worked and the sacrifices you made. You have every right to enjoy your success."

"It's not what I'd imagined. . . ." His voice trailed off.

Perhaps a jolt of reality might help. "Look how far you've come. Do you remember that apartment we lived in when we moved to L.A.? I couldn't bear to look at the carpet in that place too closely for fear of what I'd find—even though I must have vacuumed it at least four times before we moved in. To this day, I hate carpet. And the smell. It was always musty. And what about that used furniture we bought at a thrift store? Thank goodness we at least bought a new mattress."

Suddenly I grimaced. "Ugh. I just remembered we put the mattress directly on the carpet. I wonder what sorts of things joined us." An involuntary shudder rocked me.

"So, that's the reason I don't like carpet?" Tanner asked. "I guess I never noticed at the time."

My eyes widened in disbelief.

He laughed. "Hey, I'm a guy. I have a higher tolerance for these things."

"Yeah, you're right. The only way you would have noticed was if one of the creatures had crawled into a guitar."

Then I started laughing too. Pretty soon we were both laughing so hard we could barely breathe. Deep laughter, rising from the belly, and so much laughter that it gets stuck in your chest and throat so you can't make a sound, making everything even funnier. Tears were streaming down my cheeks and Tanner was doubled over in the chair, his eyes glowing with glee but not a peep issuing from his mouth.

I hadn't laughed like that in a long time. Then I became aware for the first time that these deep, cathartic laughs happen only when there is someone else around—someone to share the moment with. There is something about watching another person succumb to laughter, whole-heartedly, without reservation, that makes you laugh harder.

Tanner and I had laughed a lot like this in our early days.

My abdomen hurt. "Stop making me laugh."

"It's not me, it's your pathetic, pathological fear of carpet."

That started us up again.

Finally, out of breath, we quieted down. I grabbed a napkin to wipe my eyes.

When Tanner's hands were steady again, he poured me more

tea. "To replenish the liquids."

Then Tanner squeezed a lime slice into my glass—with no wayward spray. An eyebrow arched at me as if to say that's how it's done.

"Show-off."

And we were off laughing again.

All this talking and eating—all this prolonged . . . foreplay—had been a good idea. It had given us time to get reacquainted. Maybe rediscover a bit of that trust we needed to work together.

But even the most terrific foreplay has to end.

It was time for work.

THIRTY-SIX

Tanner and I were back in the dining room, surrounded this time by all things Jason. I missed my flitting hummingbirds.

I had retrieved my laptop and work gear from the living room where I'd left them when I joined Tanner in the music room earlier. Tanner had fetched mugs of coffee from the kitchen.

"Where would you like to start, Jessie?"

"Let's begin with the survey. You can tell me about the site."

Earlier, as we had walked through the house, I'd kept my distance from Tanner to avoid being overwhelmed by his relentless energy. But now we stood shoulder to shoulder at the table, looking down at the drawing that showed the boundaries and dimensions of the lake property. I spread out several more documents for quick reference, including a detailed topographic map and the title, which provided more information on easements and building restrictions.

Tanner was nearly bouncing on his toes, energy and excitement rolling off him. I longed to share his enthusiasm, but even with the easing of tensions over lunch, I still had doubts that we could work together successfully. Too many troubling undercurrents swirled around this project. Our past and its continuing hurt. The problematic antecedents of this proposed house—could it really make Tanner happy? That I still reacted to him so viscerally. Which emotion or wound would surface next?

Yet, I wanted to give Tanner a place where he could rejuvenate, where he could find quiet. Yes, he was no longer on drugs. Yes, he had achieved balance and health in his life. But I wasn't sure he had found peace.

So, while Tanner became more animated as he talked, I became more stoic, armoring myself in professionalism.

Despite my best intentions, though, his scent—recalling the coastline of the Olympic Peninsula, where the rainforest flirted with the ocean—clouded my judgment.

Thank goodness I only had to listen. The lot was located at the end of a finger of land lying between the open lake on one side and a cove on the other. The panoramic vista had sealed the deal for Tanner. An old dock was still in place, but the cabin, which had been in disrepair, had been razed.

Tanner pulled out his phone and showed me pictures of the site. I could see why he had fallen for the property with its sweeping water view.

I Googled the lake on my laptop to get an aerial view. I'd been expecting the area to be surrounded by houses packed together like sardines in a tin. In fact, this lake still had sparsely populated patches along its shore. Tanner focused the satellite view on his property. Because it was located at the tip of a narrow peninsula, he had few immediate neighbors. He was lucky to have found the place.

Once we finished talking about the site, we sat down. I opened my laptop and savored a long sip of coffee. I expected I would need several more cups to get through the afternoon as we were about to embark on the most difficult part of this weekend—well, except for meeting Jason. This part was too personal, too reminiscent of the dream we had once shared. My chest ached as usual; by the end of the weekend it would probably feel like an elephant was sitting on it.

Did he understand how difficult this was? Could he really think everything was in the past for me, after seeing my house?

I sighed.

"Okay, Tanner. Describe your vision for the lake house."

"You know what I want. It's what we talked about."

What the heck did that mean?

"Tanner, I'm not the same person I was twelve years ago, so I wouldn't design a house now as I would have then. Plus, it's obvious that your tastes have changed"—he arched an eyebrow—"or, if you prefer, evolved." My mouth involuntarily curved into a cheeky smile at his obvious delusion.

"I want to create a house for you that reflects where you are in life now."

"Then take all the things we talked about and update it to your current aesthetic."

Did "all the things" we'd talked about include three children? I bit my tongue, sipped some coffee from the mug that was fast becoming a prop for when I needed to breathe, and tried again.

"Pretend I have amnesia. That I have no recall of what we once discussed. We're starting fresh. I'll ask you questions about the house and you respond as you feel today. Please."

His fingers started tapping lightly on the table and that "V" formed between his eyebrows. Why was he annoyed? I was only here because he'd asked me.

"What am I missing?" I asked. Now my brow furrowed. "I want to give you the best possible design I can. But it has to be based on your present life. I know very little about what's important to you now or even how you live on a daily basis."

He scowled. "And I'm telling you I haven't changed in what I want."

Was it too early for me to throw up my hands?

"Humor me, will you? After all, I am the professional."

A slight smile wobbled at the corners of his lips.

Success, of sorts. I pressed forward. "First, how do you plan to use the lake house? Do you see yourself using it primarily for occasional vacations, for regular weekends, or do you even see yourself up there during the week?"

His lips pressed together. "A bit of all three."

Was he being serious? I wanted to kick the guy.

"You do realize that how you use the place determines the design? The more time you spend there, the more extensive the space program."

His furrow grew deeper. "Assume I'll be there a lot."

"What's a lot? Is it fifty percent of your time? Thirty percent? Compare it to your time at this house. Would you really want to be away from your recording studio here or business for a significant amount of time?"

He nodded slowly. "Okay. Less than fifty. I have to be in town for both Jason and my music. Say twenty percent."

I picked up the mug, not sure whether to drink from it or throw it at him. But who wants to waste good coffee?

"Will you be going up there to fish by yourself? In which case I'll give you a tent." He tossed me a dirty look. "Or will it be primarily for you and Jason? Or, perhaps a place for socializing—with your friends and his?"

"I'll need guest bedrooms."

I clenched the mug handle. For whom and how many? The damn details, please! Number of people to be accommodated. Types of water toys that needed to be stored. Special rooms—for practicing music, making fishing lures, storing black T-shirts. I don't possess ESP.

I counted to ten and tried a different tack.

"Give me some adjectives to describe how you want the house to feel."

Tanner stared at me. "Jessie, it's what we talked about. It's the same words I used to describe your house—surprising, open, light-filled, innovative."

That was it. Tanner and I had our chairs turned partially toward each other as we sat at the table. My right leg was crossed demurely over my left knee. Using my top leg, I kicked him—in the shin. Not hard, but hard enough to get his attention.

Tanner started to laugh. "Very professional, Jessie. I forgot what a quick temper you have."

"Trust me. That was not quick. I wanted to kick you ten minutes ago. Why are you being so difficult? You keep telling me 'just like we used to talk about.' But those are the crucial words. It was a collaboration. You wanted to know what I wanted and I wanted to know what you wanted. If you really intend to build this house, we have to collaborate."

To make sure he got the point, I added, "Plus, the home we talked about is very different from the house you live in now. I need to understand the elements of this house that appeal to you as well. I don't want to disappoint you—if I agree to do this." I threw the last words in to make sure he understood that the project rested on communicating with me.

"Okay, okay. I get it." He even grinned. "Maybe you 'kicked' some sense into me. But will you please put down the laptop? It's off-putting. I'd rather we just talk."

"Deal—as long as you don't mind me making notes on paper. I don't want to forget something."

"Sure. I just don't want the computer between us."

See, that's where we differed. I didn't see a computer between us. I saw twelve years of baggage. *You say tomahto, I say tomayto.*

"How about more coffee first?" He took my mug and rose.

My eyes followed him as he left the room. The man was infuriating—but he sure looked good in those khakis.

When Tanner returned with the fresh coffees, I asked him to describe his vision for the house any way he wanted—from adjectives to specifics.

He talked. I listened, jotting down descriptive words and phrases, but not interrupting.

It was wonderful to see him engaged. He had been clean for

years, but for me it was healing just to sit here and listen. Our last months together had revolved around the drugs—if we weren't talking about the drugs it was because he was amped up on them. This afternoon would be a much, much better memory of Tanner.

It wasn't easy, but by the end of the afternoon we had the initial space program for Tanner's house.

The list included: a great room; kitchen, with breakfast counter, partially open to the great room; Jason's bedroom plus three more for guests, all with bathrooms (and he called it a refuge?); a master bedroom; TV/game room for Jason, with space for Tanner's exercise equipment; at least one deck; a music room; a garage; and, miscellaneous storage and utility space, particularly for outdoor gear. Moreover, the house was to be innovative, unexpected, comfortable, light-filled, warm, tech-savvy, and green.

I don't know why Tanner had found it so difficult to tell me what he wanted. Had he really expected me to intuit what he needed? Or was he embarrassed by the differences between what we had imagined for ourselves twelve years ago as poor students and what he wanted now. Well, boo-hoo. It had probably been as difficult for me to hear.

But at least I could work with what we had. And the list gave him something to reflect on.

"May I email this list to you so we can print off copies for tomorrow? I'd like to talk about each space in relationship to the site while we're at the lake."

"Sure."

Finally. Now I could get ready to meet Russ.

As we rose from the dining table, Tanner again offered to drive or pick me up.

"Thanks, but I'll use Uber."

"Well, if you see lights on in the music room when you get back, you're welcome to come in."

"I'm on East Coast time, Tanner. I'll probably fall into bed."

I rubbed the back of my neck. It had been a long day. Moreover, it had been a hell of a ride, emotions jostled and shaken all over the place. But once Tanner had started talking about his expectations for the house, things had fallen into place. Could we really do this? I wasn't sure. Tomorrow I'd have to see if he continued to participate in the dialogue.

If not, at least I knew where his reboot button was located.

THIRTY-SEVEN

"Just how serious are you, Jessie?"

Russ, Sally, and I had been talking for almost two hours about a partnership. Initially, the conversation had been a bit like flirting, as Russ and I tried to gauge each other's interest.

But the more we talked, the more freely the ideas flowed.

We were at a popular neighborhood bar near where Russ lived, sitting in the back away from the noise. The place had been built around an antique, high-polished, dark oak back-and-front bar duo at least twenty-four feet long and probably made around the turn of the twentieth century. Through some trick of age, the bar's antique mirrors transformed the modern pendant lighting over the bar into the golden candlelight of an earlier era. I could see why Russ suggested this place.

We had finished off the sliders and nachos a while ago. The owners, friends of the Howards, were now keeping us supplied with coffee and yummy cappuccino cookie bars, still warm from the oven. I'd stuck to decaf, though. I was excited enough about the conversation. No need for a caffeine high to prevent me from sleeping tonight as well.

Russ was about six feet tall, a barrel-chested rock of a man. His auburn hair and beard suggested a rugged outdoors type, maybe a logger from the Northwest. In actuality he had the hands of an artist. A master builder of 3-D architectural models, he had multiple scars on his hands from sharp little X-ACTO blades.

Funny, honest, passionate, clever, and generous to a fault, Russ was a person one could trust and rely on when starting a scary new endeavor.

Stacks of index cards littered the tabletop between us. Some women carry emergency items in their purses, like tissues or stain-eraser pens, but I carry old-fashioned 3" x 5" index cards. Taking a photo of an unusual architectural feature, whether it's an innovative building detail, a surprising landscaping element, or the play of shadows on a textured surface, is nowhere near as good as drawing it.

I had been jotting ideas down as we talked—potential design niches, relevant technologies, goals, our philosophy.

Spread in front of Russ were cards on which he had been doodling. A shopping cart for a homeless person that could carry their belongings and be converted into shelter. Premade garden sheds that could be connected and turned into a house for a couple or a family who had been living out of their car. A prefabricated unit that could be shipped flat and assembled on-site within hours to provide temporary emergency housing—complete with a solar roof.

Did I have major concerns? Of course. I had a good reputation—in D.C. But that wouldn't translate easily to California. But if I moved forward on Tanner's house, that might give me some name recognition in the area.

How funny was it that Tanner may have thought my designing his house would help get me the partnership in D.C., when in fact it might help me make the move to L.A.?

But Russ and I both agreed that the best way to gain entry into the market would be to participate in as many architecture competitions as possible. That would let us give voice to our vision.

"I wouldn't be here, Russ, if I weren't serious."

"What about your partnership? Can you really pass that up?"

My mouth went dry—and I had a panic-attack-worth of second thoughts. But I stumbled on. "I . . . I love working with Evan. If I were to take the partnership, I'd commit to him. So, it's now or never. I could probably nudge Evan into some of the things we've talked about tonight, but all this"—I spread my hands out to encompass the cards—"is not his vision."

Saying that felt almost like treason, as well as ungrateful. Evan had taught me the business and had trusted in my leadership ability. It saddened me to think I might leave. But he would also want me to follow my heart, not stay with him out of loyalty. At some point, the partnership might feel like a pair of golden handcuffs.

Russ and I did share a similar philosophy about how architecture could impact people's lives and how design should interact with the environment. Already we had begun to define our vision. The focus would be on housing in all its variations: multi-family, individual, communal. Or, even better, the focus would be on "home," where people could live with dignity, feel safe, and find comfort.

(Hmmm. Hartley Howard + Housing? Or H3? H2: Housing? I

scribbled the potential names for our company on a card.)

Building small, like my team's micro-apartments, would be just one component. And a project like Tanner's lake house would be just as welcomed because of the proposed use of technology and sustainable materials to reduce its carbon footprint.

Guiding principles would include sustainability, mobility, energy-saving technology, and affordability, while the goal would be the well-being of those living in our designs, whatever the size or the situation.

Where there was crossover between these core tenets and other building types we could explore the fit.

We'd even agreed that the best location for the firm was L.A. Not everyone's life needed to be uprooted.

"I wouldn't be honest, though, if I told you I wasn't scared. So many questions. Is there really a market for what we're proposing? Is our vision too broad? Can we financially survive the first couple of years?"

Then I laughed. "Too bad we're not a tech startup. We wouldn't have to be financially successful for years."

"Wouldn't that be nice?" Russ agreed. "Unfortunately, architects live in the real world."

The real world. Yes. In fact, I needed to speak to Russ and Sally of that real world. "Uh, by the way, I should mention why I'm in L.A. Teddie Daulton"—the two glanced at each other—"asked me to design him a lake house. I'm here on recon. We'll look at the property tomorrow and see if we can work together."

"Are you back together?" Sally asked, her eyes boring into mine like some type of new lie detector machine. About a foot shorter than Russ she kept the big man grounded. Heck, she could probably keep me grounded as well. This venture would have to work for her, too, if we were to move forward.

"No, no. We ran into each other unexpectedly in D.C." Then I tried to spin it. "If I take the job with him—and I'm not certain yet that I will—I'll be designing it under my current firm, obviously. But if it's built, at least I'll have my name attached to a relatively high-profile residential project in the area. Any buzz could help us initially."

Russ rubbed his beard. "Do you think you'll take the job?"

Russ had reason to worry. He didn't want a distracted partner, or one that might be a flight risk back to D.C.

"Too early to say. Maybe by Sunday."

"Why did he approach you? There are plenty of great architects in L.A.—no offense intended."

"Believe me, I asked Tanner the same question. But he'd toured my house in D.C. and liked what he saw."

Two sets of eyebrows shot up.

"You invited him over?"

"Not exactly." I picked up some of the cards on the table and pretended to organize them, giving my hands something to do as we worked through this . . . speed bump. Would Tanner's house be a benefit or a distraction? For me, for the partnership?

"Tanner and I hadn't talked in twelve years. But, long story short, he ended up visiting."

Sally took up the line of questioning. "How would you feel about moving out here if something happened to your relationship with Teddie between now and then?"

"It's not a relationship," I said, the words snapping out a bit too quickly. "Well, it's a professional relationship. But I'm not moving to L.A. because of Tanner. The situation with Tanner is a coincidence, but a convenient one since it got me out here to talk to you both."

There were more looks between the two of them but I couldn't read the meaning. Skeptical, maybe? I couldn't blame them.

I broke off a piece of a cappuccino bar. "I'd probably worry, too, if I were in your place. But I'm committed. I'm willing to leave my firm, a partnership, and friends to move out here to start this firm. And I haven't talked to Tanner about any of this. He doesn't know whom I'm having dinner with or why and has no idea that I'm even thinking about leaving my company."

Russ collected the rest of the cards and handed them to me. "You've given us a lot to think about, Jess. I'm interested but I need to know you're fully invested, no matter what happens with Teddie D."

I met his eyes, then Sally's. "The competition served as a wake-up call for me. I'll do this even if it means setting up a solo practice. I can't be more committed than that."

Russ pressed his lips together. "We'll need more time to consider all this. And, unfortunately, I'm a little distracted right now." He stopped.

Sally stepped in. "Russ's father just had his appendix removed two days ago. Everything looks good, but his father will need assistance for a couple of weeks once he's home from the hospital. Russ's mother is worried sick so we're helping as much as possible."

I bit my lip. "I'm so sorry. You should have told me earlier. Here I am, talking on and on and you're probably exhausted. Of course, this isn't the time to make a major decision."

"Thanks for understanding," Russ said.

"But I would like to continue the discussion when you're ready."

I stacked all the index cards neatly and put them in my bag. I'd type them up and send a copy to Russ. In between his job and taking care of his folks, he might enjoy a bit of daydreaming.

Who knows? With a little faith, maybe these random ideas would become the foundation of our firm.

Arriving back at Tanner's house, I noticed lights on in the music room. For one crazy moment I thought about talking with him. Once upon a time he had been my most trusted advisor.

But it wouldn't be professional. Besides, I could talk with Nick. At this point, his feedback would be more impartial than Tanner's.

Plus, I needed sleep. Hours in a car tomorrow with Tanner? In a cramped space?

I'd need my wits about me.

THIRTY-EIGHT

Nick would be so proud.

I'd awoken early, still on D.C. time. Stiff from sitting so much the day before, I dressed and went for a jog through the just-waking neighborhood, nodding to the handful of people who were also out running or walking their dogs.

But I missed Nick's distractions as I ran, despite having plenty to think about after last night's dinner.

I had just returned to the guesthouse by the footpath, when I saw a door open on the lower terrace: Tanner heading to the pool to get his laps in early.

I stood at the window inside, watching. He paused for a moment at the edge of the pool, stripping off the T-shirt and sweats he wore over his trunks. His body was beautiful—so long-limbed and powerful. Physical memories of him—touch, smell, and taste—bombarded me. Tears spilled down my cheeks. All the emotions that I had tried so hard to keep in check yesterday came pouring out at the sight of him. Twelve years and I couldn't get past those damn memories.

Stepping back from the window, I continued to stare. He dove in and cut through the water effortlessly, rhythmically, the muscles flexing in his shoulders and back with each repeated stroke. Even from the guesthouse I could sense his energy.

I might be here in the present but I was reliving the past. Yet I'd do my best to inch that dream house into the present for him.

But it was now pretty clear that I wouldn't be asking Tanner about renting this guesthouse, should I move to Los Angeles. If I had the chance to watch him swim every day I'd never put on those damn blinders, which would be the only way I could live in this perfect little villa.

I headed to the bathroom, not wanting to intrude on his privacy any longer. As I stood under the shower head I let the water wash away the tears. If only it could do the same with the misgivings I had about the coming day.

I put on blue jeans and a jade-colored silk blouse for the trip to the lake, and, of course, another pair of dangly, beaded earrings, a mixture of green-colored beads. Then I waited until lights came on in Tanner's kitchen.

By the time I arrived, the restorative aroma of coffee was filling the kitchen. Tanner poured me a cup—unfortunately I'd need a gallon to keep my head clear today.

With his hair slicked back from the swim and the shower, Tanner looked great—recharged, as always, by the water.

"How was your dinner?"

"Fine. Can I help with breakfast?"

"Sure. How does an omelet sound? Pamela's teaching me to cook."

My eyes widened. "An omelet sounds great."

"Why don't you cut up some cantaloupe and fix the toast?"

When I finished my assigned tasks, I set plates and utensils on the island counter alongside our coffee mugs. Our morning routine in our old apartment had been slightly different: showers followed by coffee, yes, but then good morning kisses as we fixed breakfast. The meal often got delayed.

Tanner cut the omelet and slid the halves onto the plates. He had added tomatoes, sweet green peppers, onions, and feta cheese for a Greek omelet.

I speared a piece of the omelet with my fork and tasted it. "Wow! This is delicious. What else have you learned to cook?"

His face lit up at my enthusiasm. "I've pretty well mastered the egg dishes—fried, poached, soft-boiled, hard-boiled, and scrambled. If you want eggs, I'm your guy. Now I'm learning to grill. It seemed a manly thing."

"That's good. A plan B to fall back on in the event this 'music thing' doesn't pan out." A not-so-subtle reference to that first conversation long ago—and how right I had been.

He rolled his eyes, shook his head, and went back to eating.

I guessed there would be no kisses this morning—or bed to remake.

I grabbed another cup of caffeine.

As we drove off, today in a hybrid SUV, Tanner turned on the radio and we listened to the news on NPR. When that ended, he switched to SiriusXM Radio, starting with a blues station, but changed quickly to the Sinatra station. He must have remembered that I enjoyed the old standards.

Tanner never sang in a car—at least he hadn't—which was a shame. He has a wonderful voice. Not the ubiquitous tenor pop-rock voice of today but rather an earthy tone that reminded me of some of the rock artists of the 1970s, but with the expressiveness and vocal gymnastics associated with grunge. He is fearless and honest when he sings, connecting straight to his emotional core to extract the notes and sounds he needs to tell a story—a wail, a growl, a lover's sigh, or a note of lament held for what seems like an eternity. His voice never fails to thrill.

Me? I couldn't help but sing in a car. I started humming along to the old standards and was soon singing softly to myself, though I could remember only about half the words to any song. Ella Fitzgerald was scatting to "Blue Skies."

I caught Tanner glancing at me, his lips twitching in amusement.

"Hey, I know you deliberately changed stations," I said, making him aware that I was onto his joke.

His eyes back on traffic to navigate a convoy of eighteen-wheelers, he asked, "Do you remember when we drove from Chicago to California?"

"Of course." We had taken two weeks, sighting-seeing along the pop-culture remains of Route 66. A short vacation before plunging into our careers.

Who wouldn't want to see a hundred-seventy-foot-tall catsup bottle, or an eighty-foot-long concrete blue whale, or Cadillac Ranch, with its art installation of ten partially-buried Cadillacs, tail fins riding high? We also passed through odd wilderness places like the Painted Desert and Petrified Forest. And two short detours had given us Santa Fe and the Grand Canyon. The trip was perfect for Tanner, a history buff, and for me, a fan of Americana. A joyous melding of the man-made environment and natural beauty.

On that trip we'd listened to the radio and CDs and talked about music and architecture. That we were both to shape voids for our livings seemed auspicious, even fated—Tanner shaping silence with notes and words while I shaped space with matter.

For me, the trip was also a music course rolled up in a language course, where the language just happened to consist of notes and chords. Tanner told me about his music, the musicians who had influenced him, guitars and their tonal qualities, his writing process, and the genres informing his music, as we listened to everything from Robert Johnson to Led Zeppelin to Pearl Jam. I reciprocated with commentary about my favorite architects and styles.

Most importantly, though, I learned about Tanner. For the first time, I understood that music was how he experienced and processed the world, his emotions and thoughts converted into music. Music was Tanner's second language—heck, maybe even his first.

"I loved that trip out here. We were so carefree," he said, as he tapped on the steering wheel along to the beat of another song. "And I loved that we shared each other's passions."

He was right. I didn't understand music like he did; after all, I was spatially- and visually-oriented. But I could appreciate the profound power of music.

"I always wondered why you never sang in the car," I said. "Singing in the car is like sipping coffee while reading the newspaper."

"At the time, I was more interested in analyzing the music that was playing. I suppose I was working."

"So, a busman's holiday as you drove?" I asked.

"Probably," he confessed.

"Well, here's a crazy idea. Why don't you sing with me, right now? I promise, it will make you feel like a rock star."

He smiled, then actually started singing along to Frank Sinatra's "Come Fly with Me." Although we started off singing together, I stopped to listen to him, his voice smooth as Sinatra's as he harmonized with the recording.

He appeared twenty-one again, the sheer joy of singing making him as lighthearted as when we had driven here from Chicago. My heart soared, like the words of the song itself.

He glanced at me, one eyebrow cocked, so I joined back in to keep him singing. "'. . . Come fly with me, let's fly, let's fly/Pack up, let's fly away!'"

"How do you feel?" I couldn't resist asking.

He grinned. "Like a rock star."

THIRTY-NINE

Once we pulled off the main highway onto the road to the lake, I switched the radio off so Tanner could tell me about the area.

Eventually we took a right onto a gravel road, which ended in a turnaround from which led a narrow dirt track. A "Sold" sign was posted next to the lane. Tanner continued down the rutted track, the jouncing of the car on the washboard trail providing a rock-and-roll beat to the conversation.

The lot was deeper than I'd realized, with tall evergreen trees that would provide privacy from the land side, even in winter. On the left, we caught fragmentary glimpses of the lake through the trees. As we rounded a small bend in the road that skirted a man-high outcropping of rocks, the lake burst into view, sparkling in the sunshine. Tanner parked the car at the end of the lane, about fifty feet from the water's edge.

The vista was spectacular, encompassing both the lake and the cove, which extended about three-quarters of a mile to the right. Two sailboats navigated in the trifling wind between us and several small islands in the lake.

I got out of the car and stretched, breathing in the fresh air with its crisp pine scent.

"This is wonderful, Tanner. You were lucky to find such an untouched property." It was a beautiful lot—perfect for the sun-filled house we had envisioned. My eyes filled with tears in seconds and I abruptly turned and walked several feet towards the lake. It didn't seem to matter if I mentally prepared myself for these moments; I still got sucker punched by long-ago remembrances.

As I stared out at the lake, the wispy clouds above reflected as strange, creeping water creatures just below the water's surface, Tanner's voice came cheerfully over my shoulder. "My agent found this lot before it came on the market. The same family had owned it for two generations but the heirs wanted to sell. I offered an all-cash deal with a quick closing that got their attention."

I nodded, turning back to face him. "Can we walk the property first? I'd like to get a feel for the topography and views." Plus, walking would give me a chance to get my feelings under control.

We started with the cove side. I walked ahead, fallen twigs and leaves crunching under foot. "Tell me about the dock. Are you going to keep this one?"

"The dock is sound, but I'll probably build a new one at some point."

Several dinged beer cans lay on the ground in front of us. I picked them up and handed them to Tanner.

"Let's talk about the dock first then, as it may have a bearing on where we site the house. Is the current location good or would you prefer to erect the new one elsewhere? Also, will you need to run the road down to the water?"

I leaned down to pick up more rusted cans. Tanner cradled his arms and I added them to the load.

"No need to run the road down to the water. The boat will be moored at a marina about twenty minutes away by water. And when I'm ready for a new dock, I'll probably rebuild it in the same place. That way Jason and his friends can swim in the more protected cove."

I tossed three more cans on the pile Tanner was carrying.

Looking at the remaining can I still held, I asked, "Have you thought about security? People obviously enjoy this place as much as you do."

He grimaced. "I have a security company. But I wanted a preliminary site plan before bringing them in."

I added the can to his pile and then bent down for some bottles. Apparently, I wasn't hiding my growing grin well enough.

"Enough!" Tanner finally realized that I was having way too much fun. He dumped the armload of cans and debris on the ground and then wiped the dirt and leaves off his shirt. "This is the perfect job for Jason. He can run around exploring the property while picking up old treasures."

I brushed the dirt off my hands. "Well, make sure he has a tetanus shot."

"Yes, ma'am." But he smiled at my concern.

After walking the property, we headed back to the car and I turned to face the shore. "It makes sense to locate the garage to the left of the road so you have an unimpeded view of the lake on arrival. It also means we save the largest piece of buildable land for the house."

Tanner nodded.

I walked to a cleared space between where the original cabin had stood and the lake. A soft breeze murmured through the woods, background accompaniment to the squawking scrub jays peeved at our intrusion.

Tanner joined me. We were standing shoulder to shoulder again, his hand mere inches from mine.

Ignoring him, I rotated around slowly, studying the surrounding trees and views. Tanner had set the program for the lake house, but I wanted the site to drive the design.

Already the house was taking shape in my mind.

Hmmm. Did that mean I had decided to proceed with the project? Despite all the problems of dealing with Tanner, all he had needed to reel me in was to dangle a piece of land and a building program in front of me. Had Tanner known that when he had coaxed me to L.A., not accepting my no?

"I think we should build vertically to take advantage of the views. What do you think?" Plus, if we built vertically, we could keep most of the trees between this open space and the lake.

He, too, had been examining the views. Turning, he met my eyes. "You're the designer."

"Then upward it is. Now let's go over your space requirements in the context of these views. But first, which vista do you prefer—the lake or the cove?"

His right hand shielding his eyes, he considered the panoramic view. "I think I prefer the cove. What do you think?"

I looked at the two vistas, initially surprised by his choice. Then I realized the cove view turned inward, affirming the home as a refuge.

"Yes, it's more private. I'm starting to get some ideas about how to group the spaces, maybe separating your personal space from Jason's and the guest spaces. I assume the music space should be included in your area?"

He nodded.

"Is the music room primarily private or will other people use it?"

"Private."

We went through the remainder of the list, discussing each room within the context of the surroundings. Sometimes, as he had done yesterday, he would answer, "You know what I want." I resisted kicking him, though. I didn't want to be accused of a quick temper again . . . especially if I was taking the job.

FORTY

All things considered, the trip to the lake had gone well.

Before leaving, though, I needed one more thing. Having already taken photos of the lake from where the house would stand, I now wanted pictures of the building site from the lake.

Tanner and I walked out to the end of the pier. I turned around and started snapping shots of the shore. Envisioning the front of the house peeking through the evergreens, I stepped backwards for a couple more shots.

Too late, I realized I'd reached the end of the dock—but momentum was still propelling me backwards.

Tanner tried to grab me.

Feeling only air beneath me, I tumbled into the water, going under. The water was shockingly cold after the last hour of being toasted by the sun.

"Jess, are you okay?" Tanner shouted when I reemerged, as though I had already drifted miles away.

"I'm fine. Stop yelling. Would you take the camera?" I was holding it up in one hand, trying to keep it out of the water. Maybe Charlene was right; I'd drenched Tanner and now I was thoroughly—and embarrassingly—drenched by the hand of karma.

Tanner stretched down and snagged the camera, placing it safely on the dock.

Then, cannonball style, he jumped in, drowning me again.

I retaliated, flailing water at him until he was as soaked as I was. It was freeing. I felt like a kid again, on vacation in Vermont with my family, splashing around in the lake with my brother. So many emotions were released in that moment, my body relaxing after a long week of tension.

"Looked like you needed rescuing." Tanner flashed me a huge grin.

I laughed, splashing more water at him. "You came closer to drowning me than when I fell in."

He disappeared under the water. Oh, I knew this game from long ago: he would pop up behind me. I twisted around, ready for him.

Instead he reemerged where he had gone under and grabbed me from behind in a lifesaver's carry hold, his left arm across my chest.

"I shall save you whether you need it or not," he crowed as he swam with me toward the ladder, his arm across my breasts. His breath teased the back of my neck, triggering goose bumps and causing my nipples to swell.

The more I struggled to get away, the tighter he held me—like a Chinese finger trap. My nostrils were probably flaring from the firmness and intimacy of his grip.

And it wasn't just my torso he was supporting as he swam; I felt the length of his body under me, lifting me, bumping rhythmically against mine.

I moaned.

Tanner froze, abruptly releasing his hold. I sank immediately and unexpectedly without his support, taking water in through my nose. When I surfaced I was hacking and snorting, trying to get the lake water out.

"Are you okay?" he growled.

I was not okay. And it was about more than the coughing. The fervid throbbing still persisted. I wanted the man, here in the water. It wasn't like we had never done that before—the man was half seal.

Suddenly he pulled away from me, swimming for the nearby ladder. "Enough playing, Jessie." His tone was stern, like he was talking to a wayward child. "We need to get you out of those wet clothes."

He thought I'd been playing? Hadn't he felt it? I was still vibrating like one of his guitar strings. I wondered if I could even make it up the ladder—unaccustomed and unconsummated lust sapping my energy.

When I didn't climb the ladder quickly enough, Tanner grasped my arm and yanked me the rest of the way, not looking me in the eye. Then he strode off to the car while I was left to retrieve the camera.

I stood on the dock for a minute, looking out over the placid water—so unlike my emotions, which were churning massive whitecaps. How stupid was I? I thought Tanner had felt the connection. I was sure of it. Yet he had recoiled.

But more important, why had I reacted like that? I knew our

relationship was long over. And, again, the last thing I wanted was a one-night stand. Both because Tanner was like a potato chip—you couldn't have just one taste—and because it would cheapen what had been real in our relationship. Maybe he could work with me, but I was right to doubt that I could work with him.

I turned and trudged back to the car, stopping to wring water from my shirt and give my pride and stomach a chance to recover.

Tanner was rummaging through a gym bag when I approached. Still averting his eyes from mine, he tossed a towel my direction.

I caught the towel and started drying my hair.

"I've also got some sweats you can put on," he barked.

Oh, give me a break. I hadn't deliberately fallen into the water to seduce him. He needn't look quite so shocked and aggrieved.

I shook my head. I didn't want his sweats; they'd be too long for me, puddling around my ankles. "You take them. I'll be fine."

"No, those jeans will never dry. My khakis will be fine shortly."

Then he held up a hoodie and a T-shirt. "Which would you prefer?"

"The T-shirt." The idea of absconding with the shirt flickered through my brain but I quickly discarded the thought.

I headed to the opposite side of the car and stripped off the sodden jeans, rubbed my legs with the towel quickly, and pulled on the sweats. Then, taking the shirt off, I dried off some more, deciding finally that the bra needed to go as well. I donned his T-shirt and, as part contortionist and part conjurer, took off the bra. When I finished, I looked up and saw Tanner glowering at me in the side view mirror.

I was tempted to throw the bra at him but threw the towel instead. He stripped off his shirt and did the best he could with the sopping towel. I couldn't help but watch. I was still tingling from our earlier encounter. At least I could get some visual satisfaction—though it only made me want more of what I couldn't have.

He ignored me. When finished, he ran his fingers through his hair. He looked great.

Me? I must have looked like a kid playing in his father's clothes, his T-shirt hanging off my shoulders. I envisioned a Shar Pei. Could I look worse?

"Are you ready for lunch?"

Was he kidding? On the way up, he had mentioned that we'd go to the nearby marina for lunch, but I assumed he'd change his mind after this fiasco.

"Are you sure you want to?" I replied, clearly suggesting otherwise.

"We don't have options. Besides, they sell T-shirts. We'll get one that fits better."

"Do they sell clown noses as well?"

I saw a slight smile. I must have looked a sight to have elicited even that response in his grumpy mood.

"I'll check."

FORTY-ONE

It was a twenty-five-minute drive to the marina. But the strain between Tanner and me—amplified by the close quarters—made it feel like forever. And I couldn't even begin to understand where the tension was coming from. The incident in the lake seemed to have summoned up all sorts of monsters. Yes, I had been unprofessional, but he had jumped in after me. He knew I was a good swimmer; he needn't have "rescued" me—and certainly not in such an intimate and arousing manner.

After we parked, Tanner said, "Stay here. I'll see what clothes they have." He didn't bother to ask my size.

In a couple of minutes, he was back.

"Sorry, no clown noses—or floppy shoes. This will have to do." He handed me a shirt and a beach towel. The T-shirt read "Fish Magnet." How charming.

Tanner smirked.

Twisting away from him, I changed quickly in the car. Unfortunately, the shirt was tight and my nipples were firm and full from the cool air.

When I got out of the car Tanner gave me the once over, a slight upturned curve hovering at the corner of his mouth.

"I'd like to propose takeout," I said.

"No, no, you look fine."

Which I took to mean I looked hideous. He turned around and headed to the diner. I followed in his baggy sweats and the new, too-tight, puke-colored T-shirt, thinking that he had more than achieved retribution for my pouring water on him two months earlier.

When I got inside, however, my peevishness lifted.

The diner was fabulous, a time capsule from the 1950s. And by that I don't mean it was retro but rather the real thing: red Formica-topped tables with shiny ridged-chrome edges; an eating counter with swivel stools topped in yellow vinyl; black and white linoleum flooring; and, marvelous primary-red banquettes. I loved it.

Forgetting my attire and embarrassment, I asked Tanner if we could sit at a booth. He nodded and folded his long body onto a bench. Then his face reverted to the vexed expression he'd been wearing since the lake fiasco.

After placing orders with the waitress—who looked as authentic as the diner, I speculated, "Perhaps you and I shouldn't eat in restaurants together, Tanner. Or, at least, you should sit at a separate table."

That got his attention.

Tanner raised one eyebrow. "Why's that?"

"I don't seem to be at my best. First, I toss water on you. Next, same restaurant, I snort water all over the table. Yesterday I squirted lime juice in your eye, and today I'm probably ruining your rocker reputation by looking like a jester." There were only a few people in the place, but all of them had noted Tanner when he walked in.

"Well, you do keep things interesting," he conceded. "But we did okay over breakfast today . . . unless, of course, you were harboring wicked thoughts of what to do with the coffee or frying pan but were too hungry to carry them out."

He thought we had done well at breakfast? Obviously, we lived on different planets.

But I played innocent. "I'd like to think one meal could be safe, but with anything hot around I can't even guarantee breakfast."

"Then, please stay away from me tonight while I'm grilling. I don't want a trip to the emergency room."

"Ten-foot restraining order?"

He shook his head. "How about twenty? Once I'm through cooking and we're at the table I'll lift the order." His eyes were fixed on mine, but his peripheral vision danced over my braless breasts and chilled nipples.

My body went hot under his gaze, but I managed to squeak out, "Deal."

Thankfully, the waitress appeared with our lunches—a tuna melt for me and a turkey sub for Tanner.

Suddenly I was hungry.

Tanner seemed less so, picking up a French fry and then putting it down, repeatedly, as if about to speak.

Finally, with an attempt at casualness, he inquired, "So how's Nick?" His face puckered on the words, as though sucking a lemon.

I swallowed a bite of my sandwich. Why was he asking about Nick? "He's okay."

Still focused on his fries, he said, "I read his book."

My eyebrows shot up. Wasn't expecting that.

"It was . . . thought provoking. I gave copies to a few friends who I felt might be interested."

"I'll let him know," I said, even more surprised.

Tanner continued to play with the damn fries. Something else was on his mind.

Finally, his eyes rose up to mine. "How are the two of you doing?"

My eyes narrowed. "The two of us?"

"You know—friends with benefits?"

I slowly put my sandwich back on the plate and glanced around. All I had was iced tea. It was one thing to reject me at the lake—that was his prerogative—but it was another to judge my character unfairly.

Very slowly, my voice low and warning, I replied, "I never said that, Tanner. You presumed it."

His brows puckered, suddenly unsure of himself. "You didn't say otherwise," he protested.

He was digging the hole deeper. "Why should I have to deny something that isn't true? And if you believe that is how I operate—sex as the prelude to intimacy rather than the reverse—would refuting it have changed your mind?" Of all people, he should know that I didn't play at relationships.

I pushed my plate away. "Besides, with that recent tabloid story, you should know better than anyone not to speculate."

He flinched as though slapped. "I'm sorry, Jessie. I misunderstood the situation. It was just that he seemed . . . possessive of you."

"That's funny, because he said the same thing about you. And you know what I told him? That it had more to do with you two alpha males than it had anything to do with me. In fact, it was insulting—neither of you has any reason to be possessive."

Now it was his turn to be confused. "So, you're . . . uh, not seeing him?"

Was this why he had recoiled from me at the lake? He thought I was seeing someone while coming on to him? So much for respect. Any lingering lust for him vanished.

I eyed my tea. He followed my glance and grabbed the glass before I could.

"Jessie."

"Oh, I wasn't going to do anything."

"Sure."

I rolled my eyes. "Nick's a friend. I go jogging with him. He comes over for dinner occasionally and we'll watch a movie or a game. I did attend an office function with him last weekend. You know why? He said if he invited anyone else they would assume the invitation meant more than it did."

Tanner stared at me, trying to understand. "But he's a good guy, right?"

"He's a great guy. But what's he's been through in the last five years makes what you and I went through look like a stroll in the park."

"I don't understand." His face was a question mark.

I paused. I didn't have to explain Nick, but maybe it would put things in perspective for Tanner—a man who had so much to be thankful for, including a child. "Four years ago, Nick lost his only child, Sophie, who was six, to aplastic anemia. The treatment requires finding a compatible bone marrow donor. The best matches are usually a sibling, but Sophie was an only child. The doctors eventually found a matching unrelated bone marrow donor, but Sophie developed an infection after the transplant."

I took a breath. "After Sophie's death, Nick and his wife grieved in different ways. He was filled with anger while his wife refused to talk about their child's death, wishing only to move on. Which she did, divorcing Nick about a year after Sophie's passing—and remarrying two years later, followed by having another child. But Nick's still grieving."

The muscles in Tanner's face went slack, as though he was sick. "I'm sorry. I can't imagine what the death of a child must feel like. Of course, you tried to help him?"

The question sounded snarky but actually acknowledged my compassion.

I sighed. "I've suggested counseling or a support group, but he's caught up in his anger. It fuels him—and those Ironman Competitions. I think he's afraid there'll be nothing left of Sophie if he lets go of the anger. And one thing I've learned is that you can't fix someone who's not ready. But I'm a friend when he needs one."

His voice low, Tanner said, "This might sound odd, but would you like me to talk with him sometime when I'm in D.C.? I know a bit about loss and a lot about waking up angry and using it to fuel the day. But anger is never the answer."

I was surprised—and touched—by his offer. Again, he was paying Alex's kindness forward. But his loss—the unraveling of his marriages and the addiction, I supposed—was different from Nick's situation.

"I appreciate the offer. Maybe I'll suggest it to Nick if the time ever feels right."

"I mean it, Jess. My hell was of my own making, unlike Nick's, but either way, it can be hard to find your way out once you're trapped. In the darkness and pain, it's hard to imagine there's any light outside."

Damn. Maybe he could help Nick. My chest tightened—for both Nick and Tanner.

We ate the rest of our food in silence. When we finished, Tanner asked for two coffees to go.

As he opened the car door for me, his mouth curled up. "Not too many women could pull off that look." He burst out laughing.

Clearly, he was in a much better mood than when we had left the lake property.

Me? Not so much. Tanner hadn't even questioned his assumptions about me and Nick, hadn't expected better of me.

But then, to be fair, I'd had my own expectations of who he was now, as shaped by his fame, not by his character.

I sighed again.

FORTY-TWO

Steaks and sweet potatoes were on the menu for dinner. Tanner had already fired up the grill down by the pool.

The day before, his chef had prepared a chopped salad composed of sweet peppers, cucumbers, tomatoes, corn, and ranch dressing. Now I was dicing lettuce and avocados to add to the salad, per Pamela's instructions. The consistency was almost like a salsa—a smart way to get kids to eat vegetables.

When the doorbell rang, Tanner said, "Let's roll."

Huh? I'd planned on staying in the kitchen, playing line chef. Meeting Jason would be tough enough—the back of my neck already feeling a headache coming on. I certainly hadn't prepared myself mentally for meeting his mother. And I doubted Nadine would be any more thrilled to meet me.

So, when Tanner opened the front door, I hung back at the entrance to the dining room.

Jason came bounding in, talking to his dad, already in mid-paragraph. Tanner motioned me forward.

"Jessie, I'd like you to meet my son, Jason. Jason, this is an old friend of mine, Ms. Hartley."

On autopilot, I moved to the door and stuck out my hand. "Nice to meet you, Jason."

I felt disoriented. I had expected to be gobsmacked when I finally met Jason, but it was the woman standing behind him who'd caught my attention.

"Yo," Jason said to me.

Tanner looked down at Jason. "Dude, try again."

I refocused on Jason. He had the same build as Tanner and was dressed in shorts and a Lakers T-shirt. His hair was a little lighter, but the dark brown eyes were the same.

The boy rolled those eyes. "Nice to meet you, Ms. Hartley."

"Yo."

That got a frown from Tanner and a grin from Jason as he headed into the dining room, Tanner's eyes following him.

Then Tanner remembered he still had another introduction to make and turned back to the door.

"Jessie, this is Nadine. Nadine, Jessie."

Well, this was weird.

She didn't look like the Big Bad Wolf.

She was maybe five inches shorter than I and very thin, in that starlet way which made me worry about osteoporosis. But she had long, beautiful chestnut-brown hair that saved her from the Hollywood-blond cliché.

She nodded at me, her neck as stiff as a two-by-four. In that nod I read acknowledgment of who I was. I followed her lead and nodded back. She seemed reluctant to cross the threshold, standing at the far edge of the stoop, not even on the welcome mat.

"Excuse me, ladies. I need to check on Jason." Tanner left the two of us standing there awkwardly. What a chicken.

Nadine's face scrunched up, her eyes following Tanner's back. This was not the look of a woman who had been with Tanner "only to have a child." This was the face of a woman who had loved Tanner. Maybe that was the rationalization he'd told himself because he hadn't been in love with her, or maybe it was the story she'd told him to save face when they divorced.

Standing on the threshold, I realized that Nadine hadn't taken Tanner away from me any more than I had taken Tanner away from her. Our estrangements from Tanner were the result of his addiction and the failed dynamic we'd each had with him. We had more in common than I had expected.

Her wounds were broadcast across her body—her lips pinched, her arms folded tightly over her torso, the distance she maintained, all in an attempt to stay poised in this difficult situation: a conversation about the future to which she was not invited, to talk about a place her only child would be spending time. Probably without her.

"Gee whiz," I said. "Ta—Teddie can be a real dick, can't he?"

Her eyes popped wide.

I stepped down onto the porch so as not to tower over her. I wanted to tell her to get angry and move on, but who was I to give her advice? I hadn't exactly managed that myself.

Instead, I said, "You know, neither of us was able to help Teddie when he was on drugs. But I believe Jason saved him."

Nadine's eyes filled with tears, but she stood taller. She reached out and grazed my arm for a fleeting second with her fingertips, whispering, "Thank you." Then she turned and walked to her car.

I waited on the porch until she had driven through the gates and turned onto the road.

This weekend I had stepped into one very odd, very uncomfortable episode of *The Twilight Zone*.

When I reentered the kitchen, Tanner and Jason were sitting at the island counter arguing noisily about who the best baseball pitchers were—current and past.

Tanner looked up briefly.

I nodded back. I had been really nervous about meeting Jason. After all, this wasn't a photo of him, which had been enough to derail me in April; this was the real thing. But after meeting Nadine, I felt as if meeting Jason was . . . child's play. Who knew?

Nonetheless I leaned against the counter for just a moment before chopping up more lettuce, to let my brain catch up with my emotions. I didn't join their conversation, deciding it was better to let Jason get comfortable. Let him enjoy a few minutes one-on-one with his dad.

Plus, I was afraid my voice would crack.

But I watched them as I tossed the salad ingredients together. Really, the resemblance was uncanny. Tanner and his mini-me. Except that Jason's hands were flying during the discussion. At one point, Tanner rubbed the top of his son's head in affection.

"Daaad." Jason protested, his face reddening. He peeked in my direction.

Hey, kid, we've all been there. Trying to act like an adult around strangers while your parents treat you like a child.

I winked at him. He blushed even more.

Tanner looked over at me, too. But he was all smiles. Smiles overflowing with love for his son. Poor Jason. He was just going to have to endure his father's overt affection—it wasn't going to change any time soon. He was very lucky.

I was running out of keeping-myself-busy tasks, so when there was finally a lull in the conversation, I asked, "Are you hungry, Jason?"

That got his attention. Looking up at me, he said "I could eat a horse!"

"Gosh, Tanner, we're not having horse tonight, are we?"

Instead of a laugh, I got another blank look, this time from Jason. I looked at Tanner in mock disbelief. "Doesn't anybody know your name?"

"Jason knows it. He's just never heard anybody call me by it. Just so you're aware, Jason, Jessie always calls me Tanner."

I rolled my eyes. "Yes, because it's your name, Tanner."

Jason seemed to find the exchange funny, like his dad was getting schooled.

But Tanner's son wasn't above schooling me, either. "We're not having horse, Ms. Hartley. That's just an expression."

"Oh, thank goodness. Otherwise I'd be heading straight to dessert."

Tanner was trying not to laugh at the two of us. He slid off his stool, saying, "You and I should check the grill, Jason."

Tanner poured iced tea for himself and lemonade for Jason and handed the lemonade to his son, along with a bowl of sweet potatoes he had sliced earlier, brushed with olive oil, and sprinkled with a little salt. Then he picked up his own glass and his home-made dressing of lime juice, olive oil and fresh dill for the potatoes once they came off the grill, and the two headed for the garden. I was impressed at Tanner's newfound culinary skills—and Pamela's teaching abilities.

Alone, I exhaled with relief. This was going to be a tough evening. But maybe this could be that one time, like in my fantasy encounters with Tanner, when I could rise above my emotions—for Jason's sake.

Finished with my tasks, I started carrying the food and condiments outside. Tanner had just put the steaks on the grill and said he would add the sweet potatoes when the steaks had about ten minutes to go.

Jason was sitting on the edge of the pool, his feet dangling in the water, kicking and splashing. He was doing his best to get his dad wet. It was obviously a game they'd played before. Tanner had set the grill just close enough to the pool so that Jason couldn't resist trying, yet far enough that Tanner and the food were relatively safe. Every so often Jason succeeded in splattering his dad.

And for once it wasn't my fault; I was a good twenty feet from Tanner, still under my restraining order. But it seemed that Jason and I were on the same page when it came to Tanner and liquids.

I brought the rest of the food in two more trips and then sat down at the table, enjoying the outdoors and the bird serenades after the long day. The mouth-watering aromas coming off the sizzling grill were redolent of picnics and holidays, friends and family.

Meanwhile Tanner and Jason were arguing about Jason's cell phone. Jason thought the phone needed to be upgraded, complaining that he was embarrassed to use it around his friends. Tanner wasn't buying it, his jaw clenched like he was practicing for the teenage years.

I, on the other hand, was hugely entertained.

Every once in a while, Jason would throw a glance at me, a slight crease to his forehead.

Might as well find out what was on his mind. "Do you two cook outdoors often?" I asked Jason.

Feet still dangling in the water, he looked over at me. "Maybe twice a month." Then, with a sly look, he added, "How do you know my dad?"

I tossed a glance at Tanner to see if he wanted to answer. Maybe he'd even said something already. But Tanner just smiled, looking at me like he was as interested in the answer as Jason.

"Your dad and I met in college," I said. "Did you know he was a history major?"

Jason shook his head. But the floodgate for questions had opened. "Why are you here?"

Tanner jumped in this time. "I've hired Jessie. We'll talk about 'why' over dinner."

Then, with a cheeky grin on his face, Jason asked, "Did you date my dad?"

I wanted to rub the back of my neck. Man, why was Tanner leaving me to handle the tough questions?

"We dated our last year in college and for a short time after graduation. I ended up taking a job on the East Coast and now I live in Washington, D.C." A simple, clear answer. Nothing implying cause and effect or the long time-lag between the two events. Tanner couldn't have done better.

"And what about you, Jason, are you dating anyone?" I had babysat enough tween-age kids, between Charlene's daughter Isabelle and my office mate Karen's twin boys, to know how to quench the flow of personal questions.

Jason's whole body spasmed and his face scrunched up in alarm. "No! I'm eleven. I can't date!"

"Eleven. Hmmm, so you're not driving either?" I asked, as if confused.

At that question, he caught on and tried to splash me with his hands, grinning.

"If he could see over the dashboard, he'd try," Tanner teased.

Motivated, Jason went for a bigger kick-splash and nailed his father. Tanner shook the drops off his hair. Thank goodness, the food was protected by the grill cover, because I was starved.

Satisfied with his mastery of the pool, Jason sprang up and headed for a basketball half-court tucked beside the lower terrace, where he started tossing a ball at the basket.

When Jason made a shot, he'd glance over at us. I'd give him a thumbs-up to let him know I was watching. Tanner stood at the grill, watching as well, spatula in one hand and tongs in the other, a contented smile on his face. I wondered if Nadine ever saw this expression, or if it was all business when they interacted.

Jason seemed to be a normal, active kid. Tanner and Nadine had done well despite the difficult circumstances.

When the steaks were ready, Tanner called his son back to the table and lifted my restraining order.

As we ate, Tanner and I talked to Jason about those early days when mPulse had first started playing in Chicago, taking any gig they could, just to get experience and exposure.

Jason was surprised. It was a far different image than he had of his successful father. To him, Tanner had always been famous. It was probably good for him to realize that everybody has to pay their dues.

The conversation flowed effortlessly, from Chicago to music to things that interested Jason, all punctuated with laughter and lots of gentle teasing, even between Tanner and me. Maybe too much teasing. Jason kept glancing between the two of us, the slight furrow returning to his brow.

FORTY-THREE

After dinner, Tanner said, "Now would be a good time to talk about why Jessie is here, Jason. She's an architect. I've asked her to design a weekend house for us at a lake."

His son's eyes grew wide. "Really?"

"Yes. I showed her the property this morning. I'm hoping that maybe this time next year we'll be barbequing there."

"How come she got to see the place first?"

Uh-oh.

Tanner flashed me a look of apology.

"Because Jessie's the professional. I wanted to see the site through her eyes first, to make sure it could work for everything we'd need. Besides, Jessie and I were working. When you and I go up, we'll have fun. There's already a dock where you can cannonball into the water."

Guess I shouldn't mention the trash collection project Tanner had in mind. My status would take another hit.

Tanner pulled out his phone and showed Jason pictures of the property.

"Can we jet ski there?"

"We'll definitely swim, sail, and fish. Maybe even windsurf or paddleboard."

"What will it look like?"

"That's Jessie's job. She'll take all the spaces we need and design a place that's amazing."

Jason looked over at me, his eyes skeptical. Maybe he didn't think women could design fun places for boys, or maybe he didn't want me interacting with his father. And I'd thought we'd been doing so well.

Tanner continued. "It's a vacation place, so it'll be smaller than this house. But we'll have room to invite guests."

I jumped in, trying to keep from sliding lower in Jason's estimation. "Something I could do, Jason, if you'd like to invite more friends than there are bedrooms, is to provide bunk bed cubbies. They're not bedrooms but alcoves off a hallway where your friends could sleep. It's essentially overflow space. Ski lodges often use them."

I raised my eyebrows at Tanner, looking for a reaction.

"What do you think, Jason?" Tanner prompted.

"Bunk beds sound like fun," he admitted.

Then Jason launched into the gazillion questions Tanner had predicted. Sometimes Tanner deferred to me on a house question.

I poured Jason and me more lemonade while he grilled his father.

When Jason finally slowed down, I inquired, "Have you ever seen a house being built?"

He shook his head.

"Well, if your dad moves ahead on this place, get him to take you to the site periodically. Some people find the construction process interesting. I particularly like the initial building stages—when all the structural elements go up. You see the skeleton of the house first, and then the muscles and skin are added."

Jason nodded at me, his eyes wide.

Encouraged, I added, "And take plenty of pictures. When you put all the pictures together at the end, you'll have a wonderful story about your new home."

Tanner regarded me thoughtfully. "That's a good idea."

He turned to Jason and put a hand on his shoulder. "You could be the official photographer. How does that sound?"

Mini-me nodded enthusiastically, his eyes shining. "But you'll have to get me a better phone. The camera on mine is lousy."

I glanced at Tanner and laughed.

Tanner frowned at me. "Are you two in cahoots?"

"He has a point, Tanner. Or you could get him a good digital camera."

Jason jounced in his chair. He could smell victory.

Tanner drummed his fingers on the table. "Tell you what. Why don't we play a game of basketball—two-on-one—for your choice of a new phone or digital camera? Jason, you and Jessie can play against me since you two have obviously been scheming together. Whoever reaches eleven points first, wins. And don't worry—Jessie played basketball in high school. We'll have dessert afterwards."

Shoot. What had I gotten myself into? I'd played volleyball in college on a scholarship and still played in the night league with Charlene, but it was a long time since I'd played basketball. But I was competitive, thanks to my brother. And, I could rarely pass up a challenge—especially one issued by Tanner.

I raised my hand up to Jason for a high-five and was relieved when he slapped it, even though the response was halfhearted. Turning to Tanner, I said, "You're on, old man."

We headed to the half-court.

"Can we practice a couple of shots first?" I asked.

"Sure. Five shots each," Tanner offered.

My best shot was a jump shot. I managed three out of five from different locations. That wasn't bad considering how long it had been. But then, I had incentive.

Watching my shots, Jason let out an audible sigh of relief.

He and I went into a huddle. I suggested a couple of strategies. I hadn't grown up watching the Celtics with my brother and father without learning something.

To start the game, Jason would toss the jump ball. "Ready. Set," he said, lobbing the ball up and then heading to the hoop. Silly Tanner—he was waiting for "Go." I grabbed the ball and tossed it to Jason, who put it in. First blood. My teammate and I did a victory dance under the hoop.

"Hey, you guys cheated," Tanner complained, retrieving the ball.

"You have five inches on me, Tanner. Consider it a handicap."

The game bounced back and forth between us, with quite a bit of physical jostling between Tanner and me. But unlike our earlier contact at the lake, this bumping only got my competitive juices flowing . . . well, that and a little residual anger from earlier.

Tanner had a good hook shot that got him points. But I knew how to set a pick that would let Jason get to the basket. And Jason would bounce me the ball so I could take a jump shot.

And all the while, I was trash-talking Tanner, once telling him he was the poster boy for the phrase "white men can't jump." Jason giggled, but

Tanner called a technical foul, giving himself a free shot.

Jason and I objected but it was moot, since Tanner didn't make the point.

With the game tied ten-ten, I was taking a jump shot when Tanner collided with me as he tried to block the ball. I went down, hard.

He apologized, the ball tucked under his arm, his eyes stricken as he helped me up.

I dusted myself off and snatched the ball away from him. "Foul!" I crowed.

I stood at the foul line, bouncing the ball. This shot was for all the poor rich kids needing new cell phones and for all the foolish women still grieving a relationship long past. I pictured the perfect shot, then slowly released the ball.

Swish—nothing but net.

Woo-hoo. Lots of high fives between Jason and me, and in-your-face victory moves aimed at Tanner. Sure, we had cheated once or twice, but this game was about winning, not principles.

As Jason dashed happily back to the table for dessert, Tanner held back and put a hand on my arm. "Are you okay?" he asked. "I didn't mean to take you down."

I smiled smugly. "You didn't. But I should get an Oscar for that fall."

"There wasn't ever any hope for me was there?"

"Not when you didn't try to make that foul shot you had. I was merely following your lead. I'm just glad I still had a couple of jump shots left in me."

Tanner laughed. We had been playing for the same side.

As we ate dessert, brownies made with fresh raspberries and extra chunks of chocolate that Chef Lange had baked the day before, Jason waffled between getting the phone or the camera. You could tell he wanted the phone, with bragging rights to impress his friends, but the idea of a new gadget that was more adult also had its temptations.

I sat back and watched the two of them discuss the pros and cons. Tanner was sitting across the table from his son, leaning in towards him. It was like seeing Tanner reflected in a vintage mirror, the reflected image blurred, not fully realized. Two months ago the sight might have wounded, reminding me of the children we had talked of having.

But it was obvious that Tanner had worked hard on the relationship with his son. It couldn't have been easy, with all the touring, the early-on addiction, and the divorce, but he had gotten it right.

I respected him for that.

Suddenly Jason asked, "Which do you think I should get, Ms. Hartley?"

I hadn't been listening closely. After all, it was their debate. But I appreciated my teammate including me. "I guess it depends on whether there are other things you'd like to do with the camera. Do you have an interest in photography? Do you plan to travel in the future and want to take more than selfies? Document things other than the house? Or, maybe you'd like to specialize in something like sports photography and work for your school newspaper? If so, you'll want a good camera. But it will take more time to learn to use it. If you don't have the time, patience, or interest and simply want decent snapshots, then a smart phone is good enough."

Tanner and I watched Jason as he struggled: something just for fun—and status—or something that might be more consequential.

His forehead screwed up in thought. After a moment or two, his face brightened. "Dad, I'd like the camera."

Tanner seemed pleased. "Fine. You can research them and bring me a couple of recommendations. Deal?"

"Deal!" Jason turned to me, adding, "Thanks, Ms. Hartley."

I smiled at him. "You're welcome. Maybe you can send me a picture some time."

Night was settling in but we sat a little longer at the table while the two of them talked about the week's schedule. I listened quietly to the rhythm of their conversation, the give and take between them that made them family, and I drifted along comfortably in the flow of words.

Around nine thirty, Tanner said it was time to drive Jason home.

We carried the dishes up to the kitchen.

"It was fun meeting you, Jason. It's been a long time since I played basketball."

He gave me another high-five. "I'll send you lots of pictures."

"I'd like that."

Tanner said that it would take about an hour to drive Jason home and return.

I quickly put the food away and the dishes in the dishwasher. Then, exhausted from another roller coaster of a day, I hurried to the guesthouse, crawled into bed, and turned the lights off before Tanner returned.

But it was tough falling asleep.

Ever since leaving Tanner, I had worried constantly about his health, even after his stint in rehab. I'd never stopped feeling guilty about not being able to help him through his addiction. And despite attending Al-Anon for years and knowing that the addiction was his to contend with, I'd felt the failure of not being able to help him, both emotionally and physically.

But after being with Tanner this weekend—experiencing how healthy he was, seeing the tangible results of his success, watching him interact with his son—I couldn't help but think that the best thing I'd ever done for him was to leave.

FORTY-FOUR

When I woke, embryonic images of Tanner's lake house were floating around my brain—far more comforting than my realization last night of how full his life was now.

I took my time getting ready, trying to avoid breakfast with Tanner since I didn't want a repeat of yesterday's too visceral memories. If I waited long enough maybe Tanner would have eaten and I could fix coffee and toast for myself. My flight wasn't until the afternoon but I packed to delay heading to the house as long as possible.

But I never saw the lights come on in the kitchen. My stomach growling (I was ready for Jason's horse), I finally ventured out. On entering the main house, I heard sounds of a guitar drifting again from the conservatory. I turned towards the music room to greet Tanner before ransacking his kitchen.

Again, he was seated on a stool, bent over a guitar, his head, heart, and hands united in purpose. I knew immediately that he had woken with a song in his head, just as I had woken with silhouettes and volumes in mine.

Tanner had always preferred composing in the mornings. I believed there was often a holdover from sleep when he'd been subconsciously creating—I had sometimes seen the fingers of his left hand dancing while he slept. If he went to work quickly on waking, he often seemed able to tap into the latent memory.

I turned and headed to the kitchen. I knew he wouldn't have eaten anything yet, going straight from bed to the guitar, still in sweats, eager to extract the song. I found a carton of orange juice and poured two glasses. Searching further, I found several croissants and set two of them on plates and returned to the sunroom.

As I placed the juice and roll on the table next to him, Tanner nodded, noticing me for the first time. I put my food on the coffee table and went back to the living room where I'd dropped my gear.

Rejoining Tanner, I sat on the couch, yoga-style, facing him. I took a sip of orange juice and then opened my sketch pad.

Recreating the property and the view of the lake in my mind, I began exploring the form and expression of Tanner's house. I wasn't thinking about floor plans or functions, details or materials, but simply what shapes would best reflect the site and what Tanner wanted. Yesterday, as we stood at the lake talking, I'd begun to envision a three-part schema for the house: two bedroom wings and an entertaining area, all connected by a central tower.

The tower, containing the staircase, would mirror the tall surrounding evergreens while also providing a vertical counterpart to the horizontal wings. It would also allude to the vertical element in this house that Tanner liked so much, as well as to what had felt familiar about my place.

For now, though, I wanted to consider only the exterior of the house.

After completing several sketches, I stopped and flipped back through the pad. I decided to explore two of the drawings more fully to see how far I could take the forms.

As I finished the second sketch, Tanner started playing his song in full. Startled, I looked up.

The piece was amazing.

The melody flowed slowly and mellifluously off his guitar, dripping like thick molasses glistening in sunlight. Or maybe it was more like ambrosia, tasting of the fullness of life—both its joys and sorrows—and finding beauty even in pain. The music was transformational: no one could hold onto melancholy when faced with such eloquence.

I never understood how Tanner could bring forth a piece of music so complete, so perfect, in so little time upon waking. He was like a conduit for the muse of music.

Tanner's eyes were closed, letting me stare. It had been such a long time since I'd watched him compose. He would be so absorbed that I often thought him someplace otherworldly—that if I were to reach out and touch him, he wouldn't notice.

He played through the song. When the last note had faded into the silence, he looked up.

Almost afraid to break the moment, I whispered, "It's remarkable, Tanner."

Lowering his head, he played the song once more, this time drawing out the golden melody. I almost wept, though the music was far more beautiful than sad.

When he finished the song the second time, he placed the guitar in its stand.

"Will this be one of the songs on your new album?" I asked.

"Yes, though it's not the record we planned on making when we went into the studio. Instead, I'm doing something very personal—with the band's whole-hearted help."

"I can't wait, knowing this song will be on it."

He came over to the sofa and sat next to me. I inhaled his presence with its whispers of forest and sea. For an amused moment, I wondered if I might be ovulating, what with my exposure to Tanner all weekend.

"What are you working on?" he asked.

I handed him the sketch pad. "I'm playing with massing and expression."

He thumbed through the pages, examining each drawing without comment.

Worried, I asked, "If you're still interested in proceeding, there are two elevations I'd like your reaction to."

I held my breath. Either of us could make the call not to continue. But now that I'd seen the property, I knew I could design him something wonderful.

Tanner stared at me. "Of course, I want to proceed. What did you think last night was about?"

With an internal sigh of relief, I replied, "Just checking. Don't want to assume anything." Then I hurried on before he could change his mind. "These two sketches don't represent the house per se but represent two potential approaches to expressing the structure."

I showed him the first drawing. "In this interpretation, I've expressed the structure of the house on the outside—the columns are exposed on the exterior, as opposed to being covered by cladding. The visible exterior columns are meant to echo, along with the tower, the nearby evergreens, making the house part of its surroundings. The building will feel heavier, like it's anchored to the ground, thereby contrasting more dramatically with the transparency of the upper portion of the tower and the lightness of the house within."

He nodded.

I showed him the second drawing. "This one emphasizes the lightness of the house both inside and out. The structural elements are covered on the outside, producing a smooth and more traditional exterior. Consistency is highlighted in this approach, as opposed to the contrast in the other." I paused, giving him time to look at the sketches.

He flipped between the two sketches several times.

"Do you have a preference?"

He took another long look at each one. "The one with more contrast. It feels right." He burst into a grin.

I nodded. "I term that one masculine—the muscles and bones are exposed on the exterior. The other approach I call feminine because of its lightness and smooth exterior. I prefer the masculine one as well."

Then, for the first time all morning, I smiled.

FORTY-FIVE

Tanner took a shower while I headed to the kitchen to make a much-needed pot of coffee.

When Tanner reappeared, he looked refreshed, his hair still damp, reminding me of yesterday's disastrous episode at the lake, as well as all those past breakfasts. I must have done something positively wicked in a previous life to have to relive those mornings from so long ago.

Of course, some women might say I was lucky.

"What about yogurt with fresh berries?" he asked. "Also, Pamela makes an amazing blueberry and cinnamon muffin. I'll warm them in the microwave."

While he did that, I poured the coffee and started my task of setting out the dishes again, wondering if renting his guesthouse would always be accompanied by a delectable breakfast with its even more delectable owner. Maybe it wouldn't be such a bad way to start the day.

My pulse quickened.

Followed by me dropping a fork on the floor.

"Sorry," I muttered.

Tanner glanced at me. "At least it wasn't aimed in my direction."

I turned away from him to put the fork in the sink. Maybe the fork hadn't been aimed at him, but my thoughts sure had been.

I sipped the welcome cup of coffee and said, "I enjoyed meeting Jason last night." I meant it, even though it had been difficult initially. "He seems like a great kid."

Affection for his son glowed in Tanner's eyes. "Thanks. You were all he talked about on the way home—well, you and the camera. And he wants you to join us for a Lakers' game—although maybe he'll be bored by the NBA now after your devious, trash-talking style."

Heat crept up my neck. If we could just stick to the house design I'd be okay, but no, he just had to talk about other things—although in all fairness, I had started this conversation.

"Did you tell him I was a Celtics fan?" I looked down at the yogurt.

"No. Couldn't bear to disappoint him. A beautiful woman who knows how to set a pick. I think he has a crush. Maybe the two of us can convince you to cross over from the dark side. I have season tickets to the Lakers' games. We could go any time you're in town."

I stood up to get more coffee, the heat still crawling up my spine. Was this a preview of what hot flashes felt like? I poured what coffee was left in the pot into my cup and busied myself preparing a fresh pot.

"By the way, I took your advice." Tanner continued.

My brows scrunched. "What advice was that?"

"You know. More adult conversations with Jason about drugs and alcohol and the birds and the bees. I started with drugs, since Jason might give me credit for knowing something about that subject. I'm not sure I'll have the same credibility when it comes to talking about sex."

I was back at the counter, finishing the last muffin—which was delicious. "Well, you do have that rock god thing going for you," I snickered.

Tanner laughed, not taking the bait. "Then for once, I won't mind the label." He put down his cup. "Would you like to see the studio now?"

I jumped at the chance. This was something I could actually do without embarrassing myself—too much.

Tanner was right; the studio was interesting as an architectural space. It contained two isolation booths as well as the control room. And with a custom-designed ceiling of varying heights, Tanner noted that the acoustical accuracy in the room was exceptional.

Guitars hung on the walls along with scores of photos, mostly of musicians Tanner had worked with. Interspersed among the pictures were several Grammys and platinum records—but not nearly the number he'd received. A sofa and comfortable club chairs were placed at the far end of the room near a large window overlooking the backyard, the entire space being designed for utility, artistry, and creativity.

But as impressive as the space was, it was even more fun watching Tanner describe all the equipment and how he could use it, still as animated about his life's passion as he'd been on that first day at the coffee shop. This studio, along with the music room, were where his heart lay—the rest of the house mere window dressing.

Well, except the dining room with all things Jason.

As we stepped onto the terrace to collect my travel bag from the guesthouse,

Tanner halted at the balustrade. For a moment he was completely still, looking at the cityscape beyond the tree tops. As I joined him at the railing, the citrusy scent of some unfamiliar southwestern flower drifted up from below.

With his eyes still on the urban panorama, Tanner said, "At your house, you said that you no longer fully believed in love. Is that true?" His fingers tightened around the metal railing.

He caught me by surprise—both with the question and his directness. My fingers, too, tightened around the railing.

Over the last two days, Tanner and I had talked about "things" from the past—the old apartment, the house we'd dreamt of building, his rehab—but we hadn't talked about the relationship itself. With good reason.

My breathing slowed, my lungs unable to draw in air because of all the past emotions and memories shoving their way into my chest.

Cautiously, I replied, "Perhaps it's more accurate to say I believe that sometimes love isn't enough." Charlene's stark words about love not being able to save her father had stayed with me.

"Why do you prefer that version?" His voice was quiet but piercing in its intensity.

"Because if it's not that love simply wasn't enough for our circumstances—then what did we share? What we thought was love, was it just infatuation? Lust? Some type of compulsion?"

He stiffened, as if my words were repugnant. "Do you really believe it was something other than love?"

"I don't want it to be something else, but sometimes I wonder. If it was love, why couldn't it save us? That's why I come back to the idea that sometimes love isn't enough."

I thought back to the garden last night, when I'd walked to the guesthouse by myself. With the landscape lights on, I could clearly see the pool and the patio area. But at the edge of the yard—at the periphery—things were indistinct, shadowy.

Maybe that was like our relationship. Looking at it straight on it had looked like love, felt like love, even tasted like love, but at the periphery there was something wrong—something eroding it, tainting it, gnawing away at it. Maybe it had never been love.

"What about you?" I asked. "You've been married twice. Do you still believe in love?" As soon as I heard the question aloud, I was ashamed. I hadn't meant to be cruel.

He surprised me. "You know what, Jess? I do believe in love. Not because of my marriages, of course, which were about anything but love. But I know with absolute certainty that what you and I shared was love."

My knees almost gave way. I clutched the balustrade, letting it take my weight, as I stared into the distance, trying as usual to keep the conversation cerebral and away from my heart. "I guess I'm right then." I replied softly. "Love must not have been enough." I should have felt relief at his words, but I couldn't get past my disappointment that our love had been so frail.

Tanner grabbed my shoulders and turned me towards him. His face was suffused with frustration. "Your love got me into rehab. I'd hit my low point with that second marriage. I was in Las Vegas and met someone at a party. Two days later we woke to find we were married, thanks to some 'friends.' The only good thing was that she was a trust fund baby with no interest in being married. We couldn't get divorced fast enough.

"For me, though, that thoughtless, meaningless marriage was my wake-up call—I knew I had to go into rehab. I was ashamed of the example I was setting for Jason. Knowing that you had wanted me to get treatment and that Alex had believed I could do it gave me the courage."

He loosened his grip on me, his hands sliding down to grasp my upper arms more gently. Transfixed by his words, I didn't move.

"Do you know what the most difficult thing about rehab was? It wasn't getting off the drugs. That was rough, of course, and I was physically ill going through withdrawal. But that was a physical and mental ordeal—doable. The hardest part was not resorting to the drugs again to forget what I had done to you. I finally had to take responsibility." He searched my face, with anguished eyes. "I really am sorry about what happened, Jessie. I never meant to disappoint or hurt you."

I knew he meant it. I felt it in my bones. "Thank you," I whispered. A piece of me was made whole. Love had helped him.

His dark eyes, though, were still filled with the pain of remembering what his addiction had done to us.

But I had my own truth to tell. "Tanner, I forgave you the addiction before I walked out the door."

His eyes latched onto mine, searching for honesty, as if my words couldn't possibly be true.

"I know the rift between us wasn't intentional on your part." I spoke slowly so he could find the truth in my words. "I know you didn't choose to push me away in favor of the drugs—even though sometimes it felt that way. Of course, that doesn't mean that I didn't feel angry, heartbroken, hurt, disappointed, and a hundred other emotions." I gave him a small, wry smile. "But, with all my heart, I knew you hadn't hurt me deliberately."

Tanner's body sagged, his weight on his forearms as he leaned heavily on the railing. I wanted to wrap my arms around him to console him, but instead, as he had done for me with my brother, I let him stay in the moment as long as he needed.

Neither of us spoke on the way to the airport. Both of us were lost in the small kindnesses we had received: for him, my forgiveness of the addiction, and for me, Tanner's certainty that what we had experienced was love.

After pulling the car up to the drop-off curb, Tanner retrieved my bag from the trunk. We stood silently on the pavement, looking at one another as people hurried by, the wheels of their suitcases slapping roughly on the concrete sidewalk.

Finally, Tanner stepped forward and embraced me. It wasn't a hug between friends; it was a hug acknowledging loss, a hug of consolation. We stayed in the embrace for a long moment, buttressed only by the strength of the other person, grieving a relationship that had once been.

FORTY-SIX

Everyone in D.C. couldn't wait to hear about the weekend.

When I informed Evan Monday morning that Tanner and I were moving forward on the project, he gave me a huge grin and a way-to-go pat on the shoulder.

The staff, though, was less interested in the project than in what Teddie D was like. "Charming" and "funny" came up a lot in my replies. Stephanie was a source of endless questions. And she gave me a joyful trampoline move from her chair when I gave her a CD autographed by Tanner.

Charlene and I met for lunch at a gourmet hamburger joint midway between our offices. She ordered a beef burger ("Otherwise why bother?"), but I decided to try an ahi burger.

She wanted all the details from the trip, but I gave her the expurgated version, scrubbed clean of the dangerous emotional and physical moments that seemed too charged—like meeting Nadine or watching Tanner compose.

Besides, I was embarrassed by my ingrained reactions to him, undiminished by the years. I didn't need Charlene's spooky truth-seeking missiles revealing more stupid failings on my part. Plus, I didn't want to give her additional evidence of karma at work with the mortifying tumble into the lake—I'd never hear the end of it.

"When are you going on your trip with Isabelle?" I asked, redirecting the conversation.

"In a couple of weeks." Charlene dabbed at the corners of her mouth with a napkin for some ketchup that had oozed out of the burger.

"Do you have the itinerary set?"

"Yes. From Duke north to Harvard and points in between."

Duke University was where Charlene had gone as an undergraduate. Isabelle would have her choice of colleges. She was smart—just like her mom.

Nick was the breath of fresh air, less interested in Tanner than in how my meeting with Russ had gone. But then Nick was the only one who knew about that meeting.

I'd walked over to his house after work to pick up my key. We were sitting on his front stoop, catching up.

"It's not a done deal by any means, but Russ is interested. Ethically, I had to tell him about working with Tanner on his lake house and that seemed to raise some red flags. Whether he's worried that my move to L.A. might have more to do with Tanner than the company, or that something could go wrong with Tanner's project and I'd be distracted, I don't know. But how can you prove a negative—that neither one of those is the situation? That it's all about the company?"

Nick nodded. Was that a flicker of laughter or skepticism in his eyes?

"Anyway, it's a really good fit. Our ideas kept flowing all night. We have such a good rapport. I'll just have to chip away at his concerns somehow."

Two neighborhood kids—a little younger than Jason—passed by on skateboards. They were jumping their boards off the ground and trying to flip them. Thank goodness they had on helmets and knee and elbow pads, as they hadn't perfected the trick. I kept my eyes on them until they disappeared behind a hedge—just in case I needed to grab my emergency kit out of the car.

Nick cleared his throat. "Um, is L.A. big enough for both you and Teddie D if the lake house falls apart?"

So, it was skepticism. But I had wondered the same thing when I'd first settled on L.A. as the best location for the new business.

When I had relocated to the East Coast eight years ago, it was because of the constant tabloid stories and rumors about Tanner. I'd had enough. But Tanner was no longer on drugs, he had a new band—one which wasn't plastered on magazine covers as the bad boys of rock and roll, and he had a son for whom he wanted to be a role model. I suppose there would be some buzz should he ever marry again, but I'd been through all that before—twice—and survived.

I rolled my neck to relieve the tension that set in now whenever I thought too much about Tanner. "You know, I think it would be okay. We're not in the same industry so we wouldn't run into each other often.

And while we do have friends in common, they were supportive of us when we split and hopefully will continue to be. No, my problem isn't with Tanner." I turned to face Nick, giving him my most innocent, wide-eyed look. "It's with his guesthouse."

Nick's hairline and eyebrows almost collided. "What are you talking about?"

I grinned. "He has the most wonderful guesthouse. It's a one-bedroom, Mediterranean-styled villa, complete with a stone terrace overlooking the pool and garden. It's separate from the main house and has its own footpath from the driveway. And then there's this pergola with the most delicious smelling flowers—vanilla and cloves. I can't tell you how much I love the place. The only downside is Tanner."

Nick laughed. "Other women want to date Teddie D. You want to date his guesthouse."

"Yep, that's pretty much it."

We kept on laughing. It was nice to talk with someone about the vagaries of my past relationship with Tanner and the irony of the current situation. It put things in perspective.

By the end of the week, even Trish had called.

"Why didn't you tell me you were in town?"

No hello, no how are you? She was not a happy camper.

"I'm sorry, Trish. But the trip was spur of the moment. Tanner shows up in my office one day and wants me to look at a property the next." Not quite accurate, but close enough.

She wasn't interested in the logistics, only in how we'd gotten along.

"The project is moving forward," I said. "We visited the property and developed a program for the house. The time was productive. By the way, did you know he was thinking of building a second home?"

Trish hesitated for a telling minute. "Teddie told us he was looking for property." There was a thump, followed by a "rats." I never understood how she controlled those hyperactive hands when she painted. "He mentioned it over dinner about a week after he saw your place. We figured your house was the catalyst for finally building the retreat he's always talked about. But we had no idea he planned on hiring you."

So, his desire to build the house wasn't out of the blue; it was something he'd wanted to do for a long time. Once again, I had misjudged him.

"Well, you can't be more surprised than I. But as long as he wants to move forward I'll do the best job I can."

"Is it possible you won't continue working together?" She had caught the scent of uncertainty in my statement.

"We come with a lot of baggage, Trish. Even after all this time, it keeps us a little off-balance around one another." Me, anyway.

Her sigh traveled three thousand miles. "I was hoping we might see a little more of you. Will you let me know the next time you're in town to meet with Teddie, so we can get together?"

"Depends on timing," I waffled. The last thing I wanted was to put Trish in an awkward position, knowing how important her and Alan's friendship was to Tanner. "But I might be out in L.A. on a different mission in a month or two. Maybe we can get together then."

"Great."

And the two men I had gone to L.A. to see?

On the plane home, I had organized the index cards from dinner with Russ and Sally and transferred the information to my laptop. Monday night, I emailed Russ the material along with the first draft of a vision statement for the firm. Not to pressure him, but to assure him I was serious.

And the email from Tanner? He couldn't wait to see my design and already knew he would love it.

No pressure.

FORTY-SEVEN

"So what career options are you considering, Stephanie?"

Stephanie and I were having lunch at Zaytinya, a restaurant serving eastern Mediterranean cuisine. Now that she and Joe had moved into their new condo (and had repainted the master bedroom from dark eggplant to a gentler periwinkle), Stephanie had announced she was ready to focus on her future. I thought this eatery would be a more comfortable place to begin the conversation than in an office full of curious coworkers.

The two of us were sharing several small plates—mushroom couscous, cauliflower tiganites, crispy brussels sprouts, and two seafood dishes. I scooped more of the tasty couscous onto my plate.

"I'd like to do something with my Bachelor of Fine Arts?"

"Are you thinking of going straight into a job or going on to graduate school?"

"I'm torn?" She twisted a lock of her long brown hair around her left forefinger.

"How do you want to be involved in art? Do you want to create art? Curate art? Conserve art? Or do you want to be on the commercial side, working in an art gallery or an auction house?"

Stephanie scrunched her brow in thought.

Taking advantage of her silence, I speared a couple more sprouts. How did they get them so crispy?

"Here's another approach. Down the road, do you want to be dealing with the public on a regular basis or working behind the scenes?

"I like dealing with people . . . usually."

"Well, when you think about where you want to be in five years, remember it's not just how you want to interact with art, but also how you want to interact with people."

We continued the conversation as we finished the meal and then lingered over tea.

Stephanie decided her next step would be to explore graduate degrees in fine arts in the area, see if there was a program that tugged at her heart.

"While you're doing that, also do a D.C. arts job search. That will give you an idea of the opportunities out there and what qualifications are required. And when you search the Smithsonian site, check out their docent programs. Joining something like that could give you a peek behind the curtain at a museum." I wiped my hands one last time on the napkin.

"Thanks so much for all the ideas, Jessie."

But we weren't finished. I still wanted to talk about the "upspeak" and felt this conversation would be less daunting while walking—at least for me.

"You know, Stephanie, every generation has its particular quirks with language." I looked straight ahead and not at her.

She was silent, not certain where the conversation was going.

"As part of my mentoring I want to make sure that you have as many tools as possible to be successful." I shortened my stride to better match hers.

"So, I want to make sure you realize that you have a tendency to 'upspeak.'"

She turned and gave me a puzzled look.

"There's nothing wrong with letting your voice rise at the end of a sentence. It can be charming. But I want you to be aware of it as there may be occasions when it could undermine you. For example, if you're in an interview, you'll want to come across as confident rather than tentative. Or perhaps you're participating in a group project and want your opinion to be heard. Making a declarative statement will give the idea more heft and you more ownership."

Then I laughed. "I've even had women who upspeak tell me that they've offered suggestions in a meeting and a guy in the group grabs the idea and runs with it, as though the idea were all his, arising from a little voice in his own head."

Stephanie's eyes opened wide in an "aha" moment. "I've had that happen! I just thought they were being jerks? I didn't realize I was letting them do it."

"That's why you need to be aware of it. On the other hand, upspeak can come in handy if you're working with someone who's very sensitive or doesn't like suggestions or advice. It introduces an idea more gently. I'm definitely not suggesting that you change your speech pattern among friends and most colleagues. But make sure your sentences speak for you—as well as your words."

When we finally returned to our office building, Stephanie said, "Thank you. I wasn't even aware of my . . . my habit?" She had tried to make it a statement but failed at the last moment. She bit her lip in annoyance.

I patted her shoulder. "Don't worry. All habits take time to change. And the good thing is that most of the time it won't matter. But when the occasion warrants it, you'll be prepared to be as assertive as you want."

"Did you have speech 'quirks,' Jessie?"

With a father who was head of the Classics Department at Brown and a mother who taught literature and composition at the school, there wasn't much chance of that. But a phrase frequently repeated by teenage friends came to mind.

"Like totally."

To avoid interruptions from staff, I worked on Tanner's design at home in the evenings. Before settling at the drafting table, I'd put on one of his albums.

I had told Tanner it would take about four weeks to complete the preliminary design. In the meantime, he was to let me know if he had any changes to the space program.

As I explored the spirit of his house, I began to add the contrast Tanner had liked so much between the exterior and the interior to spaces within the house as well. It was a contrast reflected in his music—like the pain and beauty of the song he had composed the past weekend.

Maybe this house could bring the closure we both needed. Tanner would have the personal refuge and piece of the past he needed, and I would have atoned for leaving him—even if he had ended up better off without me.

When I wrapped up work on Tanner's house each night, I'd grab my laptop and focus on my own ongoing research project.

What did the egg freezing process entail? How many cycles of hormones would I need at my age to get an appropriate number of eggs for storage? What was the success rate for someone my age conceiving and having a child? What were potential adverse effects of the hormones and egg retrieval procedure? And, how much would all this cost—for the hormones, the cultivation and removal of the eggs, the storage, and then the fertilization and implantation of an egg when the time was right?

The journey from start to finish would be expensive. Fertility websites liked to refer to the whole process as an "investment" in one's future. But, as in any investment that involves risk, you could lose it all (for example, poor quality eggs, problems at the freezing facility, improper thawing) without having anything to show for it. And was this an "investment" I could even afford, now that I wanted to start a business?

And hovering above all these practical and financial issues were philosophical questions that no amount of computer research could answer.

FORTY-EIGHT

Over the weekend I received another email from Tanner. I clicked on it, assuming he had some additional thoughts about the house.

Jessie,

I can't tell you what it meant to hear that you had forgiven me the addiction. I had assumed all these years that you must have despised me for destroying our relationship.

Not that it changes the fact that I did ruin the relationship. But at least you realized it wasn't deliberate. Things weren't happening fast enough. The band barely broke even on those early trips and I felt I was living off you and your stipend and student loans. I was tired of not carrying my weight financially. The more I worried, the more I hung onto the idea that the drugs might help in the short-term.

So, when I got home from that last tour and found you gone, I was so angry that everything I'd tried hadn't been enough for you.

The words tore at me. No wonder he'd felt betrayed: to feel you sacrificed everything for someone who didn't appreciate it. And whereas he hadn't intended our rift, I had left intentionally. I had hoped that, with one less person to be responsible for, he might be able to get clean, and once he was clean, we could get back together.

I couldn't expect forgiveness simply because I had miscalculated and we remained apart.

After going through rehab, though, I finally got it. You chose the only reasonable option in the face of my growing dependence and manic behavior. I'm sorry I didn't see that at the time or that I didn't trust your instincts earlier about taking things with the band a little slower.

I've been reflecting on the nature of forgiveness all week. It's such a powerful word—with the capacity to change lives.

Tanner

What? He thought what I had done was "reasonable?"

Tanner,

If you think leaving was the "reasonable" option, you still don't understand a bloody thing. Of course, I didn't hate you when I left. I didn't leave because I didn't care but because I cared too much. It was an action taken out of despair, frustration, and fear for your health—not logic.

I realized at the time that you thought you were taking the drugs for us but your health was too high a price to pay. Moreover, I never suggested I was unhappy with how things were going. I loved that old apartment. I don't know why you thought I needed or wanted more. I was exactly where I wanted to be, doing exactly what I wanted. Plus, you already had the weight of the band on your shoulders; you didn't need me to worry about as well.

You and I were supposed to be partners, supporting each other, yet you became consumed with carrying all the responsibility—for everybody. It wasn't a mutual or even respectful relationship by the end and it wasn't healthy for either of us.

So, don't tell me you understand that I made the "reasonable" choice. It was a gut-wrenching decision but the only option I could see where you might have a chance of surviving by having one less person to take care of.

J

I punched Send, furious that Tanner had seen my leaving as some sort of rational, dispassionate act.

Of course, when I'd had a couple of minutes to think about it, I did a mental head slap. Why hadn't I just accepted his kind words—that he had found comfort in the fact that I knew the addiction wasn't deliberate? After all, that had been my objective. And I had been no martyr. I had left for my own health as well.

But really? How could he talk about my leaving as "reasonable?" There had been nothing reasonable about it. I'd been like an animal ensnared in a trap that gnaws its own foot off to escape—except that I had left my heart behind.

Damn it. This house I was working on was supposed to be about Tanner's present and future; it wasn't supposed to be the means for us to work out our frustrations and anger about the past.

The man was infuriating.

I went to the kitchen for a drink. Several minutes later I was still staring into the refrigerator when the phone rang.

I checked Caller ID.

Shoot. Tanner. I thought about not answering, but he obviously knew I was home.

Picking up the phone, I went on the offensive. "Let me guess. You've decided to cancel the lake project."

He was silent. Then, with exaggerated patience, he replied, "No . . . that's not why I called. I wanted to find out where to send the flowers."

Huh?

"The office or your home? Or would you prefer jewelry?"

Now I was silent, trying to catch up.

"You know. You said the next time I needed to atone for my sins—or was it my stupidity?—it meant double the flowers—or jewelry."

Ah. "Well, you wouldn't have this conundrum if you weren't so impossibly oblivious, Tanner. Really, 'reasonable?'"

"You're right. That wasn't the right word. You didn't have another choice. It wasn't like you hadn't tried everything else."

I slumped against the counter in relief at his words. "That's more like it. I even went to Al-Anon weekly when I found out about your drug use, to understand what you were up against."

"You went to Al-Anon?" He sounded surprised—or maybe shaken.

But then I had never told him—like so many other things it seemed. "Every week, at a place near campus—sometimes more frequently, depending on how you were doing."

There was a pause as Tanner absorbed my words. "Why didn't you tell me?"

"Because you didn't think you had a drug problem, because you thought you were in control of the situation, because you were traveling all the time, because we already argued too much about the drugs and your health. Pick a reason. Besides, attending the meetings became something I did for myself. The rest of the time I was focused on trying to help you. At those meetings, other people had my back."

I heard him inhale sharply as he began to comprehend what those weekly meetings had meant to me. "How could I not have had your back?"

I ignored his question, intent on trying to make him understand. "It took me eleven months at Al-Anon before I developed the strength to leave—by then I was afraid of what would happen to you if I didn't. My leaving was supposed to help you. Give you some breathing room. Let you get some perspective. Take some pressure off. A sabbatical, so to speak.

"But things seemed to get worse for you, not better." Then he'd gotten married and had a son, and the sabbatical had become forever. I shook off the thought. "I kept going to Al-Anon for a year or so after that, though, to make peace with my decision."

"Jess, when you were here I told you that you had helped me, that your encouragement got me into rehab. What I didn't tell you was that after the rehab program, I needed an NA sponsor in L.A. to help me make the transition back to the real world. I called Pete Michaels and asked him to be my sponsor."

I recognized the name. I closed my eyes for a moment, the words a balm.

Before I left Tanner, I'd finally asked Alan, as a veteran of the music business, if he knew anyone recovering from amphetamine addiction. I thought Tanner might more readily listen to a peer who understood the pressures he was facing. Alan had given me a name: Pete Michaels.

I talked with Mr. Michaels to see if he would be willing to visit. Like Tanner, he had started taking amphetamines while on the road. When we spoke, he was in his second year of recovery. He no longer toured, though, as the triggers for drug use were too strong for him when he traveled. Instead he was a studio musician in L.A. He had agreed to come over but made no guarantee as to the outcome.

The conversation with Tanner hadn't gone well. As Mr. Michaels told me afterwards, Tanner believed the drugs were benefitting him, not understanding that his body and brain were demanding them and that he wasn't the one in control. Before seeking help, Tanner would have to hit bottom, where there would be no more illusions about the destructiveness of the drugs.

That was when I finally accepted that Tanner would have to find his own way back. But the realization had left me numb. What if he never found his way home, lost to the tempting Siren songs of the drugs?

"And just so you know, Pete is still my NA sponsor and one of my closest friends."

I couldn't speak. A faucet had turned on and tears were flowing down my face. I was so grateful to the man who had helped Tanner.

"Are you okay, Jessie?"

"Uh-huh."

He realized I was struggling. "Which brings me back to my original apology and question. Flowers or jewelry? Office or house?"

I shook the sadness off. That was the past. I wasn't going to let it keep controlling me just as drugs no longer controlled Tanner.

"Getting flowers from you is like taking candy from a baby, Tanner. You owe me so many apologies I could open a flower shop. But I have a job I enjoy. Donate the money to Habitat for Humanity of Greater L.A.

instead."

Plus, Russ would approve.

"Also, send a bouquet of flowers to Pete Michaels with my profound thanks—and yours."

FORTY-NINE

It was too humid to be jogging, yet here I was, dragging myself though the streets of D.C., sweat stinging my eyes and trickling onto my lips where I could taste the salt. More annoying was that Nick barely seemed to notice the steam bath.

When we arrived back at my house, Nick said, "By the way, a friend gave me two tickets to a Nationals' game. They're good seats. Want to go?"

"When's the game?"

"Sunday, July 28. Day game against the Mets."

"Oh, good. A division rivalry. I'll put it on my calendar. If anything comes up, I'll let you know."

"Are you planning to be out of town?"

"I have to fly to California to present the design proposal to Tanner. Just not sure when."

"How's it going?"

"Surprisingly well."

He double-checked to see if I was being sarcastic.

But the plans for Tanner's lake house were going well. I really liked what I was creating—a house unique to Tanner, with few overt references to the past. I thought it reflected the man he was today—multi-talented, creative, hard-working, a loving, responsible father, and a stronger and more caring person for having survived the substance abuse.

Once we finalized the design, Tanner could work with someone else to construct the house.

That same day, I unexpectedly received bad news from Russ. His father was back in the hospital. "Probably hospital-associated pneumonia," Russ wrote in an email. With his immune system weakened from the surgery, his father had likely picked it up at the hospital at the time of his initial stay.

The family hadn't realized it, though, until after he had returned home from the appendectomy. The incision appeared to be healing fine, but his father had developed a fever, shortness of breath, and a persistent cough.

Now he was back in the hospital, being treated with antibiotics. Russ said he could be in for a week or two—and that was if he responded well to the medications.

I answered immediately, telling him to take care of his family.

Finally finding two open hours in my schedule, I gathered Eliot, Sharon, and other interested staff for a field trip to the National Building Museum to study the "Small Box" competition submissions.

We examined the winning entries first. Sharon was thrilled, taking several pictures of our submission, including one of just the second-place ribbon.

For me, though, the visit was about studying the other proposals, looking for new concepts, new voices, and new technologies. The 1922 architecture competition for a new Chicago Tribune building had such surprising modern entries submitted from Europe, unlike any office buildings being designed in the U.S. at the time, that many people felt one of the international designs should have won. None did. A traditional design from the U.S. won.

But the competition and the proposals were so noteworthy that the entries had gone on tour across the country and those losing submissions, representing the new "International Style," had far more impact on the future of architecture in this country than did the winning design, which with its highly ornate style was already losing favor.

Fewer proposals for micro-housing were submitted than I had expected. And the ones that had been submitted lacked the high-tech features and other twenty-first century amenities our proposal included. I pointed out to Sharon and Eliot that they had taken the potential for small, smart apartments further than anyone else.

And as I ran across interesting ideas on sustainability or other relevant topics, I jotted them down on my index cards. I'd share the ideas with Russ later this evening in an email. Maybe they'd cheer him up.

Towards the end of the tour, I found the entry from Dana's firm. It was a proposal for vertical farming, one of the silly suggestions I'd thrown out that night at the bar. Granted, it wasn't a practical solution for a pricey downtown site, but Ideas Competitions are about exploring issues and solutions, and local urban food production is an increasingly important subject. Dana's team had done a good job on the philosophical statement, but the conceptual building itself was derivative. I couldn't help but smile.

The following week, I was back at the gynecologist's office, sitting on the exam table.

"What's the problem, Jessie?" Dr. Bening asked.

"I'm spotting between periods. Could it be early onset perimenopause?" The possibility had me worried since the spotting had started two days earlier. Maybe I wouldn't have children, given the unpredictability of my future, but I didn't want the decision snatched out of my hands just yet.

She frowned. "It's possible, but not probable at your age. How old were you when you had your first period?"

"Twelve."

"Good. That's normal. We generally wouldn't expect to see any major changes until your mid- to late-forties. How do you feel otherwise? Any soreness? Tenderness? Night sweats? Hot flashes? Changes in your recent periods, like being heavier or lighter than normal?"

"No. I feel okay. A little tired, maybe."

She had me lie down, knees up as she prodded and pressed—more enthusiastically than usual.

"Everything feels fine, Jessie, but I'd like to schedule an ultrasound and blood work to rule out other possibilities, such as fibroids, anemia, or hypothyroidism."

Just what I needed—another appointment. Not like I wasn't busy enough. But I wouldn't get much sleep until I had an answer. "Fine. I'll set one up."

"Try not to worry."

Easy for her to say.

FIFTY

It was early afternoon, Wednesday, and I was working on a new church to be built in Loudoun County, Virginia.

When the phone rang, I grabbed it. I'd been waiting for a call from a structural engineer.

"Hi, Jessie."

My breath caught in my throat. Not the engineer. I started coughing in surprise.

"Are you okay?"

Tears dribbled from my eyes as I tried to suppress the hacking. Then holding the phone away from me, I attempted one last gut-racking cough to clear my throat.

"Uh, sorry about that, Tanner. A rather large frog sought refuge in my throat."

"Has he left?"

"Seems to have leaped out." I hoped I hadn't deafened the poor guy.

"Turns out I'll be in D.C. this Saturday," he announced. "In the morning, I'm giving an acoustic performance at Walter Reed followed by a visit to some of the personnel unable to attend. Could we get together in the afternoon? I can't wait to see what you've done."

Damn it. I said I'd call when I was ready. I had wanted to get his reaction to a complete set of preliminary drawings. Now I'd have to work the next several nights to finalize everything. And there was the ultrasound scheduled for Friday, which I'd have to postpone so I could finish his proposal.

"Uh, sure. Would you like to come to the office Saturday afternoon, after the performance?"

"What about coming to my hotel? I have a suite. That way I can clean up."

I hesitated, then decided that his hotel room would be okay. We'd survived an entire weekend together, after all. Besides, it was likely a couple of people might be in the office working and they'd only serve as distractions.

"Fine. Why don't you give me a call when you're ready?"

"Good. I'm eager to see what you've done. By the way, you're welcome to attend the concert. I could pick you up on the way out there?"

Have a chance to see Tanner in an acoustic performance? God, it was tempting—and stupid. No, I needed to remain detached to give a good presentation. It would be too easy to be transported into the perilous past if I went to the concert. My whole intent in doing this house was to move forward, not backwards.

"Thanks for the invitation, but I've got some things to take care of Saturday morning." All involving his project.

"Another time, then. See you Saturday."

What a princess. He calls and everything else has to get shunted aside. It must be nice to have people indulge him in his high expectations.

I glanced up at Teddy Seattle. If I didn't know better, I'd have said he was smirking. Something about my foolhardy illusion that I could remain detached during my presentation to Tanner.

FIFTY-ONE

The phone in my office rang around two on Saturday. I was almost too tired to answer. Since Tanner's call mid-week, I'd worked late every night at the office to finalize the drawings. Then I'd drive home and second-guess my design choices as I lay in bed. Postponing the ultrasound only compounded my inability to sleep.

Not even coffee was helping.

I picked up the phone. "Hi, Tanner. How was the concert?"

"Great. Took requests. Sometimes I'd give them the back story to a song, other times I changed the song up—making it more blues or more rock and roll. Thanks for asking."

My jitters receded a bit at the familiarity of his big heart. "Are you back at the hotel yet?"

"Yep. Ready any time you are."

"I have one more drawing to run off, then I'll be over."

"Looking forward to it, Jess." He sounded pumped—like he had slept well. Or maybe it was the adrenaline after the performance.

I headed to the restroom to check in the mirror that nothing was awry. I was wearing a navy blue blazer over a summery, short-sleeved, blue-and-white printed dress with a modest V-neckline—enjoying the contrast of feminine and professional. I looked almost like that put-together person in my fantasy encounters with Tanner—except for the dark circles under my eyes.

Printing off the final elevation, I rolled the documents up and placed them in a carrying tube. I could have walked to the hotel but decided to drive, as I'd head straight home once the meeting was over.

Plus, Charlene had called earlier, on her way back to D.C. from the road trip with her daughter, and told me "to break a leg." Charlene and karma had not been kind to me, so I decided not to tempt fate.

When first designing Tanner's house, I considered it atonement for leaving him. But as I developed the plans, the house had become much more: a tangible memory for him of the past we'd shared, like my house was for me; a refuge to keep him healthy; and, a gift of gratitude for having been able to share part of my life with him—this funny, kind, and creative man. In a way, having a chance to design his house had been a gift for me too—though I'd never tell him that.

I stood outside Tanner's hotel suite, suddenly nervous. If I hadn't been so tired, my stomach would have been churning like Class-V whitewater. Finally, I found the energy to lift my arm and I rapped on the door.

Tanner answered quickly and flashed me a huge grin. "I can't wait to see what you've done."

I relaxed slightly, looking around. Yes, this sitting room would be fine for the presentation. Yet . . . it was disquieting knowing that a bedroom lay right beyond that connecting door.

I shook those thoughts from my head and refocused, placing the documents on the coffee table in order of presentation. As I set up my laptop, a knock sounded on the door. Tanner ushered in a room service waiter who vanished as soon as he laid a large tray on the desk.

"I thought you might like some coffee," Tanner explained. "Is cappuccino still your favorite?"

Oh, there was hope for me. "Yes, thanks."

"I also asked them to send up a fruit plate and muffins."

Suddenly I was starved. I hadn't had anything to eat since breakfast. Maybe a little sugar would help.

Tanner placed honeydew melon slices, pineapple cubes, red grapes, and a raspberry muffin on a small plate and handed it to me along with the cappuccino. "Good idea," I said gratefully. "I never got around to lunch today."

"I figured as much."

Once he had a plate as well, I took off my jacket and sat at one end of the sofa while he sat in a chair I'd placed at a ninety-degree angle to me, so that the documents on the coffee table faced him. I might be tired, but I wasn't so brain-dead as to have him sit next to me.

He thumbed quickly through the drawings. When he looked up, he tilted his head, his brown eyes questioning. "I thought you were going to catch me up on where you were with the project. This looks like you finished the initial plans?"

I nodded but felt remorseful. Why did I always think the worst of him? He hadn't been a diva when he'd called; he hadn't expected me to finish the project. He had only been anxious to see what I'd produced so far. The problem was me—I kept thinking that all of his success had changed him in some fundamental way.

"No wonder you grabbed that cappuccino." He kidded. "You must have been working night and day since I called."

Blood raced to my face.

Suddenly, realizing the accuracy of his jest, his eyes softened. "I'm sorry. I should have been more explicit. Of course, you'd have tried to complete the project." His voice was low, apologetic.

"No, really. It's okay. I wanted to get as much feedback from you as possible. I was close to completion."

"Sure, you were." His voice rebounded, carrying a note of smugness at knowing me so well.

"Well, pretty close to completion," I amended.

We both laughed.

Smoothing out the drawings once more, I was about to summarize the design when my chest tightened. What if Tanner didn't like the house? Maybe it wouldn't reflect his present lifestyle. Maybe I had made too many assumptions.

But if I didn't walk him through the plans there'd be no possibility for improvement.

So, inhaling deeply, I said, "As you can see from this site plan, the footprint of the house is a slightly flattened, inverted Y."

The site plan, which depicted the outline of the house and garage in relationship to the lake and the rest of the property, lay on top of the drawings. I touched my finger to the stem. "This is your entertaining area, with the best panoramic views of the lake and cove."

Tanner nodded, his eyes glued to the drawing. His profile was so familiar—even the stubble now.

I ignored the hitch in my breathing at that realization and drew my fingers down to the two prongs. "These are the two bedroom wings. They're at an obtuse angle to the great room to maximize their views of the lake or cove.

"Two decks stretch between the two wings and the great room, like old-fashioned hand fans. This oversized one here, facing the lake, is an outdoor living room. Fire pit, space for a telescope to scan the clear night skies—whatever you and Jason want. The deck flanking the cove is for more intimate activities like dining or playing cards or board games. Plus, there's an outdoor fireplace and grill, here"—I pointed to the chimney stack—"so you can practice your culinary skills."

Tanner turned his head, grinning. "Hey. You making fun of my cooking?"

I smiled. "Hardly. I enjoyed you cooking for m—your cooking." Really, what woman doesn't like a guy cooking for her occasionally?

I hurried on. "Telescoping doors open from the great room to the two decks, so there's a seamless flow between the indoors and the outdoors. You and Jason will probably spend most of your time with your guests in these spaces—when you're not in or on the water."

I was aware of his body leaning into the drawings, his breathing heightened, and his left hand near mine on the plan.

With his right index finger, he traced the footprint of the house, memorizing its form, internalizing its reality. Then he looked up at me, eyes glistening, pupils dilated. "It feels perfect."

Relief soared through my body.

I took another sip of the cappuccino.

"We still have the details, Tanner," I warned him. But it was a good start—no, a great start. The late nights had been worth it. Suddenly my fatigue lifted.

I pointed to the wing on the right. "This wing is yours. Kitchen on the ground floor, master bedroom on the second level, and your music room on the third. All with your preferred view of the cove. The other wing contains Jason's room and the guest bedrooms on the second and third floors and a TV room on the ground floor. The soundproof TV/game room can be closed off from the great room when Jason has friends visiting."

I set the site plan aside, revealing a drawing of the front elevation.

Again, Tanner leaned in. I leaned in too, his proximity making the blond hairs on my arms dance. He didn't notice as his eyes were fixed on the façade of the house.

"If you remember in the original sketch I did in L.A., the three-and-a-half-story entrance tower ties the three parts of the house together."

He nodded, his eyes only grazing mine before returning to the drawing.

"Initially, the tower was intended as a reflection of the surrounding sky-seeking trees as well as a reference to the verticality of your L.A. home. Over time, however, the tower has metamorphosed into the bell tower of a church." Church represents sanctuary—a purpose the lake house would serve him.

Tanner's energy intensified, body taut, fingers clasped together. I inconspicuously scooted away from him while reaching for a grape. Being bombarded by doubt was one thing—I could deal with that. Being bombarded by Tanner's life force was entirely different.

"Like a bell tower in a church, the staircase leads to your music room on the third floor," I explained. "And because staircases have excellent acoustical properties, I've expanded the catwalk on the third level between the two wings to give you another space in which to practice music. It's now a bell tower in the full musical sense of the term."

"I love the imagery, Jess!" His grin stretched ear-to-ear and, in his excitement, he touched my right arm. I nearly jumped out of my skin at all that energy passing between us. Being tasered couldn't have been more electrifying.

But the shock of his touch also jolted me into the realization that I was violating my own first commandment of a good presentation: let the design do the talking.

"Good. But I don't need to give you the background on every design decision."

"But I want to know," he assured me.

I smiled at his naïveté. "Sure, now. Not so much at midnight, when I'm still chattering on about the concept behind the design."

He chortled—and nodded.

"Let's move to the floor plans. I'll point out the specifics, but if you have any questions about the 'why,' just ask."

Every so often Tanner would touch my arm to ask a question—but I was prepared. Sort of. Part of me yearned for his touch, while another part feared it would be my undoing.

"The house may be larger than you expected, but the space program we developed dictated the size of the structure. To offset that a bit, I've designed the guestrooms on the smaller side, presuming the focus of daily life to be downstairs or outdoors. Once we review the entire design, we can revisit that issue if you feel the bedrooms are too small. Your bedroom and spa bathroom are the exceptions."

I moved my index finger from his bedroom to the other side of the stairwell. "And here are the bunk bed alcoves for Jason's friends on the second and third floors."

Tanner beamed. "Jason's going to be crazy about these. I can see him and his friends using them as forts or hide-outs. Just make sure that the stair and balcony railings are high enough and sturdy enough to corral a bunch of rowdy boys."

"Way ahead of you."

Then I pointed to one other space. "Just outside your music room is a private balcony, overlooking the cove. Another allusion to your Mediterranean home, with its terraces overlooking the pool."

He sat back, shaking his head. "The balcony's wonderful, Jess. Thank you for thinking of it." His hand reached for my arm again to punctuate his reaction.

Damn. He was going to leave a scar.

The final image was a colored rendering of the lakeside façade at nighttime, the house lit from within while a firepit burned brightly on the main deck. Composed of shadow and light, the house was both mysterious and welcoming, a cozy and warm retreat from the indifferent darkness.

Tanner stared at the drawing, his breathing slowing as he absorbed the image.

I took a deep breath as well. This house had been intended as a place of serenity and a source of well-being for him. Maybe, for once, I had gotten it right.

After a further moment, I said, "That's about it, Tanner. If you'd like, we can talk now about changes you already know you want or you can review the plans on your own and get back to me."

Tanner stood, unfolding his long body, and stretched. We had been sitting far too long. I rose as well, twisting my neck to release the tension I had brought with me to the hotel.

Turning to me, his eyes crinkled in laugh lines and happiness, Tanner said, "I love the design, Jessie. You've thought of everything. In particular, I love the soaring staircase—especially the idea of it being a bell tower."

As if it were the most natural thing in the world, he put his left arm around my shoulders, gazing happily down at the elevations, already imagining a life in the house.

I stiffened. As his hand lingered I became increasingly uncomfortable. I didn't want to dampen his joy by wiggling out of his hold, but I now understood a little of how he might have felt at the lake when he thought I'd been toying with him, even though he was oblivious to what he was doing, staring as he was at the documents, simply caught up in his excitement.

The truth was that I wanted to share the moment with him. Wasn't that what I had been doing the whole time I'd been designing his place? Picturing him in every room as I worked?

I had been with him in the house as he played the guitar in the stairwell. I'd seen him on the deck with Jason, grilling fish the two had caught, the outdoor fireplace blazing behind them. I'd envisioned him working in the music room or playing a grand piano in a corner of the great room. I'd smelled the coffee as he fixed eggs in the kitchen. I'd seen the restorative view he had when rising from bed in the mornings. I had been in this house with him for every moment of its creation, to make sure that it would sustain and nourish him.

But now the house was his—no longer ours. I stood there motionless, his fingers scorching my shoulder, the rest of me numb.

Finally, Tanner shook off his reverie—and his hand.

"It's perfect, Honey."

Honey? Really?

Then, in a more contemplative tone, he asked, "Is this the house you would have designed all those years ago?"

A shiver snaked up my spine. Was this a theoretical question? I considered leaving it unanswered but, as usual, I couldn't let a design question pass. I gazed down at the disheveled pile of plans on the coffee table, however, so he couldn't see my eyes.

"There's more complexity to the structure. As I've gotten older, I've come to appreciate the juxtaposition of opposites, like complexity and minimalism or hard materials and soft. So, if you're asking how this compares with my ideas from long ago, I like this design better. It's more vibrant and interesting because of the contradictions and contrasts—just like people."

When I looked up, his eyes were gleaming. "That's a perfect description! It's the way I feel about my music now—that's there more contrast than with mPulse. Now it's dissonance with lyrical, intensity with lightness—with far more of the nuances that come with age and understanding."

After gazing once more at the plans on the table, Tanner asked, "Do you feel like celebrating? I'd love to take you out to dinner. We can talk about what happens next."

Out with Tanner in public? Sounded like a recipe for disaster. But if the option was sitting with him in this suite—with a bedroom next door—talking about the next steps, possibly over an intimate dinner, I'd prefer donning the puke-colored T-shirt and sweat pants and hitting the high spots in D.C. with him a million times over.

"Uh, sure. Sounds . . . nice."

FIFTY-TWO

I went to freshen up. As I stared at my reflection in the hotel bathroom mirror, I thought of the last time Tanner and I had gone out as a couple.

It was early December of my second year at UCLA. I was looking forward to a quiet evening with Trish and Alan, away from my studio, classmates, and any mention of architecture. Tanner, however, had started partying beforehand at a club he played when in town. As high as he was when he returned to the apartment, I had considered canceling, but he assured me he was fine and looking forward to the dinner.

Once at our friends' house, however, Tanner had become anxious and restless, a sure sign he was riding a cocktail of amphetamines and alcohol. Earlier than planned, I thanked Trish and Alan for dinner, helped Tanner to the car, and buckled him in. He fell asleep almost immediately, which was fine by me. I didn't want to talk; I was disappointed, furious, and exhausted by worry. Another evening ruined by the drugs.

Yes, the addiction wasn't deliberate, but I hated it. Not because I was tired of making apologies or excuses to our friends, but because Tanner was disappearing into the drugs.

When we'd arrived back at the apartment building, I placed my hand on his shoulder to rouse him.

No response.

I shook him harder. "C'mon, Tanner."

Nothing.

My anger and frustration evaporated, leaving only bottomless fear. I had no idea what to do. Had he passed out or had he overdosed?

I scrambled out of the car, lurching towards the passenger side in panic, legs like putty, my heartbeat roaring in my ears like a tornado. I was aware of nothing other than Tanner.

Then, as the thought of a life without Tanner pierced my brain, everything went blank and I stumbled, falling hard onto the curb, my fingers digging into the bordering sod to try to slow my descent. An incomprehensible emptiness stretched before me for what seemed an eternity, though it couldn't have lasted for more than a few seconds. Propelled by the nightmare—and a flood of adrenaline—I got up, raced to the passenger door, opened it, and pounded on Tanner's chest until I finally roused him, mumbling incoherently.

Somehow, I managed to get him out of the car. He refused to go to the hospital, so when we got into the apartment I repeatedly induced vomiting and plied him with coffee through the night, keeping him moving. His face had a sickly sheen and was streaked with sweat.

My heart was caught in my throat in fear. I couldn't breathe or think clearly. I didn't even notice the claret-colored stains of blood on the knees of my jeans until morning. Plus, my left wrist had swollen from the fall. Tanner never noticed.

By the next afternoon, Tanner had seemingly recovered physically but was in a black funk—a toxic stew of anger, paranoia, embarrassment, and withdrawal. It didn't seem fair—he barely acknowledged the events of the night before, while I was in sheer, unadulterated terror of losing him.

At that point I knew I had to leave. How ironic, though, that my fear of losing Tanner would force me to leave him. But how could I live with someone I adored beyond all reason, when he no longer valued his own life? How could I endure the too-real possibility that he would thoughtlessly deprive me of what I valued most?

When I emerged from the hotel bathroom, it was hard to believe that the man standing in front of me was the same person from that evening long ago. This man was solid, healthy, grounded by his music and Jason, and fully engaged in life.

He looked wonderful, having changed into black slacks, a light blue shirt, a luscious black leather jacket, so buttery supple it looked like it would melt under my touch . . . and a tie. I couldn't think of the last time I'd seen him in a tie.

He stared at me. "When I first saw you at Rasika, I thought you hadn't changed a bit. But I swear, Jessie, you're even more beautiful now." His gaze was almost physical—a soft caress flickering across my body, making my nerve endings flutter.

I became light-headed, dizzy.

Then I realized that he was probably just caught up in the moment. "Don't you think that we overlay people we haven't seen in a while with images of how we remember them? I still think of my father as having blond hair even though it's been white for a while."

Tanner shook his head. "Possibly. But aren't you usually surprised then when you meet up again? I'm not recalling some youthful version of you, but seeing the person you've become."

Well, he was right as far as it pertained to him. He was more compelling, more magnetic than ever.

I tried to ignore that fact as I went to the couch and put on my jacket. It was just going to be a friendly dinner, nothing more.

FIFTY-THREE

We walked to Fiola, an upscale Italian restaurant just off Pennsylvania Avenue and only a couple of blocks from the hotel. I was surprised he'd been able to get a table there on a Saturday night at the last minute, but it was on the early side—and he was Teddie Daulton.

The restaurant was a popular dining spot, with white linen tablecloths and waitstaff dressed in black slacks and ties and white jackets. Textured layers of materials—metal, glass, dark wood, and stone—created a warm atmosphere. A beautiful chandelier added to the ambience by casting a honeyed glow over the diners.

Rather than taking us to the main dining space, comprised mostly of abutting upholstered banquettes, the hostess led us to a more private spot to the left of the bar, with several detached tables. Tanner chose a table removed from the others.

I ordered an iced tea and Tanner asked for club soda.

"How's Jason?" I asked.

"Obsessed with his new toy," Tanner said with a shake of his head.

Jason had already sent me a couple of pictures from the new camera. Tanner had taken him to an amusement park and Jason had tried to capture the excitement of the place.

I'd laughed when I received the photos. Architects, being a bit obsessive, go out of their way to avoid including people in pictures of buildings unless they provide "scale." We want to admire the purity of a building. I had to admit, though, that Jason's photos, filled with people, were far livelier than mine.

I'd texted him back that I thought he had done a good job of capturing the vitality of the scene through the rides, the vibrant colors, and the animated expressions of both kids and adults.

"I was impressed with his first attempts, particularly starting with something as difficult as movement. Most people would have started with a still life, like a landscape."

Tanner laughed. "Jason's always in motion so there's a natural affinity. The camera has been fun—for both of us."

That was sweet. A new cell phone wouldn't have provided them this shared experience.

"Well, Jason may not be musical but he seems to have an artistic eye."

After we received our drinks and placed our orders, Tanner picked up a lime wedge from a plate and, of course, squeezed the juice perfectly into my tea.

"It would probably be easier if you ordered a glass of wine," he said. "You wouldn't have to deal with these pesky slices. Obviously, I don't drink, but it's not a problem when I'm out and someone else does."

Still focused on his virtuoso technique, I replied without thinking, "I don't drink."

I sensed his body tense up. When I looked up, his eyes pierced mine. Damn. How stupid was I? This wasn't Charlene I was gabbing to. I had to pay attention. I couldn't say everything that popped into my brain.

"What do you mean?" he asked, his eyes suddenly dark and impenetrable.

I tried to make light of my comment. "Nothing. No big deal."

"You stopped drinking because I abused alcohol?" His voice was a low growl. Maybe he thought this was one more thing he had ruined for me.

I needed to keep the tone of this conversation light, inconsequential. This was not the time or place for such a dialogue. Heck, there was no appropriate time or place for this conversation.

"No. It just seemed hypocritical to expect you to stop drinking while I indulged." Simple, keep it simple.

"You didn't keep alcohol in the apartment for much of that last year, but I thought it was only because of me. Why didn't you say something?"

"I didn't see any reason to."

"What about after you left? There was no reason for you not to drink then. I wasn't even in the picture."

Damn. My reason was so silly. I looked down at the table, not wanting to reply.

"Jessie."

"We don't need to talk about this, Tanner."

"Answer the question."

The problem was that the answer wasn't just about the past.

"Jessie."

I sighed.

Once again, I was going to end up looking silly over a meal. I kept my eyes on the tabletop. I didn't want to see his reaction. "This, uh, will sound crazy, but after leaving I hoped that by not drinking I could somehow send you good karma—at first to keep you safe during the addiction and then later to support you in recovery. It was—is—an admittedly meaningless gesture. But it seemed . . . the only way left to help."

I looked up and gave him a quick, apologetic smile. Yes, I knew my abstinence was absurd. Just another step in the grieving process, a bargain with the universe to keep Tanner safe.

Yet, oddly enough, the gesture had never felt ridiculous to me. I had never questioned its logic or my compulsion to do it—until I'd put it into words seconds ago. Instead it had seemed essential, something I had to do every day to carry some of Tanner's burden since I had failed him in so many other ways.

Shoot. He must think me a freaking idiot. I'm surprised he wasn't rolling in the aisle.

Instead, he started shaking his head slightly from side to side. In seconds, pain had carved its way deep into his features, though his eyes strangely revealed an inner calm.

"Jessie, I can't tell you what that means to me. That you supported me during my addiction and recovery after everything I did to you."

I stared at him. "You're not going to laugh at me? It sounds insane, now that I've said it aloud." I wanted to make his pain go away. "You know I never drank much alcohol to begin with. Now if I'd given up coffee for twelve years, that would be impressive."

The waiter came over with the appetizers. When he withdrew, Tanner leaned forward and said fiercely but softly, "Twelve years! And we never spoke once. Who would do that?"

Anyone observing us would have thought he was angry with me.

"Tanner, it was just about trying to share an intention with you every day. It wasn't as though it accomplished anything."

I placed my hands together on the table, almost in supplication. Reaching over, he grasped them in one hand. The sensation was electric, rocketing through my body and making me gasp.

"But it did, Jessie. I can't explain it, but I felt your support every day. I thought it was because you had been so hopeful about rehab. But now I know your strength in the present helped me in recovery as well."

He released my hands and I watched our physical connection slip away.

For the rest of the meal, Tanner was thoughtful, the dinner far more somber than celebratory.

FIFTY-FOUR

Outside, the evening air smelled of rain—metallic, electric, chalky. Only a short distance from the hotel, we decided to risk the walk.

Craack! Lightning sizzled overhead, silhouetted like a naked winter tree against the roiling, urban night sky, its jagged limbs on fire. In seconds we were drenched.

Tanner looked at me and then down at his own sodden clothes. He burst out in a whole-hearted belly laugh. "And here I was worried about getting sprayed with lime juice."

Stripping off his jacket, he held it over my head as we sprinted for the hotel. The rain hit the pavement so hard that the droplets splashed back up over our feet and puddles formed on the sidewalk in seconds.

Before retrieving my car at the hotel, I had to retrieve my laptop from Tanner's suite. Water was still dripping off us as we walked in. He suggested calling the concierge to dry my clothes.

"I'm fine, Tanner. I won't melt."

"It won't take long, Jessie. Go dry off and put on one of the hotel robes. I'll order some coffee or tea to warm you up while we wait."

I didn't want to stay, but the idea of something hot to drink was tempting. My thin dress was sticking to my skin and giving me chills.

"Tea, please."

By the time I'd dried off and fixed my hair, Tanner had already changed into sweats and a T-shirt and made arrangements for the clothes.

I cinched the robe more tightly. Yes, I may be warm and dry again, but I certainly wasn't safe from the elements.

Two pots of tea, along with macadamia-chocolate-chip cookies, already occupied the coffee table, cleared now of drawings. A few minutes later I slipped back into the bathroom as Tanner surrendered my dress and jacket to someone at the door.

"I didn't realize a hotel would get back so quickly with laundry at night," I commented, when I came out of the bathroom again.

"They wouldn't," Tanner admitted, "which is why I'm using a personal concierge service. When I'm in D.C. for an event I'll often need something at the last moment."

My clothes were going off-site? Something told me that they might not be back as quickly as Tanner had implied.

I sat on the sofa and Tanner sat on the chair, the same positions as when we'd reviewed the plans. At that time, I had worried that it would feel awkward to be in his suite. Now it was awkward, without a common business purpose.

I broke off a piece of cookie for something to do. Tanner had reverted to his earlier distracted mood from the restaurant. Silence roared around the room.

In a few minutes, Tanner resurfaced. "I obviously misunderstood much of what happened between us when I was on the drugs. I'm sorry, Honey."

If he was aiming for an apology, the "Honey" negated the attempt. Tanner had started calling me that at the time we met. It was an endearment rolled up in a nickname. I had loved it. But he no longer had the right to use that term.

"I thought you hated me," he continued. "After all, that was how I felt about myself. Yet it turns out you supported me every day, while I continued to do one stupid thing after another. Honey—"

"Stop calling me 'Honey,'" I snapped.

"Why?" he rejoined sharply, his eyes narrowing.

"First, you gave up the right to call me that years ago. Second, you've probably called many women 'honey' since we were together so it's lost its luster. Third, and my least favorite reason, is that my hair is no longer that same shade of honey blond."

He glowered. "I've never called any other woman 'Honey.'"

I rolled my eyes.

"I remember how you felt about endearments. 'Babe' or 'baby' was infantilizing. 'Sweetie' and 'dear' were for sarcasm. What's this really about—Jessie?" His eyes bored into mine.

"You tell me," I sputtered, too tired to pretend I was fine. "Why do you want this house? And why ask me to design it? You could have anyone."

Eyebrows almost colliding, he retorted, "This isn't about the house. You're far too pissed. It's about something else. Stop tiptoeing around whatever's angered you since we ran into each other in April."

I breathed in angrily, nostrils flaring. "You really want to do this, Tanner?"

"Why not? Let's get it all out on the table. See what's left." Only seconds before, he had been contrite. Now he sat on the chair ramrod straight, unforgiving, implacable.

"Fine." But my heart was racing with apprehension, leaving me shaky. What was I doing? He had only been offering me an apology. What if nothing was left after the conversation?

But enough with the apologies and flowers. After being stuck in limbo for years, I needed answers. Still, if this evening ended badly—which it probably would, there would be no going back to the small comfort I had found in our emails, no going back to the small comfort of being on the periphery of his life.

"You start." He leaned forward, forearms on thighs, one fist clutched in the other. His usually generous eyes hard.

I nodded, accepting the challenge. But I was angry about so many things I didn't know where to start. Then my deepest fear resurfaced and wiped everything else out of my mind: that memory of him in the car twelve years ago, when my world almost collapsed. The fear had never left me, even now, even though he was sitting here in front of me.

Hardly able to speak of it, I whispered, "How could you have valued your life so cheaply, Tanner? You meant everything to me."

With those words, I realized it wasn't only the loss of our relationship, not only the lack of condolences on my brother's death that had caused me to throw water on him in the restaurant. I had been furious at Tanner all these years. That he could have been so selfish as to deprive me of what I had valued most.

Tanner looked as if he had been sucker punched, not expecting such raw truth.

My anger made me stronger. "And after you went through rehab, why didn't you tell me you were okay? Why didn't you call or write? You knew Trish had my address and number. You owed me that. It didn't matter whether it was two years or ten years after we'd split, whether you were married or not.

"Every day for years I wondered how you were! It wasn't until I heard that solo album—more than a year after treatment—that I knew you were okay. Didn't you understand what it would have meant to know you'd sought treatment? To know you were safe?" Tears flooded my eyes, making me angrier.

Tanner's expression was grim. "I despised myself for the addiction, for what I had done to you, and for ruining our future. And, yes, there were times I didn't value my life. You deserved more than what I had to offer. So why tell you I was in rehab?

"Besides, when I came back from that last road trip, you'd disappeared.

How was I supposed to know you still cared?"

"You never once thought of letting me know?" I couldn't keep the hurt out of my voice.

Running his hand through his hair until it almost stood on end, Tanner struggled with the question. "As part of my rehab program the counselors suggested I write letters of amends to people I'd hurt—to take responsibility for my actions."

What? Was that why he had asked Trish for my address? But I'd never received anything from him. Had another letter been lost?

Tanner continued. "I wrote letters of apology . . . to everyone but you."

To everyone but me? I felt faint. I could taste the nausea sweeping my stomach.

Tanner placed his hands palms down on the table, trying to compose himself. Even so, his voice shook. "But I couldn't atone for what I'd done to you. I tried to write but never could find the words. Isn't that ironic? I write for a living, but I couldn't find a way to say I was sorry to the person I'd disappointed most."

When I answered, my voice was dangerously low. "The letter was all about you? How comfortable you were writing it? What about me—did you never think that I might need to know you were receiving treatment?"

His jaw clenched so hard, I thought he'd crack a tooth. "I'd been married twice by then. I didn't think you'd care."

That was supposed to explain everything?

"No. That's an excuse." My voice trembled. "Atonement isn't about making yourself feel better. It's about acknowledging the pain you've caused others. Didn't you think I deserved acknowledgment?" In my hurt, I lashed out. "You'd pledged your love, but it didn't even last to sobriety."

Tanner clenched his fists. "You think I didn't want to tell you that I was finally in treatment, that it was your words that got me there?" He looked down at his fists. Sweat had formed on his brow. "I couldn't send you a letter because it was a cowardly way to apologize. But . . . but after staying clean for a year I got your address from Trish and flew to D.C. to apologize in person. You were living in . . . Arlington? A townhouse."

That's why he'd thought I lived in Virginia?

"You came to my house?" I grabbed my elbows to keep from shaking.

He nodded. "You weren't home when I knocked. It was early evening on a Friday—I assumed you were still at work." He looked down at the table and his eyes lost their focus as he replayed the visit. "I waited in the rental car, thinking of everything I wanted to tell you and everything I needed to apologize for. Finally, a car drove up and parked in front of your house.

"You stepped out." He looked up at me. "I can still see you. You were wearing a black skirt with a light purple blouse, your hair still long. You looked incredible—as if time and the loss of our relationship hadn't touched you, while I felt ravaged by both.

"I reached for the door handle anyway—just as another car parked next to yours. A man emerged. The two of you laughed as you walked to your house together. I tried to recall the last time you had laughed like that with me—but I couldn't. I couldn't remember the last time I'd made you laugh, Jessie. But there you were, happy." He sounded wounded to the bone.

Where did he get off judging my loyalty? Of course, I'd had relationships—at that point it would have been over six years since our separation.

"So what? You chose the drugs over me, had been married twice, and had been partying hard for years. Yet I was supposed to remain celibate? Sit at home pining for you like Penelope for poor, god-forsaken—but certainly not celibate—Odysseus?" In fact, though, that was pretty much the truth of my limbo. "How long was I supposed to wait? What would have been reasonable to you?"

I didn't wait for his response. "That's the best you got, Tanner? You came to D.C. to 'make amends.' You were how far away from me? Forty, fifty feet? And you left? I happened to be with someone so it was no longer important to tell me you were okay? That you were sorry for what you'd put me through? Atonement is about redressing the past, not judging me in the present."

Tanner rubbed the back of his neck. "Of course, you weren't supposed to be celibate. But when I saw you with that man, I hoped you were better off. I didn't want to ruin something good."

This time I leaned in, my voice shaking with bitterness. "Who were you to make that decision for me?"

Then I recoiled. "You . . . you wrote a song about it!"

The girl with green eyes
Laughed at another man's joke;
I knew in that moment
It was time to let go.

That song had always vexed me because it reeked of disloyalty. But disloyalty six years after the fact?

"Dammit! If you cared so much, why didn't you come see me?" Tanner demanded. "You were the one who walked away."

Suddenly I couldn't breathe. This was the paradox. I tried to laugh at the irony, but the gurgling noise sounded like the death rattle of a small, dying animal. "Yes, I walked away. But I walked away because I loved you."

He laughed as well—even less pleasantly. "Really? You loved me?" Skepticism dripped off the words.

"Of course," I retorted. "Did you think I was so changeable, so mutable, that suddenly I no longer loved you? There was no expiration date on my feelings. But leaving was the only way I felt I could still help you."

"Why didn't you leave a note telling me that and that you still cared? I came back to nothing. Nothing! At night, when things were bad, I'd wonder if you'd been a hallucination."

I was growing frustrated at the inadequacy of my words—and at the inadequacy of my past actions. "I tried. I must have written fifty notes. But if you had read any one of them you would have realized how weak I was. And if you'd asked me to come back, I would have. I had to make a clean break for both our sakes.

"But talk about irony, Tanner. I never imagined the split would be permanent. I wasn't so naïve as to think that you would suddenly stop using drugs when I left, but I was willing to wait." Then, my voice shaking from my long-ago miscalculation, I said, "I was shocked when you moved on—probably as shocked as when you arrived back at the apartment from that last trip. Except that you were supposed to be shocked. I wanted you to realize what you were losing."

Tanner stared at me in confusion. Then, like a sleepwalker, he rose from his chair and walked around the coffee table to sit beside me, his look still uncomprehending. I was almost undone by the pain pouring off him.

"Your leaving wasn't supposed to be permanent?" he echoed.

I shook my head. "I left for your health. I couldn't ask you for timelines or promises—they were meaningless, given the addiction. But

I figured whenever you got off the drugs then you could decide if our relationship still mattered."

He bristled at my words, pulling away from me, his eyes gleaming with anger. "How was I supposed to know what you were thinking? And if the relationship was that important, why didn't you come see me after I went through rehab?"

"I didn't know you'd been through rehab, Tanner! And when I finally found out, I felt too much time had passed."

"What do you mean?"

He had been honest with me. I didn't want to admit it, but my excuses were as feeble as his. My anger dissipated. I drew back into the corner of the sofa, seeking shelter from his resentment, my heart broken by our failure to anticipate what the other person had most needed to hear those many years ago: for me, that he had gone through rehab and was safe and, for him, that I still cared.

I sighed. "You and mPulse had become a huge success. I figured fame had changed you, changed what you wanted. Plus, you had a new band after rehab and were making wonderful music again. You'd moved on."

Tanner shook his head as if to argue, but I continued. "A couple of times I considered flying to L.A. to make sure you were okay, but I was . . . I don't know . . . too embarrassed, maybe, or more likely too proud.

"I was afraid you'd see me as a hanger-on, someone trying to tap into your success. If you didn't already know . . . if I had to tell you that I loved you, you probably wouldn't have believed me—just like earlier tonight." He flinched. "That was what stopped me. What if I'd told you I still loved you and you didn't believe me?" I paused, the mere possibility making my heart pound and tears well up again. This time I gave in and dabbed at my eyes with the fabric belt of the bathrobe.

"Jessie, I know you're no gold digger."

"No. Not after what we'd been through. And if you had considered for even one second that I was there for any other reason than concern, I couldn't have endured it."

I hesitated, my heart starting to beat as rapidly as if I were sprinting.

"Plus, there's . . . another reason I didn't contact you."

Instinctively, I buried my face against Tanner's shoulder so I wouldn't have to look at him. He was as surprised as I was by my action but offered refuge anyway, wrapping both arms around me.

Another flaw to confess. It wasn't enough that I had abandoned him and aggravated his pain. This was my secret fear. This is what had kept me away for all these years. Overwhelmed, I started gulping in air.

Tanner rubbed my back the way one might calm a baby.

Whispering in my ear, his breath so achingly familiar on my skin that for a second I could think of nothing else, he said, "It's okay, Jessie. You can say what's on your mind. If it's something I did, it's time for me to take responsibility. I know I must have disgusted you, probably even terrified you at times. That maybe that was why you finally left?"

Still not looking at him, I said, "I was never afraid of you, Tanner, only for you—for your health, your music . . . your life." Just thinking about it filled me with panic and I gulped more air.

Tanner felt me shaking and held me tighter. "Then what could be more damning than what we've already revealed?"

I couldn't look at him. I didn't want to see confirmation echoed on his face. "There . . . were a hundred reasons to leave once you became addicted. So that you couldn't use my staying as permission to take drugs. Because you cared so little for your life, while I cared all these years.

"So how do I forget that, despite our professions of love, we never trusted in it and never really believed the other person would keep faith? I thought we had everything. Yet we failed each other abysmally."

Anger and pain spilled out of me as if our transgressions had taken place that day.

A rap sounded loudly on the door.

We bolted upright. I pulled myself back into the present, standing up and moving quickly into the bathroom. I saw Tanner struggling to make the same time-travel trip forward as I closed the door.

Several minutes later, he handed me my dress and blazer.

When I emerged after changing, Tanner was standing in the middle of the room.

Reaching out, he pulled me to him, one hand cradling the back of my head, the other supporting the small of my back. Exhausted, I melted into him. We clung to one another, trying to forget for a few minutes the chronic heartache, the magnitude of our mistakes, and the wounds we had inflicted in the name of love.

"I know you believe our actions speak of our lack of belief in the other person's commitment." Tanner paused, holding me in a bear hug as if I might flee at his next words. "But it seems to me, Jess, that our actions speak more of selflessness and sacrifice—that we tried to put the other's person's happiness and well-being ahead of our own. You were protecting me from something you feared in yourself and I believed you deserved a happy, more stable life."

I spoke into his chest. "If we tried to do the right thing, how could we have hurt each other so badly? Gotten what the other person needed so wrong? Doesn't that mean there was something flawed in the relationship?"

His fingers brushed my hair back from my face. "As you said, it wasn't a partnership at the end. We thought we understood what the other person needed, but by then we were struggling alone in the dark, just trying our best."

I couldn't accept his words, given what had followed.

Sensing my doubt, Tanner pulled away until I was at arms' length, his face pale from the night's revelations.

"Jessie, I love the house you designed."

I nodded.

"But I can't build it. I wanted that house for the joy that your house gives you."

He couldn't build it? I felt stricken. "I tried to give you everything you wanted and more, Tanner," I whispered.

"And you did. But now I would see only a house built on tears."

Then he took my right hand in his, gently wrapping his fingers around mine. My heart was breaking yet again.

Softly he said, "You don't have to protect me any longer. Your love made me strong. So that I could enter rehab. So that I could try to be that man again that you had once . . . admired."

In those words, I found relief. Love hadn't broken him; it had made him stronger. A tremendous weight lifted. The fear and guilt I'd felt all these years began to ease.

I couldn't ask forgiveness for what I'd done, but he had offered it anyway.

"Thank you," I whispered.

Then he released me back into the real world.

FIFTY-FIVE

Despite being exhausted from her trip up and down the East Coast, Charlene came over the next day to hear how the presentation with Tanner had gone.

"My god! What happened? You look like you lost a ten-round bout."

It wasn't a bad description. It was how I felt physically, though emotionally I felt better than I looked. I shrugged and handed her a cup of coffee. We sat out on the deck, enjoying the unusual lack of humidity for July. The garden looked refreshing in the heat, a cool palette of purples, blues, and reds, with white as rest stops—as in music, but for the eyes.

"I guess I don't need to ask how things went?"

"Actually, Tanner loved the proposal."

"He did?" She beamed.

"Yes, but we're not moving forward."

Her smile quickly faded. "Huh? Why in the world not, if he liked the design?"

"And it's all a bit ironic in that by the end of the evening I was wearing his bathrobe."

"What?"

Poor Charlene. Each remark was giving her whiplash.

Taking pity on her, I related the highlights of the meeting, from Tanner loving my design to how badly we'd handled our relationship.

"Do you think he might reconsider the house at some point?"

"It's hard to imagine."

"That's too bad. I was looking forward to meeting him. Can't you at least pretend there's a future?"

I laughed.

"Now tell me about the trip with Isabelle. Did she tell you which schools she liked best?"

"Of course, . . . not," she said, with a touch of annoyance. "I'm her mother. Why would she tell me anything?"

"She's also a teenager. No snark about any of them? No love-at-first-sight?"

"Only says she wants to do more research."

"Well, that's a lot better than falling head first for appearances. Right?"

She reluctantly nodded. "Sure. But I want her to talk with me about her choices. This may be one of those last big mom-daughter things I'll do with her. She'll be off on her own soon."

I scooted my chair closer to her, to reassure and comfort her. "You've got a great kid, Charlene, and a great relationship. When she's ready, she'll talk. Until then, let her spread those wings."

When Charlene was ready to leave, we took our cups into the kitchen. But when we got downstairs, she stopped before opening the front door and stood there eyeing me, as if to determine my guilt in a case.

"What did I do?" I yelped. Under her gaze, my innocence didn't sound convincing even to me.

"I know you don't want to hear this, Jessie, but it strikes me that you're letting pride perpetuate the original mistakes with Teddie D."

"What are you talking about?" Annoyance crept into my voice.

"Just that you refuse to consider a future with him because of the past."

"Charlene, we had our chance. It didn't work out. How many tries do we get?"

She sighed. "Well, for Teddie D I'd say as many as it took. But, hey, that's just me."

Later that evening, Nick called. I wasn't expecting to hear from him as he was in Philadelphia for the week to co-teach several economics and public-policy classes at The Wharton Graduate School of Business. He'd taught before joining the think tank and liked to keep his foot in the door.

"How are you?" he asked.

"Fine. Just tired."

"Rough weekend?"

"You could say that. Tanner won't be building the house."

"What?"

"Oh, he liked the design well enough but decided that it wold be a house 'built on tears.'"

"My offer still stands. I'd be happy to fly out there and beat the crap out of him."

I was too tired to defend Tanner's perfect nose yet again. "No, actually it's okay. We finally got everything on the table—the answers we both needed for closure. Life isn't perfect, and neither were we. It was just easier to blame the drugs.

"The one good thing that came out was that we tried to do what we thought was best for the other person, though we made a god-awful mess of it. But, surprisingly, I think I can move forward with that."

Tanner and I had to live with the past and our mistakes but the situation no longer had to control us, just as addiction no longer controlled Tanner. And it was long past time for me to let go of my fear for his health. He had been forged anew in the fires of his addiction and I needed to respect that.

"And you're okay with that? You can accept that outcome?"

"I can. It's actually a relief to let go of the anger and fear I've been holding onto all these years about the relationship—and about Tanner. I already feel stronger. Like I'm finally ready to live life without my foot always on the brake in case something unexpected rolls out into the street."

I deliberately let the silence hang between us.

"I feed on anger," Nick conceded.

"I know."

"It's how I hold my daughter close. I worry that if I get help, in losing the anger I'll lose Sophie. There'll just be this big hole. I feel it's the anger that keeps her with me."

I waited.

With a wisp of heresy, Nick said softly, "Maybe it's time for me to let go of the anger as well."

"It's scary, I conceded. "The anger is raw and stays fresh and seems to keep the memories alive. But I promise you you'll still have the memories once the anger is gone. And the memories without the constant pain and the anger are so much better. Trust me."

With more certainty in his voice, Nick said, "Guess it's past time to see a counselor. Time certainly hasn't healed anything." Then almost pleading, he asked, "But I won't forget her, will I?"

"Never. You're not that sort of person, Nick. Sophie will always be part of you. Your memories will just be gentler, more accepting of our human limitations—that all we can do is try our best, whatever the outcome."

Before hanging up, Nick asked, "Does the situation with Tanner change anything about your proposed business venture?"

"Nope. But it does pretty much put the kibosh on Tanner's guesthouse. Plus, he hangs around the place too much. Some of us have real jobs."

Nick laughed obligingly.

Monday morning, I gave Evan an update on the presentation. Tanner and I had agreed that I would tell Evan that Tanner liked the design but was putting the project on hold while he finished his new album. Then in a couple of weeks Tanner would call Evan to terminate the project because of the impending launch of the album and the subsequent tour. By then Evan would be focused on another project and the loss would be less immediate. Bye-bye, *Architectural Digest*.

Nonetheless, Evan was surprised. "Jessie, you know the house is amazing, don't you? The richness of the interior spaces is particularly exciting. The layering and contrasts read almost like music. I can't believe he put it on hold."

His comments at least made me feel better about the project itself.

"Thanks, Evan. Unfortunately, he's a busy man."

There was one last person I needed to talk to about the lake house.

"Hi, Russ. How's your father doing?"

"Much better. Thanks for asking. He's back home. Been home about a week."

"That's great!"

Since his father had gone back into the hospital, I'd only had sporadic emails from Russ. He simply had too much on his plate and wasn't in a place mentally to make a major decision about his future.

"I really hate to bother you with all you've got going, but I wanted to tell you something—in case it affects your decision."

"Are you having second thoughts?"

"No. definitely not," I said quickly. "It's just that when we had dinner, I mentioned I was working on a lake house for Tanner and that if we were to move forward it might help create a little buzz for our proposed company. Unfortunately, the project is dead."

There was a pause. "Uh, how do you feel about that?"

"Okay. Tanner actually liked the proposal. But as you can imagine, it's . . . awkward working together."

"I bet. Do you still want to move out here?"

"This business venture never had anything to do with Tanner, Russ. It's about making architecture that feels vital, that has an impact. So even if the only office space we find is next door to Tanner's house, I'd make it work and be happy."

"Given that we couldn't afford a place next door to Teddie, that's one promise you can easily keep." Russ laughed. "I do appreciate you letting me know about the house, but that never factored into my decision."

Decision? He had made a decision?

"I planned on calling you this weekend. It's a go."

"Go? Like we'll have a firm?" My voice squeaked on the last word and my heart started racing in excitement.

"Yep. Everything with my father made me realize I need to do what I love, not just occupy a chair."

"And Sally's on board?"

"Absolutely. Really, when might we get another chance to do this?"

"It truly seems like the right time."

"So where do we go from here?" Russ's breathless question gave away how pumped he was.

"Unfortunately, we just finished the easy part. Now's the hard part."

By the end of the call we both had assignments. I would put together a projected budget for the next two years and a time-line for setting things up. Russ would start looking for space to lease: an open-concept plan, preferably in an older, recycled building, perhaps a loft, or even a business park. Above all, it had to be well-located—and cheap.

And we would continue the discussion about our niche, our vision, and the best structure for the company.

"One last thing," I said. "I can tell you're ready to move quickly on this, just as I am. But make sure to take the time you need with your family. We both have jobs that can tide us over until all the pieces fall perfectly into place."

"Thanks. Don't worry. Mom and Sally will make sure of that."

"Hey, Russ. As soon as I hang up I'm breaking into my Snoopy happy dance."

FIFTY-SIX

I met up with my colleagues from UCLA for drinks at the end of the week. I was still buzzing from my conversation with Russ but couldn't say anything. Russ and I had taken the first step but it was still a daydream. Besides, Evan would be the first in my architectural world to know.

Six of us were sitting around a table debating the proposed memorial for President Eisenhower designed by Frank Gehry for a site adjacent to the National Mall. His submission had been the winner of a Project Competition—four years ago—and still hadn't been built. Nor did things look good. The whole process was the epitome of how not to run a competition.

Well into our discussion, Dana made her usual theatrical entrance. She pulled up a chair next to me as if we were besties. Contempt took hold of me.

As Dana began to ask her usual question as to whether I'd heard from Teddie D, I cut her off and inquired softly, so only she could hear, "What did you do with the letter Teddie left me after my brother died?"

She froze, like a deer caught in headlights, only her eyes darting rapidly around the bar, seeking an escape route.

With a twitch of her head, though, she shook off her guilt and brazenly replied, "I don't know what you're talking about."

I moved my chair in closer. "The letter you assured Teddie that I would receive."

Again, her eyes flew around the room.

"Your promises don't seem to mean much."

She realized my assertions were statements, not questions.

The excuses came pouring out. "Your relationship was over. You didn't need to get dragged back into it. Besides, he was going to be a father. I was protecting you."

The conversation was brimming with irony. Dana's pilfering of the letter to keep us apart was, in fact, the reason Tanner and I had come together in April.

My eyes bored into hers. "I didn't need your protection, Dana. What I needed at that moment were kind words from someone who had known my brother." I could have gone on, but there was no point. There would only be more rationalizations.

"Did you read the letter?" I asked quickly, hoping to take her off guard.

She averted her eyes, some spot on the floor holding her undivided attention.

"I . . . I just wanted to make sure he wasn't trying to take advantage of you while you were . . . vulnerable."

I inhaled sharply. "So, you did read it." I let the sentence hang in the air between us, then said, "What you did wasn't about concern. It was about power—over me, maybe over Teddie even. And having read the letter, you knew he wasn't trying to take advantage of me. You could have still given me the note. But you chose not to. There was no kindness in your action."

I had always tried to give Dana the benefit of the doubt. Dana's father was a moderately well-known architect and she'd hoped to emulate him. Frustration at her own shortcomings had ended up being taken out on her classmates—particularly if our designs were well-received by the jury.

To always carry around the burden of not being quite good enough had to be hard. I'd always wondered how she would have fared had she chosen a related field, like urban design, and been out from under her father's shadow. Perhaps she could have found her own way and been happier.

But, as I considered her actions, it struck me that Dana had yet to apologize for what she'd done. Even Tanner had apologized, and it hadn't been his fault. I looked at my glass; it was empty. Mark, though, had just refilled his with beer.

"Excuse me, Mark." I grabbed his glass and poured it on Dana's lap.

She gasped in shock, her eyes round. "Jessie! What the hell!"

Everyone at the table turned to stare.

"That was for Teddie," I said calmly and loudly.

Just as quickly, my colleagues went back to their conversations.

I leaned in toward Dana and said, "Perhaps if you'd apologized, I wouldn't have done that, but something you've never learned is that actions have consequences. Someday you can thank me for the lesson."

Next to me, Mark whispered, "It's about time, Jessie."

I stood up and went to the bar to get him a fresh beer, leaving Dana to scrounge napkins to clean up the mess.

She no longer had any power over me and I wouldn't regret the action for one nanosecond.

Tanner would have been proud.

FIFTY-SEVEN

Tuesday morning Evan called me into his office. Maybe Tanner had finally phoned to cancel the lake house project? For someone who wasn't in my life any longer, Tanner sure was taking up a lot of space and time.

"Jessie. I've got good news." Evan was beaming.

Not Tanner then.

"What's up?"

"Just had a call from Rich Silverman."

Richard Silverman was a major developer in D.C. He constructed office as well as residential buildings. We had never done business with him, though, as we were a specialty firm.

Evan waited a beat, keeping me in suspense.

I played along. "C'mon, Evan. Why the call?"

"Seems he saw our competition submission on display at the National Building Museum. He's intrigued. Wants to hear more."

I felt a rush of adrenaline. "Evan, that's great!" It's rare when an Ideas proposal pays off. Not that this was a done deal. But the fact that Mr. Silverman wanted to explore the concept further was promising.

"The appointment is in two weeks. We'll run through the PowerPoint presentation and then talk specifics of the site he's considering for an apartment building."

"Can't wait, Evan."

If we could secure this project, Evan wouldn't be so disappointed over the loss of Tanner's lake house. It would also be a great project for me to go out on.

And, Eliot and Sharon would love working on it.

A trifecta.

Dr. Bening called late that same day.

"I've got all the results back, Jessie. Your blood work is fine, exactly what we would expect to see at your age. And the ultrasound doesn't show fibroids or other growths."

"Early onset perimenopause?" I asked tentatively.

"I don't think so. Sometimes stress can bring on a change in menstruation. Have you been under more stress than usual?"

I almost snorted. Additional stress? Like reconsidering my entire career? Having to sell my house? Parents longing to be doting grandparents? Financial unknowns? Leaving my friends? To say nothing of having been hired by my former lover to design his house?

"A little more than usual."

"Well, that's probably more the cause than anything physical. Maybe it's time for a vacation—or at least a three-day weekend. Get away from work."

Hmmm. I wondered if a short trip to L.A. to see Russ would count as relaxing—or stressful?

"If you experience any other changes in your periods, give me a call. Also, have you thought any more about freezing your eggs?"

My heart fluttered.

"I've researched the process," I said. "I'll never have all the information I'd like to make a decision. One piece of data, though, might help. I'd like to be tested for the anti-Mullerian hormone."

That particular hormone often correlates with the quantity of eggs remaining in the ovaries. The higher the hormone level, the greater the number of eggs. Conversely, the lower the hormone level, the fewer eggs remain. Over the age of thirty-five the quantity—as well as the quality—of eggs in the ovaries decreases significantly each year. If my egg reserves tested low, I wouldn't pursue the procedure any further as it would probably require multiple cycles to harvest the appropriate number of eggs. One, maybe two cycles, I might be able to handle financially. Anything more would be irresponsible, given the changes facing me.

But if the test indicated I still had a moderate reserve of eggs, I'd schedule a consultation. If everything else checked out positively I could schedule vacation for the days I'd need to take hormones. If the timing worked out, I'd be through with the whole process—eggs frozen and in storage—before moving to L.A. Then I could focus fully on the firm. In two years I could reassess the situation and decide whether to make the final commitment.

"I think that's a good idea. Make an appointment for the test."

"Will do."

FIFTY-EIGHT

"Not that I mind a free lunch, Jessie, but what's really on your mind?" I'd invited Charlene to join me at a favorite deli near her home. The place smelled of years of grease from the grill top—not rancid but more like built-up furniture oil. I was eating a California turkey BLT. The avocado slices kept sliding out and I kept stuffing them back in with my fingers. Charlene was having a less unruly Reuben.

As usual, she had gotten to the point first.

"You know how much I enjoyed working on the competition a couple of months ago?"

She nodded, taking another bite.

"During the competition I contacted a classmate from UCLA, Russ. He and I had once talked about starting a firm together."

Charlene lowered the half-eaten sandwich to the plate.

I hurried on. "When I was out at Tanner's, Russ and I got together for dinner and talked about setting up that company. He needed a chance to think about it, but he's just committed."

"What the hell? How come you never told me anything about this?" Her voice was tinged with hurt.

"Other than Russ and Nick, I haven't told anyone. And Nick, only because I needed an objective business perspective. Now that Russ has agreed, though, you're the first person I'm telling. But please don't tell anyone else. Russ and I still have a lot to work out. Then the next person has to be Evan."

By now, Charlene's mouth was agape, her face one big emoji of surprise. "I don't believe it! You're giving up a potential partnership?

Nobody in their right mind would give up a partnership at a law firm."

"I know. It sounds ridiculous, doesn't it? But in grad school Russ and I had talked about practicing socially-responsible architecture together. While working on the micro-housing project, something clicked. I realized that in my escape to D.C. I'd chosen safety over dreams." Tanner's addiction had ultimately made him stronger, but it had made me a coward.

"Oh, jeez. Don't tell me you're moving back to California!"

"That's the plan. There's more interest on the West Coast in this type of architecture."

Her eyes narrowed. "Does this have anything to do with Teddie D?"

I laughed. "If this project had anything to do with Tanner, I'd stay in D.C."

Snapping off another bite of sandwich and gulping it down, Charlene retorted, "For crying out loud, Jessie. If you're moving to California, he'd better be part of the damn agenda."

I stopped at the grocery store on the way home from the deli, after telling Charlene a little more about my plans. When she'd asked about a timeframe, I'd told her four to six months—which sounded immediate to me, considering all the things I had to do. But I'd be in California tomorrow if I didn't have to sell my house and give Evan time to find a replacement.

As I approached the checkout line, I glanced at the magazines. Tanner's face was plastered on *People* magazine. Alongside were the words "Paternity Suit."

See, Charlene, this is why Tanner is not on my agenda—or my Christmas card list.

I grabbed the magazine and tossed it onto the conveyor belt. Once home, I fixed a glass of iced tea and sat at the kitchen counter with the magazine. Before opening it, I took some slow, calming yoga breaths and thought about who Tanner was now and about his relationship with Jason. I didn't want either of them hurt.

According to the article, a woman had come forward claiming that her eight-and-a-half-year-old daughter was Tanner's. Apparently, she and her husband had recently divorced and she was seeking child support from Tanner. A confirmed rock-and-roll groupie, she alleged they'd had sex backstage after a concert. I did the calculation: the daughter was too young to have been conceived while Tanner was still married to Nadine.

Tanner had not commented on the story but his lawyer confirmed that the two parties were proceeding with a DNA test to determine paternity.

I sat back. Only three months ago, the story would have sent me into a tailspin. I'd have been hurt and envious. But this had nothing to do with me. If the story were true, it had more to do with the drugs and the downward spiral Tanner had been on. Which wasn't an excuse, of course.

Because one thing I knew about Tanner now was that he would take responsibility for his actions. He would do the right thing by the child.

Yet I also knew this wasn't how he would have wanted to be involved. Yes, he had wanted more children. But, as with Jason, he would have wanted to have been involved in the child's life from birth. That's who he is. I was saddened for both him and the girl, in that if she were his daughter, he hadn't had the opportunity to be present in her life.

I sent Tanner good karma to support him in whatever outcome he wanted. Then I tossed the magazine in the garbage can.

FIFTY-NINE

The sky was overcast. As long as it didn't rain, though, the weather would be perfect for a mid-summer afternoon baseball game. Nick drove us to his office, where we parked, and then we took the subway to Nationals Park.

"Are you hungry?" he asked, once we were inside the stadium.

"I'm always up for a hot dog."

The only time I ever eat hot dogs is at baseball parks. Nothing else seems as all-American for the all-American sport—not pizza, not cheesesteaks, not BBQ, and not nachos. Nick bought three hot dogs, topped with yellow mustard, and we shared a large soft drink.

"These seats are great." We were right behind the Nationals' dugout, eight rows up.

"I thought you'd enjoy them."

The first time I came to Nationals Park for a game I'd been extremely disappointed. The architects had the incredible opportunity of designing the stadium with a view of the Anacostia River immediately south of the ball field. Instead the stadium turned inward, like a prison, with no visual connection to the river or the surrounding neighborhood. With great models already existing, like SBC Park on the San Francisco Bay or the Great American Ball Park in Cincinnati with a view of the Ohio River, it should have been a no-brainer to have designed the D.C. ballpark as an anchor for the proposed greenway along the river.

It was still hard for me not to dwell on that shortcoming when I went to games, but today's seats were too good to waste time redesigning the stadium in my head.

At the end of the first inning, there was no score. In the next two innings, though, the Nats scored eight runs, including a grand slam in the third.

We were just starting to hope for a shutout when the Mets scored in the top of the fourth. Oh, well, that would have been asking for too much along with the grand slam.

In the top of the fifth, Nick turned to me and said, "God, what a great double play."

Huh? My mind had wandered. In fact, it had wandered three thousand miles. I hadn't even heard cheering from the stands around me. I glanced quickly at the scoreboard but it displayed only one out.

"Made you look."

I gave him a wry smile. "Sorry, my mind was elsewhere for a minute."

He looked at me thoughtfully, then grabbed my hand and said, "C'mon," pulling me up the stadium steps.

Nick found us a pub-style table near the concession stands and then left to buy drinks. The concourse smelled of popcorn, peanuts, and beer, the mingled odors reminding me of other old-fashioned public events, like circuses and state fairs.

After rejoining me, Nick took several sips of beer. Then, staring down into the plastic cup, as though it held tea leaves that could be divined, he said, "I've met with a grief counselor."

"Nick, I'm so glad." I reached out and squeezed his hand.

He looked up and gave me a full grin. "I found a male therapist, though. Didn't want any of that emotional transference stuff going on."

I snickered. "Good idea. Not to say that you still won't have transference issues."

"Hey!" he laughed. "The point is that I'm finally doing something about my situation. What's your excuse?"

I stared at him. "What do you mean?"

"God, lately you look like a puppy that's been kicked to the curb. When we go jogging, I'm afraid someone's going to accuse me of abusing you." His eyes bored into mine.

"I'm fine."

"Does fine mean 'lovelorn' these days?"

The problem was that Nick wasn't wrong. I thought I could accept what had happened between Tanner and me once I had answers. Instead, I yearned for the chance to set things right, to try again with all the knowledge we had now in hindsight, to be there for him unwaveringly going forward, and to always let him know how much I treasured him. Things that had once loomed so large and insurmountable—a drug relapse, his fame, my loss of privacy, the lost time—no longer seemed relevant. A life with him far outweighed any hypothetical problems.

And, I missed hearing the details of his life. I wanted to know how the album was coming, what Alan thought of it, how the talks with Jason were going, whether they'd started talking about sex yet (and how much Tanner was sweating it), and how Jason's photography was coming.

I wanted to talk with Tanner about our work, sharing things that spoke of who we were—like that first day at the coffee shop. I wanted to complete the lake house for him, a house built on joy, not tears. And I wanted his counsel on this company with Russ that was proceeding from daydream to reality.

I needed the intimacy of his touch, the thrill my body experienced when he stood near me, the way he looked at me—still his Achilles' heel, the goose bumps erupting on my arms when his breath kissed my skin, and the way his presence warmed my blood. And, dammit, I wanted knock-your-socks-off-life-affirming-sex with him in that lake—and any other place I could get it.

I would never tire of Tanner: the sight of his body, the sound of his voice, the power of his music, the scent of north woods and ocean, the real—not imagined—sensation of his beard against my fingers and body, and the chance to share in his love of life again.

It wasn't that I needed Tanner to feel complete. I was whole again, with a rich, satisfying life. But Tanner added the shimmering golden threads to the tapestry of my life. And I wanted to bring the same wonder, excitement, and laughter to his life.

Besides, it was a physical imperative to feel his energy in my bones and my heart every day so I could help him stay balanced and be comforted by his steadfastness in return. And I wanted his steely resolve—to beat his addiction, to be a good father, to pay kindnesses forward—fighting for us every day. No, our love hadn't been perfect as I had once imagined, but it was . . . enduring.

"No," I told Nick. "'Fine' means I plan on talking with Tanner."

His eyes widened. "You are? When?"

"In the next couple of weeks."

He snorted. "That sounds vague."

"No, really. I just need to decide how. I don't want to have the conversation over the phone, which means I'll have to fly out there. The question is when."

"Jessie, get your phone out right now and make a plane reservation to L.A. for Saturday."

The guy was persistent.

"I can't do that. He might not be in town."

"And when you call and he asks why you're coming out, what will you say? You just insisted you didn't want to have the conversation by phone."

I searched the concession area—at the people talking too loudly at the table next to us, kids noisily swarming the T-shirt kiosk, the bright neon concession signs, the food vendors heading into the stadium—but couldn't find an answer.

"Uh, that's the problem. I don't want to talk to him on the phone, but I can't just fly out there. He might not be in town, he might have Jason for the weekend, or he might be in the studio. But in a couple of weeks I'm going out to see Russ, so I thought I'd call Tanner then and ask if I could drop by."

"So, the conversation with Teddie would be secondary to the business discussion?" Nick cocked his head.

Which was annoying. But his simple question made me realize how asinine my plan was. "Damn it, Nick. Of course not." The discussion with Tanner would probably be the most important conversation I'd ever have—life-changing, for sure . . . maybe even heartbreaking. "But what if he's not in town?"

"Then you call Russ." Nick raised his eyebrows, smugness oozing from his voice.

He was right. The conversation with Tanner was the paramount one. I laughed at his wisdom. "I gather your Ph.D. was in Lovelorn Studies, Dr. Parris?"

He grinned. "Economists are a dime a dozen. I needed a specialty."

Resolute, but with shaking hands, I grabbed my cell phone. Checking flight schedules for Saturday, I purchased a ticket that would get me to L.A. around ten in the morning . . . in six days.

A roar went up in the stadium. The Nats had scored another run.

SIXTY

What the heck was I doing? What if Tanner wasn't in L.A.?

But I had no choice. Just as it had been so many years ago, I could no longer imagine life without Tanner. And what I wanted now was no longer driven by fear for him, but love.

I turned my phone off and prepared for take-off from Reagan National. Once over the Potomac River, I leaned my head against the cool window and tried to let my mind go blank. Instead, it went into an endless loop of what could happen. By the time the plane touched down in L.A., my stomach was in shreds.

But I had to try. Charlene was right; pride had already kept Tanner and me apart for too long.

After picking up a rental car, I drove straight to Tanner's place, arriving a little before noon. I pulled the car in front of the gate and got out to ring through to the house. No one answered.

I backed the car out and parked in front of the high wall. I knew the code for the gate from my prior visit but I didn't want to freak Tanner out by parking an unfamiliar car on his property, nor did I want any of his service people, like a lawn guy, to find me sitting in the car, uninvited, inside the gate.

Tanner could be anyplace this time of morning—with Jason at a summer league soccer game, at an NA meeting, at the studio, maybe even having an early lunch—or a late breakfast—with someone.

I decided to sit in the car a while longer. If he didn't show up, I'd break down and call, asking if I could stop by later—provided he wasn't out of town.

But I didn't want to stay parked too long—one of the neighbors might call the police. Wouldn't that be funny? When I finally reached Tanner, it would be to ask him to bail me out. He might get a chuckle or two over that.

I turned my phone back on and checked the time. I'd give myself another half hour and then I'd call Tanner. As I waited in the warmth of the car, I found myself nodding off.

The shrill ring of my cell phone roused me. I checked Caller ID. Tanner. I gazed around quickly in case he had driven up. Nope. No car. No Tanner.

"Uh, hi, Tanner," I said brightly.

Tanner didn't bother to greet me. "Where are you?" he barked.

"Did a neighbor call you?"

"Why would a neighbor call me?" he growled.

"I'm . . . well, I'm in L.A." But in case he was about to careen around the corner in his car, I added, "I'm . . . parked in front of your house. I thought maybe a neighbor had called you about a suspicious car."

There was silence. I didn't hear joy echoing around in the vacuum.

"By any chance, are you going to be home soon?" I asked.

"No. I'm in Washington." His voice sounded like fingernails on a chalkboard.

He was in Seattle? "Are your parents okay?" I asked with concern.

"What?" His voice grew raspier with each remark, as though he was trying to retain control of himself but his voice was having none of it.

"You said you were in Seattle. I thought maybe one of your parents was ill."

"Washington, D.C."

Oh.

"What are you doing in D.C.?" I was thoroughly confused.

"I took the red-eye from L.A. Got in a couple of hours ago at Reagan National."

"Oh, that's funny. I was at Reagan this morning, too."

"You find that amusing?" He didn't sound like he found it amusing.

"Sort of." But that was only because I was having a problem putting all the pieces together. "Why are you in D.C?"

"Who doesn't like taking the red-eye to the East Coast? Or maybe I'm here for the sheer enjoyment of sitting on your stoop, waiting for you to get home from whatever errands you're running, and trying to call you only to find your phone turned off."

Oh-oh.

"I won't be home for a while," I confessed.

"I gather as much, since neighbor Nick enthusiastically told me that when he got home from the gym. I don't know if I'm more annoyed that you're not here, or that he was so full of glee when he told me you were in L.A."

No wonder he was testy. I'd treat the question as rhetorical, though, in order not to worsen his mood with the correct answer.

"As soon as Nick told me where you were, I made a reservation for a flight out of here that gets in to LAX about eight thirty tonight. Do you think you can stay put?"

"I can't stay here in front of your house. Eventually someone will report me to the police as a stalker." My brain seemed stalled in first gear.

"I didn't mean literally. Go to Trish's, go to a movie. Just don't get on a plane. I've got to go. I'm about to go through security."

I snickered. "Don't enjoy the security frisk too much."

"Jessie." He sounded as if he'd had all he could take for one day.

I might as well add to his travails.

"I love you, Tanner." Me, who didn't want to have this conversation over the phone. My throat went dry. But I couldn't wait any longer. I was already so anxious that I hadn't been able to sleep—or eat, now that I thought about it. Maybe my stomach would stop doing cartwheels now.

There was silence again. Followed very emphatically by another growl. "Do. Not. Leave. L.A."

"Aye, aye, Cap'n."

I heard his eyes rolling madly in their sockets, three thousand miles away.

Then the connection went dead.

That had gone well. But then I was probably delusional given my lack of sleep. At least I'd told him. He wouldn't be blind-sided once he got to L.A. He hadn't responded, of course. Heck, maybe he didn't even know how to respond. But he had a long flight during which he could figure out an answer.

I felt almost perky. I was counting on the fact that Tanner had seemed far more in the present these past few months—from the emails to our last conversation at the hotel—than I had. And he seemed far more accepting of our failures, rather than regarding them as mortal sins.

And best of all? Despite his two marriages, he still believed in love—and believed that what we had experienced was love. Not an illusion, not infatuation, not lust. Love.

Seven hours to kill.

Despite Tanner's suggestions, all I wanted was to sleep with the relief of having said what I'd come to L.A. to say—whatever the outcome. I called nearby hotels until I found one that accepted early check-ins.

Once I registered and was in the room, I set a wake-up call, turned on CNN softly for white noise, and fell soundly asleep. I had not one single dream—not about Tanner, not about architecture.

SIXTY-ONE

After taking a much-needed shower, I donned a pair of clean jeans and a short-sleeved, azure silk blouse, and called room service for a light supper. While waiting for Tanner's call, I checked emails, in case he'd sent a message.

He hadn't.

The longer I waited to hear from him, the more anxious I became. I'd been able to sleep because time had stopped—Tanner was in flight. Life had been suspended. But time—and nerves—were starting up again now that Tanner was almost back in L.A.

The cell phone rang. With shaking hands, I picked it up. Then dropped it. I tried again.

"Jessie." Tanner's voice was still a growl. My heart jumped into my throat. Guess the flight hadn't helped.

"Uh, hi." I could think of nothing to say—that hadn't already been said.

"Are you in L.A.?"

"Stayed as ordered, sir." Shoot. He was growling and I was returning his edge with snark.

"I'm at the airport. Could you meet me at my house?" Then, as an afterthought, he added, "Please?"

"Since you used the magic word, sure."

"I'll be there as soon as possible."

"Hey, safety first," I replied more gently. I did want the man to arrive in one piece.

Dusk was turning to evening as I drove back to Tanner's.

Why was he so cranky? I tried to remember if he had been testy before I told him I loved him but couldn't recall; I'd been too surprised to hear he was in D.C.

Given that he had been sitting on my porch when Nick found him, he had obviously come to see me.

Shoot. What if he had decided to move ahead on the lake house? That would explain why he hadn't called Evan yet. And it would also explain his irritability—he decides to move forward with the lake project and I blurt out I love him. Yeah, that might make him a tad irritated with the hired help.

So here I was, parked outside his house for the second time in one day. Now that it was almost dark, though, it was creepy sitting alone in the car. Quiet and creepy. I started imagining strange, diabolical things lurking in the shadows and bushes. Coyotes. Tarantulas. A valley girl.

Headlights shone behind me and a car pulled around mine and into Tanner's driveway, the gate sliding open. With relief, I quickly followed his car in.

I parked to the right of his car nearer the garage but remained seated—I couldn't get my legs to work. I imagined getting out and sprawling to the ground. Taking a couple of deep breaths, I tried to shake off the strain of waiting all day to see him.

Tanner appeared at the car door. I unlatched it and stepped out slowly, testing my legs. Too slowly, apparently, as Tanner grabbed my wrist.

"Come on."

I resisted, remaining in place, my legs needing to readjust to gravity. "Can I get my bag?"

"Of course." He sounded slightly less feral. Or maybe he was just tired, as his face looked pale in the glow of the garage lights. "I'm sorry. It's been a long day."

"Believe it or not, I know."

That elicited a slight smile from him but it didn't ease the tension controlling his body.

"Uh, Tanner, before we go inside, did you, uh, hear everything I said on the phone? There wasn't static or something on the line, was there? You were able to hear everything I said?" I didn't want there to be any misunderstanding or a compounding of my stupidity, if what I said had been inappropriate. Of course, if he hadn't heard my confession he wouldn't be the wiser about what I was dithering on about now. But I wasn't sure I could say it again without some reaction from him first.

"Of course, I heard you," he snapped. He hadn't released my wrist yet. I wondered if he thought I was going to flee. Straight into the arms of those coyotes? I think not.

"Would you like to hear more?" I hoped his answer would confirm what he'd heard.

"Not unless you want me to take you on the ground, here and now."

A jolt of electricity flashed down my spine. For a second I was rooted to the earth, unable to move. Then I was set free, catapulted by the sheer exhilaration of being given a second chance at love, at life. My heartbeat roared in my ears.

Tanner took me in his arms, pulling me tightly to his chest, my forehead resting on his cheek—and that now familiar beard. I experienced him with every sense.

He strewed kisses like flowers through my hair, then lowered his aim to my neck, going for a spot just behind and below my ear that he knew would leave me delirious. The warmth of his breath on my skin was enough to send blood racing madly to more demanding body parts.

But I had one more question to ask before hitting the point of no return.

With my left hand on his torso, so I could feel his heart and the truth of his answer, I asked, "Why were you in D.C.?"

Tanner pulled his upper body away from me, his face expressing surprise. "To woo you, of course. Why else would I be there?"

I didn't even realize I'd been holding my breath. "It, uh, crossed my mind that perhaps you were there to tell me you wanted to move ahead on the lake house."

"I could pick up the phone to do that, Jess. No, I had decided to give you a month to come to your senses after our last conversation.

"That evening at the hotel I knew you only saw failure in our actions. But what I saw was a love that had survived my addiction and years of heartbreak, disappointment, anger, neglect, remorse, pride, and misguided self-sacrifice. It was astonishing. I want that love—its immensity, its passion, its fierceness, and its constancy—in my life every day. If you hadn't called within a month I was coming a-courting." He smiled at the old-fashioned words.

I nodded, tears in my eyes. It was what I wanted, too. "But it's only been three weeks," I whispered.

"Oh, I got tired of waiting. I thought you might have gotten lost in the past again. Besides, I came a-wooing with a gift I figured you couldn't refuse." The tilt of his head screamed cockiness.

"And what was that?" I asked, laughing. Assuming he meant his delectable body, I moved my hands lower in the spirit of cooperation, his body responding enthusiastically.

Tanner grinned. "If only I had known it would be that easy. No, Jessie. Your gift is the new album."

"You finished it?" I almost forgot my ongoing exploration. Almost. "What do you think of it?"

Tanner ignored my wandering hands. "The question is what you'll think of it. I wrote the album for you."

"What?" That got my full attention.

"It's the letter I never wrote you in rehab. The album is entitled *Making Amends*. It won't compensate for all these lost years, but I hope it will help you understand what you've always meant to me. And that song I wrote when you were here? I titled it 'Honey.'"

Of course. The notes had drizzled like liquid gold from his guitar. Tears splashed down my cheeks. He had finally found the words—and of course it had been through music. Tanner leaned in and started kissing the tears away. Then he headed to my throat.

"Can . . . can we listen to it right now?" I stammered.

"Nope. It'll keep. You'll start blubbering, I'll get soaked, and then I'll have to run out to the drugstore to buy Kleenex for you. The evening would be ruined." He smirked.

"Hey." I poked him in the chest. But he was right, I would be a mess and there were other things I, too, wanted more.

"First thing in the morning?"

"Maybe not first thing—but in the top ten," he teased.

"I certainly don't want to ruin your evening so maybe this gift will help." I slipped my hand into my jeans pocket and extracted a packet.

I handed it to him.

It was a condom. "Until we get tested."

He chortled. "Only one?"

I elbowed him. "It's a start. Plenty more in my bag."

"I like the way that sounds."

Tanner wrapped his arms around me tightly, immobilizing me. I felt his heart beat, strong and determined. For a second, I thought it my own. Maybe it was—maybe we shared a heart now.

Tanner groaned, his voice a whisper, a light flutter on my neck, sending me nearly over the edge. "Please, come with me to the house. You won't enjoy the gravel."

Heat flooded my body and my knees gave way. Tanner grabbed both my elbows, steadying me.

The tables had turned and he knew it. Laughing, he said, "You're playing with fire, Jess. Don't forget, I know everything about your body. Exactly how you like being caressed . . . and nibbled . . . and kissed . . ."

Of course, he had to demonstrate. I went weak with anticipation.

"And don't think I haven't already thought about what I'll do to every inch of you. You gave me plenty of time to reflect on the plane home."

Great. I had been sleeping and he had been planning a full-scale invasion.

Then he growled, "You'll beg for mercy, for that moment your body arcs in ecstasy."

My heart raced and my nerves started misfiring.

Laughing, Tanner took advantage of my loss of words and grabbed my hand again, slinging his bag over a shoulder and picking up my overnight case.

I thought I remembered how potent sex with Tanner was. But I hadn't. For it wasn't just the sex; it was the emotional component Tanner brought to the physical that took my breath away, stripping me to my most vulnerable and impassioned self.

"Forget the house, Tanner. I can't wait. How about the lawn?"

A teasing grin lighted his face. "It's your fault for asking too many questions—and for giving me a hard time. And no. The sprinkler system is bound to go off. I'm not taking the chance."

Instead, he pushed me forward to the house. When we reached the door, he unlocked it and we walked in together, hands entwined, over the threshold.

SIXTY-TWO

My fingers tightened on Tanner's. After twelve years, I was terrified.

"Uh, do you think it's possible we could . . . spontaneously combust?"

Tanner's eyes laughed. "I believe we could . . . but what a way to go. In fact, I could probably burst into flames just holding your hand and thinking about what we're about to do. To share a life with you again. It seemed too much to hope for."

He pulled me rapidly up the staircase but at the top of the landing he stopped abruptly, his expression transforming to concern.

"I have to tell you something. Before we go any further. It might change your mind." He paused, struggling to find the words. "A woman recently came forward, claiming I was the father of her child. I—"

I cupped my palms gently on the sides of his face. "I know. I saw the story. What's important is that you'll do the right thing whatever the outcome of the paternity test. I just hope it's the outcome you want."

"Jessie." He pulled me into him. He was stronger for his ordeals—yet he was accepting my support. Which is how it had to be—a true partnership again.

"I have the results of the DNA test."

I looked up at him, my eyes not wavering from his. I—we—could handle this together.

"She's not my daughter."

I nodded. "Are you okay with that?"

"Yes. I didn't think it was likely. Groupies weren't my thing. And, as I told you, I had learned my lesson about unprotected sex."

"Then, I'm glad. Because if she had been your daughter, I knew you'd be upset you hadn't been part of her life earlier."

"Thank you. But does this change your mind? All these stories you'll have to endure?"

"Sorry. You're stuck with me." I burrowed into his chest as he enfolded me in his arms. We hadn't been derailed.

He kissed me on the forehead and lifted my chin up. "Before we get more distracted, I want to make this clear. I love you, Jessie. I've always loved you."

"I love you, Tanner. I'll always love you."

"You are the only person I have ever wanted to share my life with. You're my soul."

I was overwhelmed. By his words, his touch, his physicality, and the promise of what was to come tonight and the years ahead.

"I'm going to do everything I can to make this long-distance relationship work so you won't even notice the miles between us. We've been through far worse and our love has remained constant. Constant, Jessie. We can do this."

Oops. All cards had to be on the table. I squeaked, "Uh, what if it's not long-distance?" There might have been a note of panic in my voice.

He sighed. "I wish I could move to D.C. I'd do it in a second if not for Jason."

"No, no. I mean what if I were to move here?"

He shook his head. "You can't do that. You have a partnership waiting in D.C."

"I do. And I love my firm and Evan. But do you remember that dinner meeting I had when I flew out here?"

Tanner nodded but looked puzzled.

"I met with one of my old classmates that night. Russ Howard. Do you remember him?"

"Of course," he said, though his tone was still perplexed.

"Russ and I are establishing a firm together. A company focused on social- and environmentally-progressive architecture. The firm's a better fit for the West Coast."

Tanner's expression was blank for a second. "Here?"

When my words finally made impact, his eyes blazed and he pulled me back into his arms. Maybe we'd never make it to his bedroom tonight. That was okay. I was content just to be enveloped in his arms.

"Nothing would make me happier, Honey, if that's what you want. But we'll make things work even if you'd rather stay in D.C."

My nickname sounded like nectar on his lips. "This company is what I want." Then I added quickly, "But it won't be immediate. Russ and I have a lot to work out. Maybe six months."

"Sounds like an eternity. But I want you to do what inspires you, wherever that leads."

"I'd hoped to talk with you about it this weekend—if things got that far between us."

"Oh, things are way past that."

Suddenly he inhaled sharply, as the idea of me moving to L.A. sank in.

"Do . . . do you still want children?"

My heart missed a few beats. "Uh-huh."

Joy swept across Tanner's face. "How many?"

Like so many years ago, I raised two fingers, my heart fluttering erratically like a baby bird learning to fly. A house filled with light, happiness, and three children.

Tanner clasped me tighter, leaning his head against mine. His breath tickled my throat as he whispered haltingly, "First born, boy or girl. Alex?"

My chest filled—not with sadness at my brother's name this time but with joy.

"It-it-it's perfect," I squeaked. And my parents would love it.

Guess I owed Russ another phone call to let him know there might be a few more changes in my life. But with Russ or without him, I'd start the new company.

Then, for the first time since we'd encountered each other three-and-a-half months ago at the restaurant—that dinner with Charlene I had almost canceled because of my grumpy mood—Tanner took my face in his hands and kissed me. Why it had taken so long this evening to get to this point, I don't know. Maybe things had needed to be said first.

Once we started, though, we couldn't stop. His hands cradled my head, the fingers of my right hand coiled through his hair, my other hand curled around his neck. We kissed slowly at first, finding our way home, then more intensely, seeking our old intimacy. I felt more alive than I had in a long, long time.

I couldn't believe how familiar he felt or how familiar he tasted after all these years. Tanner was the ocean, his lips touched by the salt air, his energy surging like the tides.

Once again, our kiss was filled with promises and dreams but this time the kiss sealed our commitment—our fates forever allied.

With wonder in my heart, I whispered, "I never found the antidote to that first kiss, Tanner."

"Thank god, or my heart would still be broken."

Picking up the bags again, Tanner nudged me along. Two doorways to bedrooms at the back of the house opened off the landing. Turning a corner, we entered a hallway. Two more doors on the left led to bedrooms overlooking the front yard. At the end of the corridor was a final doorway.

I came to a halt at the sight of that open door, looming, pulsating with possibilities.

"Jessie?"

I stood, transfixed on our future.

Finally losing patience with all the starting and stopping, Tanner dropped the bags, picked me up in his arms, and started carrying me down the corridor. I was thrilled—and annoyed.

"Put me down."

"I've no intention of putting you down. You're dawdling."

"I'm not dawdling . . . I'm nervous."

Tanner halted, with me still in his arms. Concerned, he said, "I'm sorry, Jessie. We can wait. I just had too long on the flight back to think about what you'd said. It was a long and very uncomfortable flight home. We have the rest of our lives. I don't want you to regret moving too fast."

"Thinking of me was uncomfortable? How romantic."

He chortled suggestively. "Very uncomfortable—and very romantic."

"Well, I certainly don't want you to be 'uncomfortable' any longer than necessary. You promise we'll have plenty of time to talk?"

"Years and years, Honey."

I trusted him completely.

As he gazed at me, I felt once again like his Achilles' heel. This time, however, I would not fail him.

I whapped him on the chest. "Then what are you waiting for? I'm nervous—not crazy."

Tanner laughed, a little too heartily. "Glad to hear that. These last few months I haven't been entirely sure. But we really can wait."

I did my best harrumph. "Maybe you can, but I can't. For some reason, though, this seems like the longest hallway I have ever encountered." I leaned in and pressed my lips against his, followed by tongue, quickly answered by his. The brakes came off.

For more incentive, I ran one finger lightly up and down the nape of his neck while undoing the buttons of his shirt with the other. With only one hand, though, I wasn't having much success.

"For crying out loud, pop the damn buttons off. I don't care."

By the time we got to his bedroom, there was a trail of buttons in the hallway and I had his shirt pulled out from under his belt. I placed my head against his bare chest, taking in the taut muscles and scent. Man, I was definitely ovulating.

He lowered me onto his bed. His bed. My head went woozy. There definitely wasn't enough blood flowing to my brain.

Leaning me back onto the mattress, Tanner straddled me. I took my hand and brushed my fingers across his lips, imagining the sea. Then I caressed the stubble that had seduced me months ago. This time it did inflame my body.

Tanner caught my hand in his and kissed the palm. The kiss, even though as light as a butterfly landing, sent another shot of electricity through my body. I wondered how many jolts I could take and remain sane.

Tanner's other hand traced the curves of my body as if memorizing—or rather recalling—its shape.

Then both hands cupped my breasts, still covered by my shirt. Through the material, he kissed and nipped at them, knowing I wouldn't be satisfied as long as there was anything between us. Grinning at my near swoon, he deliberately returned to caressing my body.

Since he was now otherwise engaged, I unbuttoned my own blouse with fumbling fingers. When finally finished, I sat part way up and slipped off the shirt, followed by the bra. My nipples were swollen in response to Tanner's practiced tongue and fingers.

Meanwhile he was slowly unzipping my jeans. Then, hooking the top of the pants with one finger, he teasingly started tugging them off my hips, bit-by-bit, kissing the skin on my abdomen as it became exposed, heading lower and lower.

I whimpered. Damn, the man was going to make me beg.

I turned slightly to the side to toss my shirt clear of the bed.

It was then that I saw it.

I bolted upright on the mattress, the blood rushing from my head, leaving me faint and trembling. Tears started pouring as I gulped in air.

Focused on my jeans, Tanner was slow to realize something had happened. Only when he felt my body shaking did he look up, his eyes registering panic. "Honey—"

He followed the direction of my eyes. When he saw what I was staring at, he relaxed, joining me on the bed and enfolding me in his arms, murmuring repeatedly, "It's okay." He gently kissed my tears, my hair, my throat, my bare shoulders, to soothe me.

When Tanner thought I had calmed sufficiently, he stood up and crossed over to the dresser. There on its top, perched a lone teddy bear. The bear was outfitted in an astronaut suit, complete with helmet. The visor was up, thank goodness, so the poor thing could breathe.

Tanner retrieved the bruin. "This was the bear I picked up for you on that last trip—the one when you left. I got him in Houston on our way back from New Orleans." His smile was brimming with joy as he handed me the bear.

I clasped poor Teddy Houston tightly to my heart. I was never letting the bear go. This bear who had watched over Tanner all these years while we were apart. I would strap him to my chest with duct tape or put him in a baby carrier across my torso or stuff him into my bra. Tanner had kept this bear for me for twelve years. Twelve years. When we finally consummated this evening—or maybe "if," at the rate we were going—I was going to be clutching this bear. I wondered if Tanner had accounted for that in his invasion plans.

These bears meant everything to me—Tanner's love, our reunions, homecoming sex, a connection with him when he was on the road, and most of all, his safe return home.

"I can't tell you how lonely that bear has been," Tanner added, one hand tight on my naked shoulder and the other grasping my hands cradling the bear. "On that trip home I had told him all about the new friends waiting for him in L.A."

I started hiccupping as I gasped for oxygen in between the tears.

Then, hugging me hugging the bear to my heart, Tanner said, "Now you finally have Teddy Houston and that long trip is over."

Elation bubbled up my throat—along with more of the damnable hiccups.

Odysseus and his faithful bear had returned home safely from years of wandering and adversity.

— The End —

Jessie's Playlist

1. Brighter Than the Sun—Colbie Caillat
2. I'm Beginning to See the Light—Peggy Lee
3. These Are Days—10,000 Maniacs
4. Addicted to Love—Florence + The Machine
5. Wise Up—Megan Hilty
6. Tainted Love—Gloria Jones
7. Give Me One Reason—Tracy Chapman
8. The Ice is Getting Thinner—Death Cab for Cutie
9. When It Rains—Paramore
10. Good Thing Gone—Elle King
11. River of Tears—Bonnie Raitt
12. (I've Got to Use My) Imagination—Lizz Wright
13. I Almost Do—Taylor Swift
14. Listen to Your Heart—Roxette
15. Something's Got a Hold on Me—Etta James
16. All That I Need—Tedeschi Trucks Band
17. I Feel the Earth Move—Carole King
18. (Your Love Keeps Lifting Me) Higher—Jackie Wilson

Tanner's Playlist

1. I've Got a Rock "N' Roll Heart—Eric Clapton
2. Start of Something Good—Daughtry
3. Love is Alive—Joe Cocker
4. I'll Follow You—Shinedown
5. Wire—Third Day
6. It's Been Awhile—Staind
7. Call Me When You're Sober—Evanescence
8. When the Spell Is Broken—Richard Thompson
9. Old Love—Journeyman
10. Different Shades of Blue—Joe Bonamassa
11. Somewhere I Belong—Linkin Park
12. Gravity—A Perfect Circle
13. Can't Stop Thinkin' 'Bout You—Lenny Kravitz
14. The Reason—Hoobastank
15. Best Is Yet to Come—Frank Sinatra
16. Without You—Eddie Vedder
17. Your Arms Feel Like Home—3 Doors Down
18. Every Morning—Keb'Mo'

Printed in the USA
CPSIA information can be obtained
at www.ICGtesting.com
JSHW072035261023
50905JS00008B/26

9 781939 917355